The
RIBBON

The

RIBBON

Sisters of the Porcelain Doll • 2

CARA GRANDLE

ASHBERRY LANE

THE RIBBON

Ashberry Lane
a division of WhiteFire Publishing

13607 Bedford Rd NE
Cumberland, MD 21502

ISBN: 978-1-941720-87-5 (print)
978-1-941720-88-2 (digital)

You have seen me tossing and turning through the night.
You have collected all my tears
and preserved them in your bottle!
You have recorded every one in your book.
The very day I call for help, the tide of battle turns.
My enemies flee!
This one thing I know: God is for me!

~ Psalms 58:8-9

To my daughters;
Two I've loved since their first breath.
And three more that I've prayed for just as long.
You're all so uniquely beautiful.
You bring me such joy.
You're in my heart forever.

Chapter One

*J*ust before dawn, Heather had kissed her ma's cold dead cheek for the last time. Now, only two hours later, she stood frozen while her new husband kissed *her* cheek. Her soul nearly caved in on itself with the weight of emotion and the strangeness of it all as the two moments converged into one. The sadness of the funeral and death-touched morning, with what was supposed to be a happy wedding day.

Guilt churned heavy in her belly. Riley, faithful neighbor and friend—and now husband—was rescuing her, and here she was crying all over his boots. She needed to get out of this church, away from all the watchers, and out of town.

"Sorry, Riley." A woman shouldn't be sobbing on her wedding day.

Riley took his family Bible from her and put a hand on her back, offering support. "I understand. This was my idea. I've had weeks to get used to it. You've only had since last night. I should have asked sooner. But your ma…"

Ma hadn't been awake enough to talk to for weeks.

So many things had changed as Ma's declining health finally got the best of her. Four long years of sickness, struggling as the lump in her belly—having grown large enough to tent her dress out—consumed her. Then, in the wee hours this morning, Ma had gone.

Just…gone.

The smell of wood polish the pastor's wife must've used to clean the church mixed with the lingering smell of the herbal poultice Heather had used to ease Ma's pain. The clock in the back of the room sent shudders into her heart with each tick.

Ma had no ticks left.

Heather tried to swallow her tears as she and Riley remained standing before the pastor. They'd already spoken their promises to be man and wife. Before a handful of friends gathered around ready to cheer them on, they'd recited their vows to forever love each other. But instead of a warm glow, she felt cold. Numb.

Closing her eyes, Heather tried to fix a younger, healthier image of her mother in her mind rather than the sick-ravaged face and form of Ma's last moments. Her mother wouldn't want her dwelling on such things at her wedding.

Riley had been nothing but a good neighbor to them both since Pa left them to fend for themselves. He was older than her and willing to help with the chores that needed a man's strength. Heather had been fourteen when Pa left, and Riley seemed more older brother than sweetheart. She was nineteen now and no more prepared to make her way in this world than she was back then. But that didn't stop the fact that she couldn't afford to stay in her home anymore. She had no way to support herself, and farmer Hershey was already moving his foremen into her home. Now, she didn't even have Ma to advise her.

Heather raised a hand to rub the back of her neck, fingers brushing the ribbon she'd woven through her coiled braid. Ma's ribbon, one of a pair made of sky-blue satin with tiny roses down the center. It told of another life—another love—another time. Ma had been happy once. Happy with her husband and then happy with her, their only child. The weight of the ribbon, the weight of real love and better times, wore on Heather's head like a crown of brick and stone. Heavy and unbending.

The ribbon brought her hope, though. Its match lay resting inside Victoria, the doll Heather and her three best friends used to seal their sister-pact a year ago. When they'd opened the back of the doll's soft body and hidden their treasures inside, they'd made a deeper promise to witness each other's lives as best they could. They'd solidified their pact for every day they hadn't yet lived. The promise she, Cora Mae, Rebecca, and Rose made was the only thing that kept Heather from crumbling to a heap on the spot.

The pastor finished talking. Riley moved his hand to her shoulder, turning her, before dropping it again. They walked side by side, but not arm in arm, out the back of the white church. Heather's boots clicked the fresh, polished floor as her skirts pressed against the foot of each pew they passed. The wedding was over.

Over for a moment. Married for a lifetime.

Heather couldn't look into the eyes of the people who stood with smiles on their lips. They were either concerned about her well-being or, worse, overflowing in pity. These generous folks were the same ones who'd carried her mother's simple pine coffin to the graveyard this morning. A coffin Riley had built without Heather knowing. *Again, he protects me. I should love him.*

At the back of the church, a crowd of ladies waited—their hems wet with the morning dew from the journey between the grassy graveyard and the altar where she'd just pledged her heart.

Cora Mae came as close to Heather's right shoulder as Riley had her left. Their eyes met and held. There was strength in her gaze, and a wealth of compassion. Heather drank in both, grateful for her friend's presence. Their other two friends hadn't been able to attend on such short notice. Rebecca was in Eagle Creek, Oregon Territory, with her new husband. Rose was stuck at the mercantile working, per usual. Heather understood, of course, but their absence only made her more grateful Cora Mae was here. She wouldn't have made it down the aisle without at least one of her friends present.

Heather, Riley, and Cora Mae stepped in unison down the church's front steps.

"I left the wagon ready," Riley said. "Everything is in order."

Heather nodded, content to walk past all the people watching, all the way to the wagon Riley was leading her toward. It would be their new home for this trip across the Oregon Trail. Riley had contacted a reputable guide. They'd followed his advice to the letter and would continue to do so as they found their way to Oregon Country along with the many others doing the same.

Her mother's ribbon, the one in her hair, blew in the breeze and tapped her cheek, mocking her—continuing to press down with all that used to be, and all that could have been. All that would be.

"Don't worry about tomorrow. Tomorrow is chocked-full of its own troubles."

Ma's voice whispered in her mind, a one-sided conversation encompassing snatches of chats from years gone by. It had happened several times during the last few years as her mother quit speaking, each time bringing with it an ache in Heather's heart.

Riley helped her climb into the wagon and settle on one side of the buckboard bench.

"Thank you," she whispered.

The ribbon tickled her cheek. Heather was glad she'd woven it into her hair, even though it came with the burden of her parents' true love. It was also a reminder of the sisters she'd chosen and the sister-pact they'd made. Riley might have helped her find her seat, but her sisters were the ones who truly settled her heart.

All the memories of meeting with Rebecca, Cora Mae, and Rose during sewing bees came back to her. Precious times when they were all still together. When they could see each other, witness each other's lives…when Ma was still alive—before Rebecca had to leave.

Tears began anew. Rebecca had left a year ago. Now Heather was leaving. Would the four of them ever be together again, sharing in each other's lives?

The wagon rocked on its traces as Riley put something in the back. Then, thoughtful as always, he reached up to wrap a blanket around her shoulders, bracing her from the cold March wind.

If only it would warm her on the inside.

At least she could pretend she would be meeting up with Rebecca since she was heading that way. She'd never see her Ma again.

Riley placed his family Bible on the wagon seat beside her. It was important to him. His mother had been gone long before their families had met. The Bible carried the names of many generations that came before. Riley was only two years older than Heather. They'd need every scrap of their shared wisdom to get through this time. Riley's pa was around, but no one wanted a pa like him. Did he even know his son married today? Heather was too tired to ask—weary deep in her bones.

Riley adjusted the Bible and let his hand slightly brush her skirts as he did so. He always seemed to know the quiet ways to lend her strength, ways found during the last five years. Ma's declining health and Heather's need for assistance had given Riley plenty of reason to avoid his own home. And father.

Father?

Could a man like that even be called by such an endearment? Could hers?

Pa left them five years ago, his wife's pain and struggle too much to watch when he loved her so deeply. Heather understood his reasons. Even while hating him for it, there had been many times she'd wanted to do the same. It was exhausting on so many levels standing by, day after day, as a loved one wasted away, but she would *never* trade those last sweet days and years with her ma. Not for anything, not even a moment's reprieve.

But that part of her life was over. Now it was time to leave. She needed to unfreeze her heart. She needed to be out of the house and home where every corner held precious memories.

"To be absent from the body is to be present with the Lord. I think He wrote that one just for me."

Ma's sweet voice inside her memories was only an echo of the real sound. *She doesn't hurt anymore.*

Jesus was holding her now. That was what Heather needed to be thinking on. Not the fact that neither of her parents were here to hold her. She wished she knew where Pa was, though. Wished she could tell him about Ma's passing. She'd written a letter for him and left it at the post office. He would find it if he ever re-turned home.

Her trunks were already in the back of Riley's overly stocked wagon—their wagon.

He fussed with a few things. Cora Mae stood at her side with one hand resting on Heather's leg, continuing to offer silent support. She'd offered to have Heather live with her, and save her this marriage, but Heather couldn't accept. Cora Mae lived with her father, who was intent on getting his daughter married to a man of his choosing the day she turned eighteen. Heather would only be a burden.

Riley returned to his side of the wagon. "Let's go find Rose. She'll want to say good-bye."

Heather swallowed more of Riley's goodness. "That would be good." Tears continued to pour down her cheeks and drip from her chin.

Cora Mae squeezed Heather's thigh and stepped back when Riley climbed on board. His thick legs and shoulders bunched on his stocky frame as he settled on the seat and flicked the reins to set them moving. Cora Mae walked beside them.

Heather didn't look back.

"Don't cry for me, child."

Ma's often repeated words of the last months caressed her like the brisk March wind on her damp cheeks. She let the words and the winds dry her face to match her withered soul. She would obey. Not another tear would splash down.

She wouldn't look back toward the square-built cabin that she'd been born in—that she'd experienced everything in her life to date in. She wouldn't look back to Meramec—this town, the little church, her mother's grave—the place that branded a hole in her soul clearer than the seared scar on the oxen's rump that rocked back and forth with heavy treading steps ahead of them.

Ahead.

That was the only thing she could dwell on that didn't make her feel pulled and weighted. Forward was the only way to move. There weren't any reasons to cry in tomorrow.

Not yet.

Riley sat silent beside her, solid and strong—leaving his only home too. He'd never been anything but kind, and simple, and quiet. He would keep her safe from harm on the outside and the inside, as best he could. He would provide for them both—she was sure. A twinge of guilt fluttered where love should reside.

It didn't matter. *Riley knows I don't love him.* Likely he didn't love her either. Not like that. She cared for him, and he her, and she would let herself cry if she lost him. But that was where the emotions would stop.

Riley was familiar and worn, like a broke-in pair of leather boots—a good fit with no rubs. A simple love might grow from respect, but it would never turn into the raging flames her parents knew.

Good.

That kind of love killed you and wrecked you when it was lost. No sir, Heather never wanted to love Riley so much—or anyone else for that matter. Love like that was a living death sentence.

The wagon rolled slowly down the main street. Bumping heavily in the puddles left from the last rain.

She looked at the side of Riley's square face, not far above her own, as they rolled past first the doctor's office and then the blacksmith's. The wrinkle lines creasing his brow already carried deep concern for her. She would be a good wife to him. She knew how to do that. Knowing how to keep house and home was one of many gifts Ma had given her. Using those gifts would become her new purpose—her way to still feel connected and whole.

The farther they pulled down the main road, the more sucking grief clutched at her chest. The force was so great she wished she could fold into the same dark ground she'd buried Ma in this morning. She bit back a sob—*no more tears*—but Riley must have heard anyway. He reached over his mother's Bible and touched her hand with the back of his. She jolted at the merest brush, but quickly relented and let her hand settle close to his—only bumping when the wagon hit more ruts and puddles. He was her reality. The grief would lead her nowhere—nowhere good anyway.

His voice was soft, just above a whisper. "I understand, Heather. Better than you think. Don't forget this wedding was my idea. Leaving and going to Oregon Country—mine as well. We both need a fresh start. We just hafta keep going until we get to the other side of the Trail. Take each concern as it comes."

She closed her eyes and let his words soak past her fears. A new beginning. It was what they both needed. Her *and* her new husband.

Husband. Riley. The two words together sounded so strange, much like his chaste kiss on her cheek from the wedding. She'd made the right choice, she knew that, but would it ever stop feeling so awkward?

They were almost to the mercantile—to Rose.

She would miss her porcelain doll sisters that still lived here in Meramec. She would miss them almost as much as she would miss her mother. Her heart felt like it could quit beating at any moment with the losses that piled on. They were heavier than the flour sack in the back of their wagon. She hoped and dreamed the Oregon Trail would take her close to Rebecca. Her brave friend had left on a similar start-over journey.

She was glad a letter from Rebecca made it back last fall, before Heather had to leave. She knew where her friend was, sort of. Well, she had an address. If life turned out half as blessed as Rebecca's with a new home, Heather could stand tall in the face of losing everything.

Riley gave her his hankie. Heather fingered the sturdy tick fabric, grateful, again, for his quiet care.

They rolled to the mercantile doors and pulled up. Rose came rushing out, her long legs easily closing the distance to the side of the wagon where Cora Mae was. She thrust a packet of papers into Heather's hand, clinging when Heather would have let go. "I don't know what I'm going to do with both you and Rebecca so far away. I can't stand this."

Heather bent over the side of the wagon, blanket slipping from her shoulders as she gave Rose the biggest hug of her life. Then, sitting back up, she clutched the papers to her chest and smiled at her two friends. The first real smile of the day—wedding included.

"I never could forget. It's part of me. You're part of me. Forever." She didn't think it possible to bury her mother and smile in the same day but her friends had always been precious to her. "Victoria holds all our secrets now; she will hold all to come."

"No matter what?" Rose asked. She grabbed Cora Mae's hand.

"No matter what," Heather promised. "I'll write like Rebecca. I won't keep anything back. If you guys don't witness my life, who is there to care?"

Before either of her friends could answer, Riley's father stormed out of the mercantile, slamming the door and making the windows of the building shudder.

He shook his fist in their direction. Heather put a hand on Riley's family Bible—the one thing he'd asked her to carry on their wedding day—her way of trying to protect Riley from this new onslaught. Could she give him strength she didn't have?

"Get down off that wagon seat this minute, boy! You ain't leaving! You have responsibilities—chores back at the house!"

Riley stiffened beside Heather. The oxen balked at his tightening of the reins. Riley clicked them forward, ignoring the curses his father spat at him.

Heather turned to her two friends, jogging to keep up beside the wagon. This was her last time seeing them. She couldn't let Riley's pa take that from her. "Thank you for this," she said, waving the papers.

Cora Mae's face was flushed red with more than the fast pace. Tears glistened in her friend's eyes. "We'll write back as soon as we know where you are." Her voice wobbled.

"Yes," Rose agreed. "I filched the paper from my brother's supply box. He'll never miss it. He's too worked up about the last town meeting. Not a single person listened to his chest-puffing."

"I'll write. I promise." Heather hugged the papers Cecil had unknowingly donated, careful not to lose her seat in the swaying wagon that was rolling faster and faster as Riley tried to leave his father behind.

"I know you already have it, but I put Rebecca's address in there too. We can't be too careful. We need to keep in touch as much as possible. We have to." There was so much concern and longing in Rose's eyes, it almost brought another round of tears.

Heather had cried so many times during the last year—even more in the last day. Tears never seemed to help much. She sniffed and let the frigid breeze dry her lashes as she clutched Riley's hankie in her fist. The wagon pulled ahead.

"We are sisters. I won't forget it," she called to them, waving.

Riley's pa caught the oxen's reins, tugging them sideways. "I told you to git home. Stop and face me like the man you think you are."

Confused, the oxen stopped. The wagon rocked and wobbled.

Riley flicked the reins out of his pa's hands. "No, sir. I've answered to you for long enough. I ask for nothing that's yours. I take nothing of yours. Kindly get out of the way. I'm leaving."

His pa spat and then uttered another string of curses. Heather's cheeks flushed as folks on the boardwalk stopped and stared.

Heather was glad when Riley ordered the oxen to move again and the wagon rolled forward. This town would always hurt, even with Cora Mae and Rose in it. Leaving was best. The only solution left for her was forward and away.

She called out reassurances to her friends and to herself. "It will be all right. I assure you. I don't know what tomorrow brings, but I know Riley will see me safe."

Riley's pa heard her words and bellowed his own reply. "Riley won't see you safe. He's dumber than a sheep fallen over in a ditch." His face mottled and spit flew with each harsh word. "Too stupid to figure his numbers or his letters, that boy is, and too stupid to travel half a mile without help. You'll see. You'll regret sharing his saddle before the sun sets."

Riley kept his face forward. His hands were white on the reins as he answered back, directing his words to her not his pa. "Those things are true, about the learning, Heather. I'm sure that's no surprise to you. I don't pretend to be what I'm not."

Before he could shrug or make any more excuses, she put a

hand on his arm. "It's a hard day to be happy, Riley, but I'm content. I don't regret my decision." She turned back to her friends, waving a final goodbye. "I'll miss you!"

They both waved their own good-byes. Heather sealed the image of them clinging to each other as she held on to the thought of the porcelain doll and all their sister-promises.

She waved until they were nearly out of sight.

The town shrank behind them as they made their way toward Independence, the starting point of the Oregon Trail. Heather couldn't picture what her future home would look like. She tried to remember how Rebecca described her new place. The more Heather thought about it, the more it didn't really matter what her new home would look like. If she had any say in the matter, they would aim to get as close as she could to Rebecca.

Eagle Creek.

That was the name of the town. She would keep going until she was close to that. She would do her part to cover as much ground as possible, each day, before the wheels on the wagon stopped turning. Would her new husband agree?

Husband.

Her husband.

She glanced back into the wagon bed, at the slim pallet that covered most of the floor between the barrels and boxes of supplies. She swallowed, refusing to even look at Riley.

What had she done?

Chapter Two

Auburn, Oregon Territory
July 1847

*D*avid Vickner sat straight in the oak chair across from the lawyer. He smoothed a callused free hand down his freshly manicured, red beard. Every resource of strength was required for him to sit and look content and settled—nothing out of place— all poised and under control.

He drew up every rich tone he was capable of and added it to his voice. "Thank you for making time to see me. I'm willing to make a cash offer on the estate of Mr. Price. I'd hate to see such a stately home fall into disrepair. Price Mansion has stood as a testament to this town's strength and tenacity to survive for far *too* long to let it slip into decline." He waited and watched the lawyer's jowls and ruddy face to see if he held his attention.

This is the last apple to be plucked before my basket is full.

This project needed to fall into perfect place, or all the other apples would topple and fall. He'd used every trick in the book to land his current bank job. After a year of scrubbing his nose on the backsides of this city's people of prominence, he'd found a way to serve himself. His groveling was nearly over.

My future secure.

Price Mansion would be his crowning jewel—the leverage he needed to finish his masquerade—a plan constructed and built to last generations. He'd never be looked down on again.

David studied his groomed nails, and then went back to watching the lawyer. He wiped his face clean of expression—no better poker face than his, and no one was on to him. He was smarter than Auburn's smartest. His goal within reach. *I'll never want again.*

He already owned two businesses in Auburn to prove his skill at duping the idiots that trusted their money so easily.

Nothing bold.

Nothing too hasty.

Slow and steady, as he'd done before, only better. He liked the challenge of bending the town's leaders until they thought nothing about trusting him as if he was as long standing and generous as Mr. Price himself.

He could see himself in Price Mansion, glass of malt liquor in hand, as he surveyed this town from its upper balcony. His kingdom. He would decide which pawn to move and where to move it next.

He would win.

The lawyer's voice intruded his musings. "It's not for sale."

David nearly came to his feet. He checked himself just in time. "Not for sale?" His face dropped its serene mask. If the lawyer was looking at him, then, instead of at his ledger, the game would be up. He swallowed and tried again. "Not for sale? I would imagine the town of Auburn would embrace the money provided by its sale?"

"I'm sure they would, if that sale was legal." The lawyer smoothed a crinkle out of a paper on his desk, brushing a few stray crumbs to the floor.

"Legal?" Would the buffoon get on with it? David needed the facts. The chess pieces didn't always move the way you expected. He needed the information that would set his next piece into motion. There were no other options for him. Price Mansion needed to be his. *Now.* He would have the house.

David rearranged his face back into normal lines before the portly lawyer was done coughing up what seemed like a week's worth of road dust.

His mind spun, testing several options—to find purchase.

What had changed? He'd checked and double-checked for a

will before he told Jasmine to increase the arsenic. It had to be for sale. "It's my understanding that the estate is empty. With no will. There is no probate. The house will be sold at auction. Correct? Assuming of course, no one steps forward to stake a claim. Isn't that what this town has done in the past?"

If it wasn't for sale, how was he going to shape and influence the investors of this town without it? *Unthinkable.* They needed to see him *in* the grandest estate inside this budding city's limits. He needed the town's trust to finish building the structure of leadership and respect he'd started. *The mansion is the cornerstone to the whole balance.* He needed it to swing the deal with the mercantile in his favor. All his work pinned on things coming together. Sweat gathered at the base of his neck. He needed Price Mansion. He felt like he lived five days in the space it took the lawyer to begin explaining.

"Very right. That is the town policy." The lawyer cleared his throat a final time, dabbed at his flushed cheeks with a wadded hankie, and then pushed the hankie in his breast pocket. "Never had a reason to do anything other than that, when there is no will."

How could that be?

"You found a will?" David nearly groaned but held fast. *I checked with Price myself.* Had someone double-crossed him at his own game?

He thought of Jasmine. *No.* She isn't that smart. She trusted David. He'd already put his mark on her, like Mother taught him. There was no way she would betray him. His mind made laps around all his options as he waited for the lawyer to spit out the next detail. He wanted to throttle the man and then shake him until he spilled all he needed to hear.

"Not only was there a will, the will was read a few hours ago. If you'd like to buy it, you'll have to consult with the new owner. It's off my desk."

David put on all the false charm his years of being the bastard child of a prostitute taught him. "Interesting. I asked Mr. Price if he had a will just weeks ago, and he denied having one."

The lawyer didn't respond as he glanced at his lunch hamper in the corner and then proceeded to set order to his desk as if he was about to leave the office for an important meeting.

Nodding toward the hamper, David tried to rein in his scowl. "Don't let me keep you from your lunch. I'm sure you have important things to do this afternoon and I wouldn't want to be an imposition."

"Nice of you. I think I will." The chair groaned and creaked as the lawyer leaned to the side and snagged the food basket's handle without getting up.

David wanted to squeeze all his frustration out on the lawyer's fat neck. If he'd met the man in his office instead of here in the lawyer's, it might have been a possibility. But now, too many people knew—too many people were watching.

This simply can't be. Up until now, everything had come together beautifully. He had to find a new way. Price Mansion was supposed to be his.

He'd taught Jasmine how to play her part to perfection. She didn't even object when he had her slowly poison the old man. What was it all for—now?

The house would be lost.

The lawyer scanned the contents of his basket. "Thanks be that you inquired about Mr. Price's will. It must've made a difference." He wheezed and coughed.

A difference in what? David wanted to grab the squab's face and make him swallow his too-slow tongue. The lawyer was messing with him. *Him.* He was Scarlett's son. "Pardon?"

David may have been born in the back room of an upstairs parlor in the house of ill repute and he may have spent many suppers tucked away with the cook, the maids, and whatever gutter rat was working off his tick while his mother plied her trade, but because of those experiences and what Mother taught him, he would and could bend any man, any situation until it suited his purpose. He'd learned from the best, and the best always began with patience. He would see this through. Again. He would see this through, now.

The man across from him seemed to be out of breath from his coughing, like he'd run across the busy streets of Auburn and back rather than reaching for his lunch. "Without a doubt. You must've motivated him, where I could not. I've been trying to get him to write a will for the last five years. Without a will, his estate would've been scattered pell-mell. I'm so glad you persuaded him. This is 1847. Things have to be done legal, right and tight, so I keep telling my clients, wills are important. Things shouldn't be left to chance."

There is no such thing as chance in my life.

Did my questions really turn Price? Bile burned the back of David's throat. *If only I hadn't asked.* Was he his own trip up? Still close to the desk, David clutched the edge of the piece of oak furniture that matched the chair he was sitting on, making sure to grip the desk below the lawyer's line of sight. If he squeezed hard enough, David could pretend it was the man's jowly throat. Not that that would fix anything.

But it would feel good.

Price Mansion should have gone up for auction. His name at the top of the list—no contenders. He'd made sure of that. But now?

How could this have happened? "Who did the deceased name as heir again? What was his name? Did Mr. Price have any family to speak of?" David knew the answer with Jasmine feeding him inside information, but the lawyer didn't know that.

The lawyer dabbed a little sweat from his forehead with the dratted hankie he'd just coughed into before he pulled out an orange from his basket.

One that probably cost the lawyer a pretty mint to have shipped in this time of year. *Fool.*

"He didn't have much family. None he wanted to leave the mansion to anyway. That was why he wouldn't write a will, at least that's what he always told me when I tried to get him to."

David asked, "Price had a couple single fellas renting rooms from him? Do they know of any family?"

The lawyer peeled his orange in one long strand—chubby

fingers focused on the fruit before he went on. "It's them, Price gave it to. The two fellas boarding with him got it all. One more than the other, for what reason I couldn't tell ya. The first got a few odds and ends, a family Bible, and Mr. Price's three smoking pipes."

He slid a peeled wedge between his lips and chewed while he continued. "The other fella gets the house and all the furniture and assets. Though the house is pretty much the only asset. Not sure how the old fella intended to stay living in it—as big as it is—and its slowly run-down state. Lots of blunt required to keep up digs like that. Might be a mercy that he went on to be with the Lord when he did. Zeke, the new owner, might be willing to sell to you with all that to consider. I don't know how flush in the pocket he is. But you'll have to consult with him."

David wanted to scream in the lawyer's face. What did the lawyer care if the old man lost the house to death or to selling. The vein in David's neck pulsed heavy. His mind figured faster than an accountant does math. There had to be a way through this. There had to be a way to get ahead of this. Maybe the room-mate, Zeke, would give him something to work with.

David would go see him.

He would be made to come around. He knew who Zeke was around town. He knew most everyone. That was just good busi-ness. But what was Zeke's character? Was he the dirt, truth, and hard work type? *Those were the easiest kind to move out of the way.* Maybe this would all turn out for the better. "You say Zeke, what was his last name, I didn't catch it. You say he picked up his copy of the will this morning?"

"Yes, and the deed. Zeke Bradley. Nice fellow. He won't have to move or anything, since he lives there already. Pretty conve-nient. He was heading home after he saw me, as far as I know. I still need to notify his roommate, Patrick, of his inheritance." He laughed. "If you head over to the mansion and you see Patrick, would you let him know I'm looking for him. Save me a trip?" He stuffed a third of an orange in his mouth at one time.

"If I see him—"

The door to the office banged open. "Fire!" A man ran past in a blur, opening doors and shouting as he went.

David tensed. The lawyer started, dropping a hunk of orange he was about to shove in his mouth. Then, David beat the out-of-breath lawyer to the door and looked toward the commotion.

A dark cloud plumed. Men scrambled from every direction and women stopped to watch with a hand on their children's shoulders. Snapping and popping and a pulsing wind could be heard above the din.

Horses were being let out of the livery one at a time. People cleared the street to stay out of the way of the animals' wild exit. David stayed on the wood walkway and watched as the red glow ate the livery that *he'd* fronted money for just weeks ago. Money he'd gleaned from his fellow bankers without their knowledge or permission. Would this knock a leg off the chair of his carefully constructed life? His mind shifted and planned and replanned and shifted, running through options with the same speed as the frightened horses found their way out of town. Only he wouldn't let the terror of it all show in his eyes as the horses did.

Down the street, the blacksmith shop, next to the livery, was barely visible through the smoke filling the area. David's feet stayed rooted to the boardwalk. He wouldn't budge until he knew what to do. Flames chewed away across the street, consuming their way from the livery toward the meat house. The butcher shop was also an investment property that he'd managed to wrangle since he and Jasmine came to town. The longer he stood there the more folks showed up to work on putting the fire out. They would have it in hand soon, but would the second leg of the chair he was standing on burn to ash too?

While his mind whirled, light, booted steps ran down the boardwalk and stopped beside him. "What are we going to do?" Jasmine's hand fluttered in the direction of the fire.

The quiet whisper was only for his ears, but he checked for eavesdroppers anyway. "Shh. I don't know yet." But if the livery and the butcher shop went for long without an income, then they wouldn't have enough money to land the mercantile. If they couldn't claim a piece of the mercantile then there wouldn't be enough income to rebuild the livery after this—assuming the butcher shop didn't need to be replaced as well. And Price Mansion was the pinnacle—the glue that would hold his whole façade together. *The town needs to trust me long enough for all the income to catch up with what I have borrowed.*

"If they do burn, can you get more money the way you did last time?"

"I can't skim that much without being noticed, and it doesn't make sense that we muddy the waters of the town we want to stay in. This is where we want to live." He wiped sweat from his brow. "You better go. We shouldn't be seen talking."

"But if you don't have any money, then I won't be able to stay at Mollie's for much longer. Maybe we can finally let go of this pretense, and I can come to you."

"None of that now. Stick to the plan." He sliced his hand down but didn't look at her. She would be wearing the same black dress he'd stolen off the clothesline as they crossed the miles to get to this town when they began their plans. The fine fabric was beginning to fray at the cuff. No one seemed to pay it any mind, but it bothered him. If she wore through the dress, he'd have to buy her another or let her come out of mourning. He couldn't let that happen. She was his.

If she wasn't in mourning, then the fellas would come around. He clenched his fist and let the length of his neatly trimmed nails bite into his flesh.

The crackling from the fire grew louder and the scent of the smoke on the wind started to smell heavily of burnt meat—was it coming from the butcher shop or the livery? What move should he make?

Jasmine stepped past him, letting her elbow graze his stomach. He wanted to grab her to his chest and hold on until the worst of this chaos passed. Was he doomed to forever be surrounded by an upset apple basket? Would he ever be still and at rest—without having to watch his back and move the pawns in front of him?

Not now, it seemed, not when all they'd fought for, all they'd killed for was given to Zeke Bradley or burning up in the fire alongside beef and pork. It was his move. He was the only one with all the pieces. He would win the board, but he had to get out from under this. He had to think faster and smarter than all the others, like he always did.

A wagon rolled by, heading away from town. Unnoticed by all but him.

David grinned. He had it—an answer sweeter than a secret night with Jasmine presented itself, and he wasn't a man to pass up a divine gift. *A near miss but not a checkmate.* God bless his mother for teaching him how to think outside the lines.

He whispered to Jasmine. "Watch where I go and follow me in ten minutes. No more and no less."

David took a few steps down to the bank office. Jasmine matched his steps. "You have to wait here." He bent down and hefted one bar of the loose railing from the handrail where he worked. Two yanks and the wood dowel fell from its place with a crack. He looked around. No one noticed or cared. All were running to or away from the flames.

The rounded wood looked like every other railing lining the town's boardwalks. It would do perfectly.

He knew what to do. He tucked the doweling under his coat and looked at Jasmine directly. "I'll take care of us. I promise. Ten minutes." *He won't know what hit him.*

She stepped to the side.

This time he made to leave and let his arm brush across her front as he passed.

Chapter Three

Standing in front of the new mound of fresh dirt in the main cemetery in Auburn, Zeke Bradley tried to understand the old man's generosity. He'd read the will again and again, and it was no help either. He stuffed the papers deep into his pockets, crinkling the will and the deed. The deed to his own property. *I own a house.* Would it be a home without Price sitting in his old stuffed chair? Would it be a home since neither of his parents would ever see it.

The lawyer explained all the ins and outs of Price's will, but he left out the whys. Why him? Why not Patrick? Patrick was a boarder, same as Zeke.

He kicked a hill of dandelions. The white puff of seeds scattered all around his boot. Did Mr. Price feel sorry for him after he told him about his parents' deaths? A pity gift might make sense. But it sure didn't sit well. Zeke thought back through all the conversations they'd had. So many pleasant evenings spent talking about everything from crop rotation to the love of their mamas long since gone.

Maybe it was just that, he'd sat and talked the evenings away with Price for months—with Patrick too. The three of them would enjoy Miss Jasmine's fine cooking and then Price would light one of his three pipes.

Those memories, as comfortable as worn leather, were why he couldn't think about the mansion without Price, especially while he was in Price Mansion. Sitting in the big living room that still smelled of Price's tobacco smoke kicked him in the gut every time.

The fresh grave before him brought no comfort, but at least the raw dirt wasn't steeped in memories. What was he going to do? The two-story white house with rooms he could never fill was his. A wraparound porch, an oversized balcony, looking down over Main Street was all his—his home. There was no one to sit in the second rocking chair. None to look out over Auburn with him. Would Patrick even stay without Price's stories and charm?

Today, Price would have smoked his today-pipe.

I should keep that in mind.

Only thoughts about today allowed. He could still hear Price's voice in his head. *"I wait for weekends for the yesterday-pipe and the dream-pipe. You need to be careful with how often you smoke those two or they can spoil today."*

Zeke didn't smoke. Patrick did. *Was that why Price gave the pipes to Patrick and the house to me?* He shook his head. Pipes and a house—not the same at all.

But since he couldn't figure out why he was given the house, he would keep thinking with Price's pipe principle. Today wasn't about remembering and trying to figure out why Price died or why he'd left him so much. Today was about trying to figure out what he should do with his new estate.

Did he want to live in Auburn?

Would he make enough money as a surveyor to keep it up, or would it be like putting a Sunday dress on a working mule? The today-pipe would help him focus. *I'm supposed to live right now and move forward with what's right in front of me? How do I do that when I don't have anything or anyone to move toward?*

The plain truth was Mr. Price had become his friend—a solid listening ear. He'd cared about the insignificance stuff in Zeke's life. Did anyone else even notice?

He wasn't ready to shake off his grief. Sorrow was sure to stick to him like skunk stink for days. It wouldn't leave him if he left the graveside. Moving forward meant facing the empty mansion. He should leave this place of the dead and walk toward the beautiful, two-story tomb.

He sucked in a deep breath and looked around at the headstones of all shapes and sizes while he built up his nerve to face the house. The barkeep Zeke had seen around town stood a few rows of headstones over, next to an isolated grave. Without any words, turning his back on the barkeep, Zeke walked behind Price's headstone before he left. He reached up and pressed his black, cowboy hat more firmly in place before he slipped a coin out of his pocket and placed it on top of the marker. He paid his respects, and he would come and pay them again and again until he understood why Price had given him the mansion.

His parents could never have given such a gift. They died like worn oxen pulling the load until their bodies broke. His parents worked harder than anyone he'd ever met. For what? They had less than nothing to begin with and barely nothing at the end. Did they even have their pride? He could envision his father's slow nod.

Yes. Father had his pride and would be proud of Zeke—Ma too. He loved and honored the Lord, was kind and worked hard, and Zeke didn't owe anyone anything. He could stand tall and face his father someday on that score. He walked a free man. He wasn't indentured by a bad decision like his parents. He didn't have to carry a written pass from his owner to prove he wasn't running away everywhere he went like his folks. He was truly free.

And he was truly alone—besides Patrick.

Patrick was a new friend. They'd only met when they boarded together this past year. They'd shared a lot of stories to pass the winter. He liked what he'd found in the man, but who knew if he was just passing through. Who knew if either would still be around in a year.

Zeke missed being a part of a family. He missed home where people cared what happened to you. No matter how hard he worked, he couldn't make a family appear. How did you become a part of a family when you had no one? His job as a survey-or wouldn't lead him to lasting friendships. It was solitary work traipsing about the hillsides taking the measure of the land.

He thought of Jasmine and her long, soft yellow hair. Maybe she would be his beginning. She was sweet. She never spoke about her family or her history. *She must have come through hard times too.* Now that Price was gone, if she was potentially going to be *his* family, then he needed to invest in her. There needed to be more to it than enjoying the meal she cooked and admiring her trim waist each time she served Price, Patrick, and himself.

That's where I'll start.

That would be his today-pipe.

Jasmine was his today.

Price would be happy with his decision. And maybe she was a piece of his dream-pipe too, if he handled things well enough.

The road to town, not much more than a wagon rut, ran along one side of the cemetery. When he crossed the thick, green grass to meet it, he chose to walk away from town, away from the noise, away from the people—away from the mansion.

He wasn't quite ready.

He didn't think Jasmine would come by Price Mansion until evening.

He could put aside his surveying projects for the day and keep walking until he sorted himself. The blue sky and chattering birds wouldn't mind his gloom. He could walk out his grief in solitude.

He rubbed the back of his neck and tried to think what he would say to Jasmine next he saw her. The morning dew hadn't dried on the grass blades. His boots were slick with it, but his feet were dry.

Age held Price confined to the big house for the whole of their friendship. It had been several years since his friend had walked down a lonely road on wet grass.

Zeke kept walking.

His parents had been dead and gone next to forever. Even so, his memories of them were as present and real as the breeze on his face. His life's legacy, their gift to him, was wrapped up in the oft repeated words, *"Don't give your life away. Owe no man anything. Don't repeat our mistake."*

Working off their debt wore them down like a nub-pencil until there was no life left.

Price Mansion would take more money than he had to maintain it. If he sold Price Mansion would he tarnish his good friend's memory? The gift, the house itself, seemed to bring prosperity with it. It seemed to represent good standing in the community to all. The smile and handshake he'd received at the lawyer's office that morning wouldn't be the only one of its kind.

Did he need the town's respect, if he was going to turn around and lose it by losing the house since his money wouldn't hold out? Should he double his work efforts to pay for the big house's upkeep and repair? Was there any difference between working himself to death to get out of debt, like his parents had, and working himself to death to pay for something that was too big and too much, just to keep the townsfolk looking at him with an air of privilege?

He could possibly rent a few rooms like the one Price rented to him. Ideas and figures and future chores and projects vied for his attention with each step he took away from Auburn. And always the thought of Jasmine behind it all.

Zeke didn't pay any attention to the wagon standing crossways in the ruts just ahead. He didn't realize it wasn't moving until he could nearly touch it. When he did focus, he noticed the driver slumped and hanging over the side. Red spilled from the back of his head in a thick sheet to the nape of his neck.

"Dear, Lord!" Zeke ran to the man's side, lifted, and supported him down to the ground. The still man was warm in his arms, but the vacant eyes told their own story.

Boot steps scuffed in gravel.

Zeke could see them from where he crouched. A man came around the front of the wagon. "What on earth?" David Vickner, the town investor, darted toward Zeke and snatched a wooden stick from the ground beside the dead man. "Hold it right there. Don't you even think about running away."

"Run away? I found him just a moment before you came around the corner." Zeke still held the dead man as he tried to figure out why the banker was even out here on this road during business hours. None of it made sense.

"We'll let the sheriff decide if that's true. I can only tell what I see with my own eyes. And that is you sitting here with blood on your hands and this weapon beside you, while the town is on fire. What is this anyway—a piece of railing? Did you bring this from town?"

"On fire?" Without letting the man go, Zeke twisted so he could look over his shoulder at Auburn. Sure enough, a black cloud as big around as his new mansion roiled and billowed up into the clear blue.

A gasp came from behind.

Zeke jerked around. The black hem of a familiar dress came around the end of the wagon the same way that David had.

"Jasmine?" Her shocked face convinced him that his troubles were real. She would understand once he explained—she had to. She was always such a great listener. "It's not what it looks like. I was trying to help him."

Jasmine shuddered and turned pancake-batter white. She pivoted away from him and hid her quivering mouth with her hand. The paisley shawl she always draped over her shoulders shifted and almost fell to the road.

And before Zeke could say anything more, David stepped toward him. "I hereby take you, Zeke, under arrest for whatever this is. Until the sheriff can account for your acti—"

Zeke lifted his arms to block the swinging stick a moment too late, delayed by his grip on the dead man. Pain exploded in his skull. Blackness darkened his vision as his ears rang. He tasted dirt and blood before all went silent.

David kept Jasmine from touching Zeke's body as she clucked and fussed. "You didn't have to hit him that hard."

"Mind your peace, Jasmine. I didn't ask *you* to hit him, did I?" David placed the stick beside the dead man in the exact way he had the first time. He stepped over the dead man, ignoring his staring eyes, and shifted Zeke's heavy weight.

He kicked Zeke's black cowboy hat aside when it fell free and rolled in his way. He tugged and pulled until the hulking man, who was at least a half-a-foot taller than him, was next to a tree the size of a fence post. Then he went to the wagon bed and pulled out a rope.

"What's that for?"

"Pole-justice. I'm tying him up. We'll bring others back here and see him arrested."

"But why? You killed that other man, shouldn't we run?" She pointed behind her where the still cooling form lay. "Don't even think about leaving me in this godforsaken town. Things won't be any different than when we came here—if we must start over. You promised this time would be different."

"For heaven's sake, Jasmine. Shut your mouth. Anyone could come along and overhear you. I ain't leaving you. I'm making it so we *can* stay. And maybe even stay together—eventually."

That silenced her.

She came close and watched as he finished his knot. Zeke was still unconscious, lying facedown in the dirt with his wrists stretched out and secured together around the base of the tree.

When David was done, he went to Jasmine and pulled her to his chest. He could still feel the impact of striking both men's skull as it reverberated up his arm. He kissed her rough, pouring all the power pumping through his veins into where their lips met, knowing full well she would recognize and meet his passion.

When he released her, she came up for air, red-lipped and mussed. "Didn't you want me to be with him?" She pointed at Zeke.

"That was yesterday, darling—a million years ago—yesterday. This is what's happening now. We need to get back into town. In the next few days watch for me to give you the sign. I want the full waterworks. Ham it up real nice. Make them believe you are grieving this murdering madman and it will help you get one step closer to us, together, out in the open."

He tucked his shirt back into his pants and adjusted his chain watch that had come swinging free when he swung the piece of railing. He slicked his hair into place with both hands and tugged his vest down. He had to be neat. He had to be the banker—Auburn's trusted leader. "Come look at this." He grasped Jasmine by the upper arm and steered her toward the front of the wagon, crossing around to the side Zeke never quite made it to.

With a glance over his shoulder, he made sure Zeke was still facedown. He could have left him face up and spared him breathing dirt, but why? If David had his way, the man would be breathing his last breath in as short of time as he could manage.

"I had to think fast." Things couldn't be more perfect. Too bad there weren't any big trees in the nearby area. An impulsive lynching could have worked. But now, without that option, it would all have to be legal, right and tight—just like the fat lawyer told his clients. "The fire made for great cover. Sure, we lost the livery and at least part the butcher shop. And as you know, there is no capital left to rebuild." *Those businesses were bringing in the rents to hold up the others, giving me time to get on my feet.* "They will probably close from fire damage at least for a while." *I'm in dire straits for sure.* "Who would have thought that the fire that took so much would also give this?"

Jasmine wasn't looking, she was still staring at the dead man. She wasn't listening to the best part. "Won't someone suspect? It's obvious someone killed him."

"But no one but me knew he had something worth stealing. Townsfolk will be left to believe whatever we tell them." He reached behind a barrel and brought forward a dirty-looking sack. "This is why we are here. That guy brought this sack of gold to me to be valued late last night. I told him the assayer wouldn't see him until this morning. I don't know why he decided to leave town. But it's good for us that he did. I saw him head this way while everyone in town was focused on the fire."

"So, you took his gold?"

David smiled. He lifted the sack. His Jasmine was a sweet peach. Not a trace of accusation in her observation. No squeamish tears and fainting fits. She had pluck and she trusted him— *God knows why.* "Had to be done. If we didn't do something, our gig would have been up in less than a week's time and you and I would both have to start over. I didn't want that to happen. Too much invested. Plus, I like it here."

After checking to see if anyone was coming, he squeezed and rubbed her neck. He wished he could kiss her again or better yet, bring her to his bed like before.

But they couldn't risk exposure. There was still the big house to think of. "I want that house. I want that house with you in it." He looked around again, checking for other witnesses. Taking the risk, he kissed her hard a second time.

She pressed into him like the old days, before he'd rescued her and made her respectable. There was so much about killing the man, taking the gold, and tying Zeke up that made him feel alive. He wished he could bottle the feeling, instead he poured it into Jasmine.

When his blood ran hot and he hit his limit, he pulled her arms from around his waist. "Patience." Speaking as much to himself as to her. "Soon enough we will own this town. You'll have to do your part. This is what has to happen." He explained what he thought would play out.

Once she was caught up, David bowed over Zeke one last time to make sure his chest still rose and fell. He didn't need two bodies to explain away. *That's a cow pie I won't step in twice.* Then he and Jasmine started back toward town with the sack hidden as best as possible.

Chapter Four

"This small cabin will be nice after sleeping under the wagon all these weeks," Heather said to Riley as she settled into her pallet of quilts, glad at least not to be walking in the morning.

They were in Milford. A tiny town in wide open Oregon Country. The pitter-patter of rain outside was complimented by the *ting-ting-ting* of drops falling through the shabby roof into the few pots and pans they possessed.

Heather could see evening light through one of the bullet-sized holes in the rotting wood of the roof. One of at least fifty leaking culprits. *Is this better than sleeping inside the wagon?* Probably not, but she would never have said. She didn't push away when Riley snuggled closer to her under the quilt—the space was so cramped, he wasn't encroaching her space, because there was none to take. He'd left her alone—free to grieve and think. He hadn't pushed her for more all the long months of walking, but the shack was so small he was forced to be *too* close.

Riley was so excited to be here—to be done with the Trail life. "Our first place. Who would have thought? And the rolling hills stretch as far as the eye can see out there—dirt as brown as tree bark—green and growing things in all directions. I'm glad we kept walking to the end. I'm glad we made it here. This is turning out better than what I expected."

She'd never seen him with this much joy and energy. And this was better than what they planned to find, because they had no plans except to leave Meramec and find a place to start over.

Heather listened as Riley said the same thing once every half-hour since they arrived at their new home that morning. It was a beautiful sight. They were nestled in the flat bottom of a valley. Lush meadow in every direction for them to farm and graze, surrounded by hills that rolled off into the distance until they met the massive white cap of Mount Hood.

She lay perfectly still beside him, but her insides still swung side to side, imitating the clunky sway of a wagon plodding over ruts. How long before they stilled?

She would soon find out. This was the first night of many not spent in a swaying wagon. They were home.

Home.

She tried to taste it in the deep places. It didn't fit, but she couldn't do anything to force it to. Who had built such a tiny place? "I wonder who left it."

"Postman said it's been empty for over a year now. Abandoned. And, when a Land Claim is left fallow, then someone else can claim it and prove it up." Riley tucked the thin blanket up to his chin. "It's like it was here just for us."

Riley was never anything but sweet and positive…*and dull.* She stiffened. Why did she have to go on and ruin this almost comfortable moment? He'd done nothing but his best by her for months and he would continue to do so as long as he drew breath.

The least she could do was be civil, even in her thoughts. If he hadn't intervened, she could be homeless, penniless, and helpless, stuck in Meramec, even on her way to being destitute.

"Does that work for you? I won't leave you to fend for yourself for long."

"What's that?" She needed to pay better attention. She would hurt his feelings if she continued to drift off in thought when he spoke.

"I'm gonna start pulling trees tomorrow where the other own-er left off. This rain will make it a little easier. I hope the oxen will have a few hours work in them by then. They've ate their weight in grass today. Their feet don't seem to be so spread flat already."

"It won't take them long to recover around here. I never knew there was a place this green—this late in summer. I'll start the garden."

"A garden is a good idea. The postman said we could put a little store by before the cold weather hits, if we hurry. I want to clear some of the stumps before the fall rains come, to be ready for next spring."

"Do you think he's right about the garden?"

"The postman said most years he harvests all the way through October."

She could almost hear Riley smiling.

"Anything you grow in your garden will help us this first year. It's raining in July—which the postman said happens most years. That makes things easier. Although he said the heat would be back soon." He reached an arm out from under his blanket and pushed a pot so it caught two drips instead of one.

A garden. She would plant the garden and hoe the weeds. Hoe the weeds until she'd grown enough to cook dinner and for meals to store. She placed her hand over her heart in the waning light, needing to feel it beat. She was alive. She still couldn't feel anything. *Yet…*

Why did that "*Yet*" seem almost as daunting as walking for weeks on end, wiping dust out of oxen noses, and burning oxen dung chips to cook their food each night?

Ever since her mother drew her last breath and she rolled out of town, she couldn't seem to draw a full breath. How would she manage to run a home? A home Mama never laid eyes on, that Mama never would see? How would Heather ever begin to be a *real* wife to this man? She'd kept him at arm's length for months now. Survival wasn't supposed to be *this* hard.

How did you do it, Mother? All those days of misery and pain. Never once complaining.

"*I'm not living on borrowed time. I'm living on given time.*" Her mother's words came back to her. Meant to encourage, they only weighed her down with loss. Even when the memories felt like picking a scab, she didn't want them to go away. She wouldn't forget. She would carry them, bearing them. She needed them to guide her into each unknown day.

The long miles of the Trail were a convenience of sorts, now the real work would begin. *I need to come back to living.* Lying here in the cramped space beneath a soggy quilt was not how it was supposed to be. The hollowness in her chest made it easier to let one day pass into the next without more effort than putting one foot in front of another—literally.

Her heart was still so numb. She'd become unfamiliar to herself. Each night when the wagons had circled up, the meal was done, and the fire smoldered, she'd climb into the wagon to sleep. Riley hadn't followed. She could barely miss Mama and breathe—let alone find room for Riley. For a husband. She wished she could write a letter to her friends back in Meramec— or even to Rebecca in Eagle Creek—but that too squeezed the numb-yoke tighter around her chest.

"I'm sorry, Riley. I can't seem to shake it. It's like someone else is living in my skin," she whispered just a little louder than the dripping, surprising herself with voicing her pain. Riley was so patient. So kind.

Riley turned on his side. Without looking too closely she could tell his ratty, long-underwear were even more holey than the ceiling. She could darn them. She should darn them, but he'd have to take them off for her to do it. She swallowed hard. She didn't say anything. She waited the slow minute it always took for him to form his words.

"It will take time. We have that. Not much else, but we have that."

"But what if I never shake it. We walked through it all—deserts, powder alkaline, creek beds, and lava rocks. We saw wagons crushed to bits when they careened down the mountains, the Zuckers got sick, and the Nuits' babies—"

"Shh. Cholera is nobody's friend. We couldn't see all our enemies on the Trail. Here, with you, we know what ails you. Time will fix it." He shifted again so he could see her better.

He carefully pinched a strand of her hair from his pillow and inspected it like it was gold in a creek bed before he tucked it behind her ear.

He took such care and yet never trespassed her space. She had to begin. *Mama would scold me for hours, if she saw the lack of effort I'm putting into my marriage.* It was time to be a wife—if she could just wake her heart from its hibernation. But how to start?

Riley spoke, "When I shared a bunk with my brother, he would hog up a lot more space than you. And he didn't smell so nice."

She smiled. His blue eyes were the handsomest part of him.

"I used to sleep on my side like this." He laid his head on his shoulder like it was a pillow and his arm stretched out above his head nearly touching the shanty wall. If she stretched out her toe, she could touch the wall at the bottom of the bed.

"Slept like that for most of my life. And almost every night I'd wake with a numb, throbbing arm. It always felt cold and heavy, like it was someone else's arm got left out on the porch for an hour. I'd shake it and rub until all the feeling came back, but it took a while."

He rubbed his arm. "I figure you're like my arm always was. You need time. Pretty soon you'll wake up and start rubbing and movin' till the prickling comes. Then once you grieve you can rest easier and move on." He shrugged even though he was lying right next to her.

It jostled them both. "We'll wait." Then he flung the quilt back, dodging the pots and crossing to the tiniest crate that sat next to the smallest river rock fireplace she'd ever seen.

She wouldn't let herself look away from his red, long johns-covered backside. She was his wife. She rubbed her damp palms on the moist quilt.

He seemed so large next to the tiny fireplace. But he wasn't that big of a man—he was more squat than tall. He said they would build on and add a proper-sized cookstove, but how was she supposed to bake in that in the meantime? She didn't think any of her pans would fit if there was kindling and wood in the space as well.

Riley grabbed something and stood with his prize in hand. He slowly unwrapped a china cup he'd rescued from the side of the path on the long walk. "At the beginning of the Trail, this little cup was surrounded by goodness and other dish company of the same sort. Then its world came crashing down around it, leaving behind nothing of the life it knew. But guess what?"

"What?" Heather tucked her bottom lip between her teeth. He never stopped being sweet and caring. Riley struggled to know things, like book learning, but if there was a job or income to be earned for simply being good, and gentle, and nice, he would be a master.

"It's still a teacup. Still beautiful. Still holds tea, and still has a lot of life to give."

"Clever," she said.

He beamed.

Could it really be so easy to delight him? One nice compliment, and he stood inches taller as he placed the teacup on the only shelf in the kitchen. Displaying it as a prize, like he did her.

There was really nothing for it. If she didn't want only the sounds of her mother's scolding voice to echo in her memory, she would have to make an effort toward this kind man before her. *"Better not put off until tomorrow what you can do today."*

Her mother's words again, always perfect for the moment, always painful to her heart. But this time she would obey. "You should leave off your long johns so I can mend them."

He whipped his head around so fast she thought he might strain a muscle.

She wasn't much of a blusher, but at that moment her face was probably the color of his long underwear, and her stomach was as tight as the plank board she lay on. But she couldn't think about anything other than the fact he was taking slow steps back to the bed—*their bed.*

If she survived the next few hours, then she would survive

this lonely country, this home with its tiny fireplace, and—this gaping grief.

Lord, help me.

Water filled Zeke's nose until it burned and streamed down his cheeks. He woke shaking his head and coughing. Still lying on the ground, his arms tied around the base of a tree.

"Good. I didn't know if you were going to come around. What happened to you?"

"Patrick?" Zeke yanked his hands back to try and break free, scrubbing his wrists raw against the tree bark he was bound to. "Untie me, Patrick. The fool David Vickner thinks I killed that guy."

"Pretty grisly." Patrick, who was already untying Zeke, slowed his efforts to study the wagon and the corpse behind them. "Did you know that man?"

"Never seen him before." Zeke scrabbled to his knees and jostled his wrists so Patrick would get back to it. He used the tree trunk for leverage and balance. "David hit me with the same stick that whoever killed that man used."

"Did *he* kill him?"

"I don't know. I came upon things after they were all over. But no one else was around."

"I don't like the feel of all this," Patrick said.

"How do you think I feel about it? David accused me of murder and stormed off to tell the town. Jasmine was with him." Thoughts of sweet Jasmine's face as she looked at him with horror made bile rise and burn the back of his throat. She couldn't possibly think that ill of him that fast, could she? He had hopes that their friendship would turn to more—turn more to family. He was well on his way to loving her, wasn't she the least bit aware of that?

Zeke tugged on the ropes holding him captive.

"Hang on there. I'm working as fast as I can. If they tied you here, there is no way they're gonna leave off accusing you." Patrick continued to work the knot. "None of this seems right."

The knot gave and Zeke sprang to his feet, ready for anything. "I agree."

"I don't trust him."

Zeke nodded. "He was saying words like a sheriff would. I think he was trying to arrest me. But I didn't do it. I was over at the cemetery." Zeke rubbed the lump that pulsed on his temple as he searched the ground for his hat.

Patrick studied the wagon, the dead man, and the road. "You didn't see anyone else here or back at the cemetery?"

"The barkeep was visiting a grave a few rows over. I was there visiting Price after the lawyer said I inherited the house. You inherited stuff too. You're supposed to go see the lawyer. It's all here." He pulled the will and the deed out of his pocket. It was a little rumpled but, other than that, no worse for his lying face-down on it. He found his hat, pulled it out from under the wagon, dusted it with a whack to his thigh, and pushed it back on his head, maneuvering it to miss the lump on his forehead.

"If it was me, I'd keep those papers close. If this isn't about that poor bloke over there, then it might have something to do with the will. That paper has Price and the lawyer's signatures, right?"

The paper crackled and dirt smeared the corner where Zeke unfolded it. "It does. Still can't believe he left me the house."

"David could've been after this poor guy, but if he was after you, and it's the house he wants, it's good that someone saw you in the cemetery, at least."

"The barkeep only saw me leave. But other than that, no one. That's not gonna be enough with how David was acting." Both men looked around at everything, trying to take it all in.

I was walking to clear my thoughts when I saw this whole mess." Zeke waved at the wagon. "Then I tried to help him, David was there." He paused. "He couldn't have known I was coming. I didn't know I was coming." He looked to Patrick, glad for his input. The two only knew each other for less than a year, but Zeke trusted him. "And why was Jasmine way out here?"

"Good question." Patrick reached for the will and the deed and looked them over. A moment later, he looked up, sniffing the air. "What's burning? I smell smoke." Patrick paused and looked around.

"Look there." Zeke pointed behind them to the plume of smoke coming up from behind the tall trees. "David said the town was on fire. Must've happened when I was in the cemetery. You didn't come from town?"

"No. I'm coming through on the way home, back to town, from work. If I'd left sooner, I'd have seen this happen, or at least stopped David from clobbering you." Both men looked to the smoke. Patrick said, "They'll probably have it handled already. For sure by the time I get there." He rubbed his thick paunch.

Patrick was built like a bull with a healthy roll of extra flesh. He was strong. His arms nearly as round as Zeke's thighs. He would've plucked the stick away from David easily enough.

Patrick ran one hand through his hair. "I don't like the possible outcome of all this. There isn't an acting sheriff, and David has some pull in this town. If he wants something, he usually gets it. I wonder what any of this has to do with these?" Patrick handed him back the will and deed. "If he slants the details in his favor, you could lose the mansion or—" Patrick turned his attention to the dead man.

"My thoughts exactly." Zeke's gaze flitted back and forth. He felt an invisible cage dropping over him. He didn't want to think of his parents at all—the shame from either outcome would've killed them, if they weren't already dead. He stuffed the papers back in his vest pocket.

"Here." Patrick reached into his pocket and pulled out a few coins and folded bills. "It's all I've got. Take a trip. Go somewhere."

"But then they'll think I'm guilty, and I'm not."

"What choice do you have? If he killed that man over there, he is coming for you. He will pin the blame on you faster than a rattlesnake strike. He's probably already bent the ear of some. And it will be a strategically chosen some. He is looking to keep his neck out of a sling by putting yours in it."

Auburn was a law-abiding town, but with more folks coming across the Trail, that was changing. Zeke wasn't the only one who thought this basin surrounded by beautiful, white-capped, mountaintops was a pristine treasure. The town was so new, incoming folks believed what they were told as much as what they'd seen with their own eyes.

Zeke had no family here. No ties…besides Jasmine. And apparently David would try to muddle that. He could leave today, but it nettled. He hadn't done anything. *Where is the justice?*

And why did I even ask that question. I know better than anybody, justice isn't always in the cards you're dealt. If it was, his parents would still be alive. His parents would be prosperous farmers—landowners, facing normal things like drought and flood. As it was, they'd worked hard enough to pay off two farms and had nothing to show for it, not even their freedom. All because they were born to poor parents on the other side of the sea.

"You need to go. I'll do the work for you here. I'll stay in the house, listen, and learn all I can. Go someplace far. I'm sure David will have you tracked, so you best hurry. Send word to the barkeep when you're settled. I'll find a way to let him know to expect a letter for me. I'm sure I'll be watched. We don't want any interference."

"There's gotta be another way."

"Might be, but by the time you think of it, you'll be done for."

Zeke stood there, stunned. Was this really happening? He tried to think. His thoughts logjammed. Was he torn about leaving? All his things were back in the house, even his surveyor's tools. He knew he could trust Patrick to keep track of them. He also knew he couldn't use those skills and stay hidden. David knew what kind of work he did.

Being forced to leave town made him feel the all-too-familiar lack of home, family, and connection like nothing else ever had.

He nearly groaned double. Besides Patrick, no one cared enough to stand up for his reputation.

He needed to find the way through to real family and home where he was known. He would be starting over wherever he went. He would be starting over with a dark secret that would keep him from what he wanted most. He'd have to choose not to belong. Not to be known, in order to stay hidden from David, to stay alive. But as long as he chose his own path, he could convince himself that the wife and family and roots he wanted were just around the bend—only a few decisions away—once the air was cleared of this injustice. Home and family would be put off for a while, but that didn't mean forever, did it?

He rubbed the sore lump on his head under the rim of his hat. How hard had he been hit? Seemed like the impact knocked his normal life off balance. As always, life was unfair. He was being exiled.

He was alone.

He needed to run.

"Here, take this." Patrick unhooked his gun belt and revolver. "I'll use yours until we meet up again. Something will shake free eventually. If David is a killer, then we need to make sure this is his last piece of handiwork. And if he's not, then we need to find out who is and why. Go. I'll fill you in on what I find as soon as you settle and give me an address. Head toward the coast and see the ocean for us both, while you can."

Zeke put the gun belt on. The belt sat too low on his hips. He was several sizes smaller around the waist than Patrick. Not to say he was scrawny; Patrick was just thick everywhere.

Before he could decide which way to go, Patrick embraced him and thumped a meaty hand on his back. "It's gonna take all your strength to leave and not come charging back here to sort this mess. Hold strong. It will work out, especially if we work this from both ends. We simply need more time than David's pole-justice will afford. I know the sheriff in the town over. I'll go to Baker, and he'll know how to go about it. I'll ferret something out of all of this." Patrick pressed Zeke's back in the direction of down the road. Then, last minute, he gave him the canvas satchel that held the remnants of his working lunch. He'd seen him empty and fill it with Jasmine's cooking many times during the last year.

"No. No. I don't need that." But Zeke took it with a nod of thanks the whole time his eyes were looking at the tree he'd been tied to. It was like a line was being drawn in the sand of his life—before this tree and after. He determined right then and there that if he lived through the next season of his life, he would come back and prove his innocence. He would pick up the pieces of his reputation that were sure to be shattered like the glass after a rock is thrown through a window.

He would make his own justice.

He would take fair into his hands and force it. He wouldn't give up like his folks. And he would find home—whatever and wherever that was.

"Who knows what you're going to come across before this is over. I wish I had more to offer. Here, take this too. Use it as a blanket until you get one." Patrick took off his heavy, woolen jacket still warm to the touch.

Zeke could easily put it on over his coat. "I'll head West. When I find a place to settle, I'll write."

"Don't write in the next two weeks—too suspicious. And remember, write the barkeep. The house will keep till you get back."

Patrick ran a hand over his face and blew out a breath. "The house will probably be watched, especially if they want your papers. You keep those papers with you always. I'll be sure they know of that, once they figure out you still have them—if that's what this is all about."

Zeke knew he should leave. It was the smart thing to do. There wasn't really another choice—Auburn was unsafe for him. If he stood a chance of holding his head high and preserving his reputation, he had to go. And eventually returning a free man, he had to go.

"And I'll try to speak with the lawyer as soon as I know he isn't in on this too. You best get along. I want a closer look at what happened here before someone comes looking for you."

Zeke left but only because Patrick left him first. History was repeating. He'd left his parents' town after that last awful winter to get away from the stink of influenza. He'd worked his way across the land, picking up a skill along with his Gunter's chain and compass. If he left without his tools, was he even a surveyor anymore?

He broke into a faster walk, feeling hunted. He nearly ran. Several miles away from everything he knew and wanted, he walked under a large tree. Not the right kind or shape for a hanging, but his neck itched nonetheless. He'd better get a good horse as fast as he could. He could work and replace the chain and compass eventually—if he decided it was safe—but a horse was necessary to create distance. It stuck in his throat to do it, but for now, he needed to run away.

Chapter Five

After a long, hot, dusty ride, Zeke was ready to pull his horse to a stop. He'd paid for the bag of bones in trade for farm chores. The animal was nothing to brag about, but he couldn't afford to be choosy. He wished he could tip his hat over his eyes and sleep straight through till sunup, even though the sun was still high overhead. The days since he left Auburn were long. And the ride in the saddle longer.

On the horizon, he could see a stand of trees. His plodding horse would appreciate the break as much as he would. Shade was his goal. He kicked his slow horse into a trot and patted the worn-out animal's neck for doing the work of closing the distance between him and fresh water.

A good wash, supper, and sleep.

The horse stepped steady through the sage and rock on an old coyote trail, nearly lulling him to sleep by the time he was amongst the trees. Once there, he let the horse pick a path into the deeper cover as he inspected all the trees and brush around him—not expecting to find anything.

Zeke brought the horse to a stop by an old firepit with a tumbleweed nested in the middle. A path through the scratchy, scrub led away from the firepit and, hopefully, to water deep enough to bathe in.

He inspected the camp in each direction. He'd been stupid enough to let David get the jump on him back in Auburn. That still stung. He didn't want a repeat. He lifted his hat and wiped sweat from where David had hit him, lump still sore.

Two weeks had passed, but Zeke would never forget.

He sure wasn't about to be caught unaware again. His wrists still burned with the shame of being tied to a tree like a common criminal.

And Jasmine?

What could she possibly think of him? Would she believe David's lies? Had she been around Zeke long enough to know his character? The sight of finding a man clutching a dead man in the road would rock anyone's beliefs.

If Patrick didn't find anything out in Auburn, Zeke may never get the chance to clear his name. Pa always told him his reputation was worth more than any education or trade. What would Pa have done in his shoes? David was stealing away his good name, and there was nothing Zeke could do except chase his thoughts in circles. He dismounted and banged his hat on his thigh, knocking the dust free. The cool breeze on his sweaty brow was worth something. He set his hat on a nearby branch.

After taking care of his horse, he massaged his heat-thick hands together until they loosened. Refusing to chase his thoughts round again like a silly pup chasing his tail, Zeke forced himself to think what would've happened to him, if he'd stayed—if Patrick hadn't come along when he did.

He was glad to be alive.

That had to count for something. If nothing else, it inspired him to keep moving, and living, and breathing until he found his way back. If it hadn't been for Patrick's fast thinking, he'd be swinging from a tree by his throat—turkey vultures and ravens picking his bones.

And even if Patrick didn't find something to go on, a lead. Even if he would be left to wander wild country for the rest of his life—it beat the other outcome.

He rubbed his neck, front and back, growling low in his throat.

I can't control a thing.

There was nothing for him to do, except exactly what Patrick said. To get away far and stay safe until they could settle this mess. He was safe enough but staying sane was being sorely tried. Waking up tied to a tree, replayed through his head yet again.

He scanned the camp.

Nothing but the wind in the leaves.

Beautiful aspen trees in full yellow caused him to stop and stare for but a moment and then he was back after his tail—chasing his thoughts round in circles. Hindsight wasn't helping him one bit.

The sooner he got to the logging camp the better.

Patrick couldn't update him until he sent a letter. He'd decided to be a logger after spending the evening with the broken-legged farmer who he worked with to gain his horse.

The ocean was too far—too far to return to Auburn once Patrick had news. Besides, he needed a way to make a living. He could admit that it might take months and years rather than days to sort it all.

He built a fire first, then banked it and put on a pot of coffee. He would let the coffee work up to a boil while he bathed. A fresh wash sounded marginally better than a full belly. And he was about to get both.

Thanks to the farmer's wife, he had plenty of food options.

With her husband laid up with a broken leg, she'd been so grateful for his help around the farm that he couldn't stop her from refreshing all his tack—*or rather giving me some to begin with*. He continued to find things stashed in his extra pockets. Some he suspected where hidden by her children—the tiny, tin soldier he found the giveaway.

He untied his bedroll and kicked it until it rolled out flat. The blue cloudless sky was letting go to the purples and oranges of evening. A couple early stars would be next. He would stay dry enough this night.

Clean first, then full belly, then he would watch as the entire space above him filled with stars so big they seemed to compete for brightest.

At least the stars know I'm innocent.

Would Auburn have supported him, if he'd stayed and walked

down the street, going toe-to-toe with David? If he told folks what happened…and in so doing called David a liar, would they have believed him?

He flipped through his pockets and found his shaving tack and soap. No reason to hurry. He could take his time and save himself the hassle of a shave in the morning or he could leave the beard, hot and itchy as it was, to hide behind.

After double-checking the balance of his coffeepot as it heated, he scanned to see his horse's hobble would hold, before he followed the narrow trail to the small lake, hoping the blue-green water would cool him before the anger set in and stole the beautiful moment.

He shook his head. David wasn't here.

David wouldn't care a whit that he'd stolen more than his reputation. Zeke wouldn't let David have his peace this night too—even if it took all his concentration to wrestle his thoughts down.

He came through the brush to the lake. It was small enough he could throw a rock from one side to the other. Still enough to see the aspen trees in perfect reflection. He could spend a whole day sitting on the bank studying it, listening to the birds about their business.

He sighed, knowing he couldn't give this place one extra minute. He needed to reach a logging camp and get settled. He needed to send a letter that could find Patrick, so he could hear news. That was the same frustration he'd carried each night when he stopped and each day he wanted to stay instead of go on. But underneath that, Zeke's belly turned in embarrassment. Every time he closed his eyes, he could see the disappointment on Jasmine's face.

He pulled off his boots. *Why was Jasmine even there? What brought her so far outside of town?*

Jasmine cared for Mr. Price for as long as Zeke had been in town. He'd tried hard not to make her work uncomfortable by being too forward, since he was a boarder in the house where she worked. But she'd been there, every evening, when he came home from surveying. He was sure she timed it that way on purpose.

He thought she was watching and waiting for him as much as he was for her. *Wasn't she?* She was so gentle and friendly. How could he keep something that sweet and kind from climbing into his heart?

But why was she there on the road with David?

And why hadn't she been afraid of David as much as she was of him?

The further he came away from that day the more the little questions piled up—How much of the town burned? Did his house, Price's house, still stand? What had Patrick found out? Who was the man killed in the road? Why was he killed? Was Jasmine meeting the dead driver, or was she meeting David, or was she simply out on a walk? Auburn was safe enough, or so he thought.

He rubbed his head again where the bruise was fading. Even after the pain went away, he would carry the mark.

How could Zeke *not* question David? Why hadn't he questioned right then and there? Zeke finished pulling off one boot at a time and then stooped to wash his hands in the water.

His thoughts may be a mucky mess, but at least his skin would be clean. He rose to stand and tug his shirt over his head, grabbing the collar at the back of his neck. He had it half off when he caught movement from his right. In the time Zeke took to suck in his breath, he knew he was a dead man.

So much for staying safe.

So much for not being taken by surprise again.

The warmth of a second body, skin, pressed close. He turned into it. A bowie knife scraped cold against his neck. The sting of a paper-thin cut held his whole body stiff and still. He worked his fingers to finish removing his shirt so he could see. His shirt dropped to his bare feet.

Time slowed. Zeke heard every breath the man with the knife took.

The biggest, darkest-skinned man he'd ever seen stood so close behind him, the water droplets hanging off his shoulders. The giant man blocked Zeke's arm from gripping his revolver.

This is it. I'm dead.

He would die without any answers. Patrick would never know what happened. Any minute now, his throat would spill his life in redness on the dry ground beneath the golden trees.

Cicadas chirped as he waited.

Every one of his muscles flexed taut.

Each nerve screamed for the man to hurry and kill him while he soaked in the beauty—either that or take another thirty years deciding.

His lungs stilled. He couldn't have spoken, even if he could think of something to say. He felt the gulp of his throat press against the knife with each slow swallow.

The man stepped back with his index finger to his lips, shushing him.

Zeke followed the other man's every move while the breeze cooled the sweat dripping down his temple and neck. He clenched his fist, wishing he could reach for his revolver.

The stranger, naked as the day he was born, with the exception of his boots and gun belt, watched him back.

More water droplets sluffed off the man's chest and shoulders. Shoulders crisscrossed with the deepest pinked and bunched scars Zeke had ever seen. Not a single patch of skin was free of them.

What had happened to this man?

And why hadn't he already slit Zeke's throat?

Zeke watched the man's eyes for any indications of his next step and was met with wary and watchful coal-black eyes that didn't blink.

"I caaannno aaaakkkk." The muted sounds of his speech rolled into each other.

What was that? "What?"

"I caaaannnno aaallllk. Nooo tooongggg." He held up his hands, one gripping the bowie, to assure Zeke he wasn't drawing down on his gun and he wasn't going to rush him.

Then, the naked man reached for his saddlebags tucked into the dried grass behind him. Water flung off his fingertips as he retrieved a bundle of paper.

"Hhherrre." The strange voice was awkward yet understandable, if you listened.

Zeke slowly took the wad of paper and found a finely printed sentence.

I can't speak well. I have no tongue. I mean you no harm. How many times had this man had to field an introduction to a trigger-happy loner without a voice to holler hello? "I hear ya. Sorry to barge in unannounced. I'm the friendly sort. You can relax." Zeke tried to set the example and take his own advice. But instead of taking the rest of his clothes off to bathe, Zeke pulled his boots back on. "And you should feel free to put on some clothes."

The man grinned for a split second giving away uneven teeth, but he still watched Zeke with the darting eye of prey, not hunter. Prey that held him at knife point.

The bare-chested man outsized Zeke's six-foot frame by at least half a foot. He would be crushed if they grappled. But the furrows and valleys of the scars on his chest and arms made all of Zeke's defenses temper.

What kind of long nights had this man lived through?

Several circle scars, that could only be cigar-stub or pipe-ash burns, danced along the underside of his arms and neck. The man turned his broad back to Zeke, giving him a full account as he collected the rest of his things from the brush. The man's scars and hind-end disappeared as he headed along the path back toward Zeke's firepit away from the water's edge.

The scars weren't fresh, years old perhaps, but still—so many.

Zeke had spent the last several weeks bellyaching about the fact he'd been clobbered with a stick and tied to a tree for all of one afternoon. The injustice, anger, and humiliation of being tied to that pole may be his to face every day, but what did this stranger carry?

Before he had time to pity him, the big man was back with pants on and his shirt opened down the front. He pointed in the direction of Zeke's camp and gestured like he was going to join him and drink coffee with him.

"Yes. It's fine. Save some for me. Is the water nice?"

"Brrrrrr." He ran a hand over the tight black curls that covered his head. Water droplets splattered and misted in the fading sunlight.

Zeke tried not to notice that the "r" in the word was made from his top lip coming forward like the beginning of a horse nicker due to his absent tongue.

It was hard to turn his back on this stranger. He hadn't killed him…yet. Zeke walked away, trusting the man with his back as he moved to the lake's edge. He needed a few minutes to consider, and he might as well bathe. *How am I still alive?*

And what would it be like to hold conversations with a tongueless man? His ma would raise from her grave and tan his hide if he insulted this stranger. But how was this supposed to work?

So much for a relaxing soak.

He splashed around and was clean in record time.

The tantalizing smell of roasting meat reminded him of the second thing on his list for evening activities. His belly rumbled and protested its empty state. He came back into camp cautiously, sure to make noise as he came up the path. He went to the fireside, straight to his bedroll and put away all his things. His hair was wet, so he took his hat off the branch where he'd left it and placed it on the horse blanket that he was using with his saddle.

A couple grouse sizzled and hissed over a makeshift spit. Food was on the way. His stomach gurgled an amen. "Thank you. You snare those?"

The other man patted a slingshot that ran through a loop on his hip.

"That's handy. I made one of those as a kid. I was never any good at it."

"Heeerre." The man held out a tin plate with the white meat of the bird and black beans and something green. Steam billowed up from it all.

"Thank you. That looks good." Zeke found a perch on a rock that must have served as chair for this campfire. The man left his own plate beside him while he flipped through the pages of a well-used notebook and found the page he liked. He turned it to Zeke.

Name is Moses Giddings.

"Nice to meet you, Moses. I'm Zeke. I'm just passing through. Headed West. Coming from Auburn. Planning on trying my hand at logging up that way. Heard about it from a farmer I worked for. You ever been?"

Moses nodded and knocked his pack over, reaching for a different pad of paper. A leather-bound book fell out alongside the one he was trying to collect. It tumbled close enough to the fire that Zeke darted a hand out and caught it before it burned, without tipping his precious plate of food.

He turned it in his hands dusting the ash from the page on his thigh. Before he flipped the pages closed, he had just enough time to see writing.

Please forgive me. Please forgive me. Please forgive me.

Written a hundred times or more, the words covered every nook and cranny of the page. There wasn't a white space as big as a wheat kernel left. What was Moses sorry for? What had this man done? Did it have anything to do with all the marks lining his body?

"Shh." Or what sounded like a *shh* came from Moses. Moses was waving for his attention as he looked through the end of a shipman's spy glass. When had he gotten that out?

And why?

Moses snapped his fingers and pointed in the direction he was looking through the glass. Several tall trees blocked their view, but if they gazed to the right, they could see the land on the other side of the trees through the dimming light.

A rider.

"I see him. Just one?" He asked it aloud to include Moses.

Moses nodded.

Zeke made sure his handgun was hanging from the right place on his hip. He'd never had cause to pull it. Everyone knew you better not draw unless you intended to shoot. But weeks in the desert traveling alone had his nerves pulled tight as barbed wire.

He would use it if he had to. He wouldn't be pushed around again. He would be ready this time.

Moses tapped the notebook he was still clutching. Zeke gave the other back to him. Moses tucked it into his bag and began collecting his things to move on. Was the man on the other side of the trees coming for Moses, or was Moses always ready to run?

"If you stay with me, I'll do the talking for us. If things get hairy then you could do the shootin' with me."

Zeke looked in the direction of the coming stranger. He didn't care what Moses decided, but he didn't want to watch him make the decision.

Moses pushed his notepad into Zeke's chest and pointed to his small writing. The precise lettering, the same in his please-forgive-me journal, was as tight and square as what you would find in a newspaper print shop.

Careful. He's up to no good. Fast horse, guns at the ready, checking his back trail as if someone's hunting him. Checking his front trail as if he has something to find.

How had Moses written all of that so fast?

"Good to know. Stay ready. But settle back and eat. Let him think he's come across two unsuspecting travelers. If I can move him along without upsetting him, all is well."

Zeke ate the food on his plate without tasting it. He didn't get to savor his bath or his food.

Was this his last meal? *Will I live to see the stars tonight?*

"Hello, the camp!"

"Hello, rider!" Zeke waited for the new rider to come closer. "Your timing is a might poor. We just cleared our plates. We have a splash of coffee left, unless you're in a hurry?"

The scruffy stranger came closer and closer, looking them both over. When he scanned Moses, his hand shifted a little higher up his thigh in the direction of his gun.

Zeke kept both men in his view. Moses looked as wary as the stranger. His scars less visible now that his shirt was buttoned to his neck. The scars on the top of his neck, cheeks, and the back of his hands were there for anyone to see.

"This here is my friend Moses. We're thinking about hitting the timber, trying our hand at logging. You know anything about logging?" Zeke moved with slow easy strides as he spoke. He picked up the coffeepot and lifted it for the new stranger's inspection.

The stranger was still focused on Moses, his hand was even closer to his revolver.

"Don't worry yourself over Mo. If you ignore the fact that he never stops watching you even when you sleep, he's an easy enough guy to get along with. Cooks great vittles." He picked up his almost empty plate and showed it off to the newcomer, hoping to settle him in.

Zeke stepped toward the guy's horse, still offering the coffee, hoping Moses was a good enough shot if things went sideways. The stink of nervous sweat emanating from the rider only confirmed the stranger was running from trouble for sure. "You got a tin?"

The man would either slide out of his saddle and they would be in for a long night of watching and not sleeping, or he would move on and find his way.

Zeke kept talking to cover the tension. "Next town over, the one we came from, is full of nice down-home country folk—they were bragging on their new sheriff. He wrangled a few crooked arrows out of town when we were there. Quite impressive. Whole town is proud of him. The sheriff is little more than a kid, but he has the courage of a bull. That the way you headed?"

Would it work? Would he take the hint?

The man looked in the direction Zeke had ridden in from. Then he whipped his head around behind him. "I have business to the West—searching for family. Looking for a wagon party. Did you see any as you came from that way?"

"No. Sorry."

"I'll take some coffee and be on my way."

Zeke was so close the man could grab the coffeepot handle himself, if he chose. Zeke left no room for the man to dismount between him and the campfire. Moses was enough of a stranger for one night. And anyone who wrote, "*Please forgive me*" hundreds of times was more trustworthy than this shifty-eyed nervous sort.

The rider released the tie on his saddle pack and pulled out a coffee tin.

Zeke ignored the drop of sweat that dripped down between his shoulder blades. He hadn't stood up to David. He was still paying for that, and who knew how long he would have to pay.

He wouldn't repeat that mistake.

Zeke poured coffee enough for both men. The man lifted the cup in salute before he took a scalding sip.

Zeke heard Moses shuffle behind him. He hoped Moses was clearing a path for a better shot. The man eyed Moses long and hard.

"I'll be moving along. Thanks for this." The stranger raised his tin. "Boys. Mo." He took another sip, turned, and rode off in the direction they would go, toward Oregon City, holding the cup to the side, not a drop spilled.

Zeke didn't think it was an accident that the stranger pulled behind the first tree he cleared. Nobody enjoyed the thought of a rifle, or in this case a revolver, pointed at his back.

Zeke understood standing there with his back to Moses with the small cut on his neck still smarting. He turned to the fire to face Moses. "That went better than expected. Do you think he'll keep moving on?"

Moses moved his hand away from his Colt, nodded, and then pushed the paper before him. *Watching you in my sleep?*

"Sorry. It was the best I could come up with. I wanted him to be a little worried, but not enough to shoot us dead on the spot. I wanted him to think we knew each other." He sipped his coffee.

Moses tapped his notepad again.

Zeke read. *I've been to the West where you're going. Beautiful country. But I've never been a logger. Know anything about it? I might join you, if you think there is work enough. Been wandering the flats long enough.*

While Zeke read his note, Moses used his shipman's spy glass to check the horizon for their departed visitor.

"You've been there? That will help. What I know about logging would fit in this coffee cup. What I know about the country we'll be in, and the company of men we'll find would fill the same."

Half true. He was a surveyor and knew his way around the land. He would adapt just fine wherever he ended up. As long as he didn't have to look over his shoulder forever. "I can't promise there will be work, but you're welcome to join me."

What was he doing? Was he crazy? Was he as much of a simpleton as his father always was? You don't partner up with perfect strangers. And you most certainly don't partner up with a man the size of a grizzly that wrote, "*Please forgive me*" over and over again. It wasn't done.

"More beans?" Zeke offered to pour a second helping of the man's own food onto his own plate.

Moses bobbed his head. He seemed meek enough. Suppose it couldn't be worse than traveling alone. "We'll need boots, ones with the spikes on the bottom for tread. The farmer who told me about Camp 13 Logging Company told me that much. And that's it. That's all I know."

Zeke scooped beans on both his plate and Mo's. He was determined to sit and savor this food. He stretched across the fire to give Moses his.

Moses nodded his thanks and made a show of standing and pulling a small stack of folded paper from his pocket.

He fanned the papers out. Six or so different wanted posters passed under his nose. Moses was leaning across the growing fire, unconcerned if he was too close to the flames, pointing at Zeke and then to the poster, tapping his pointing finger back and forth between the two.

"You mean, do I have one of these? Am I in one? No. I'm not a wanted man, though trouble is doggin' my heels enough to make me trot away for a spell. It will work out though, I'm sure. How about you? You wanted?"

"Nnnnnooo." Moses's answer bent and warbled.

"Good. With that straight, let's talk logging. If you've been there, what is the country like? How many days of travel are we talking?" It was nice to have a new conversation, even if it was stilted.

He shoveled spicy beans into his mouth. Alive to every flavor—almost dying made food taste better. Even as he watched Moses scribble fast words, his thoughts didn't leave off thinking about David, the burning town, and Jasmine every living-second.

He needed to get to the camp and send his letter. He needed information so he could go home.

Moses thrust a paper under his nose. *We could be there in less than a week if we ride straight through.*

"That's what we'll do then," Zeke answered.

Chapter Six

avid stood hidden in his future home. He'd been unable to stay away from the mansion—from the search. So much was riding on what Jasmine was looking for he had to come help. She didn't know he was here. He watched Jasmine's loose blond curl rest on the back of her neck as she reached for another set of four books from the bookshelf. Without a sound, he slipped up behind her in the dark and placed his hand over hers.

He clamped his free hand over her mouth to keep her scream muffled. She squealed into his hand and bucked and kicked in his arms. He expected that and tried not to take pleasure as he squeezed her to his chest. "Shh. It's me. Any luck?" He was a little disappointed when she quit fighting him. She may be the only thing he could subdue—at the moment.

She turned in his arms and swallowed up what little space there was between them. "You scared the life out of me." She wrapped her arms around him and nuzzled into his chest.

David wanted to give in to the warm, softness of her. He wanted to turn into her breath on his neck, but he had only one chance to get this right. The scale was tipping the wrong way, and he needed something to put it to right.

"Did you find the deed yet? That fat lawyer said he gave the will and the deed to Zeke. I need it." *It would tip my hand.* "It must be here." *Unless Patrick took it for Zeke.*

"I've looked this house over twice. Every possible nook. I can only use the excuse of cleaning Price's estate so long before they will suspect me. Why do we need it? The gold from the guy in the wagon is enough to fix the livery and plan a barn raising for the meat house. Everyone would come from all around to help us rebuild. Especially since our two businesses were the worst hit by the fire."

"Shh." David stepped into her until she could only either be dependent on him or fall. He grabbed her face in one strong hand and clutched her pretty cheek until she objected, bracing her tight with his free arm. Her small squeal of pain thrilled him more than he cared to admit. "You can't talk about the wagon or the blessing it brought. If we are suspected, our entire ruse will go up in flames faster than the boardwalk."

He let her go. Let her settle back onto his chest.

No one was here in this house with them.

Patrick was at work, wherever he worked, and wouldn't be back for several more hours. "If I can get the deed and it is in Zeke's name, then I can force him to sign it or forge it—we get this house, and our future is set. We'll own our place in this town. People will respect us. We will have what we want, when we want it, always. But I gotta have that paper. The lawyer will know what the original looks like."

He pulled her curves closer more gently this time. "If it's in Zeke's name, then it can still be mine. The town already suspects he is a murderer. If he's not willing to sign it over, we will fuel that belief, track him down, drag him back here, and witness his hanging. Either way, I will marry you and give you new dresses, pretty as any in London, and we will be the king and queen of this town. We're so close. But we *need* that deed."

"Can we get married now? I want to be with you. I'm tired of hiding, tired of wearing black, and tired of sugaring up to *Zeke* or anyone that's not you."

He was glad she said Zeke's name like she swallowed a mouthful of sour milk.

If she even considered falling for Zeke…

David's face and neck grew sweaty and hot in a heartbeat. He clamped his jaw tight against the anger. "Soon," he said, running his hand up and down her soft back. She was more real than any plans he could make. He pulled her and smothered her curves to his.

She was as delicate as Lily had been. It would take nothing to crush her as he had Lily. But Jasmine faced him like he was the rising sun. That was worth something in all of this. She knew his worth. She reminded him with those adoring eyes of hers that he was worthy.

She was as much a part of his ruse as the house. What grand man about town didn't have a sweet little wife at home. He would shelter Jasmine from his worst humors—she wouldn't end up like Lily—as long as he had use for her. She would be pressed into the role of loving, doting, future wife.

He rubbed his hands up and down her arms. "I have nothing real to offer you, yet. This all goes away, if I can't find that paper and get it signed. We need this house. No one would ever question anyone living in a place like this."

"I don't need a place this grand. Besides it will take a lot of money to fix it—I searched it twice. It took forever. I don't need this place—I just need you."

She didn't understand. Without the house it would be like standing in an investment meeting with farmer's clothes on—no one would listen—no one would take his advice seriously. He wanted to be the orchestrator of this town's investments and he would do it from inside this house. This place would be like a preacher's pulpit or a judge's bench. It would give them their final stamp of authority. "I have them all fooled right now. Did you look in Zeke's bedroom?"

"I did. But swiftly. Zeke doesn't have much in there." She went back to searching, pretending to dust.

It had to be here in the house. "The lawyer said he gave it to Zeke, but maybe it could be here in Price's room."

"That's why I'm in here." She shivered before she opened the lid of a wooden box with loops and leaves carved in the top. She pretended to dust it as she flipped through the letters inside. "I don't think it's here. I've looked everywhere. Did you search Zeke? He might have had it in his pocket."

Her back was to him. She didn't see him tense.

He hadn't searched Zeke.

One detail missed.

A detail he'd thought of and chastised himself for a thousand times already. That whole day was planned on impulse. He didn't have time or a chance to make it right. But if he'd had a chance to plan, he never would have made such a grave mistake.

He felt along the underside of linen-lined shelves with Price's folded clothes tucked there, wishing for the feel of paper. He'd used the fire to cover the murder easy enough. An act of random fortune. He'd been looking for Zeke when the wagon with the gold came past his burning livery. It took a great man, with presence of mind, to put all the moving parts together the way he did. And the fact that Zeke stumbled upon them at just the perfect time was providence, if there even was such a thing. He'd have killed Zeke if he'd seen him first—gold or no gold, to get the mansion. This way was unexpected but better.

He wished he could truly savor the sweetness of his plan.

He should have searched Zeke.

David crossed Price's bedchamber to keep searching. Jasmine said she had been through, knowing he wouldn't find anything. He could trust her for that because she wanted this charade to be done more than anyone. She wouldn't leave anything to chance. But he had to check for himself. He shuffled through the box papers on Old Man Price's nightstand that she'd already gone through, just to be sure. More convinced with each new paper that the one he sought was with Zeke.

He pulled up the edge of the exposed feather tick mattress. Jasmine had stripped the bedclothes the first day. They were piled in a heap in the corner along with the heavy quilts Price had used. Would Zeke have slept in the dead man's bed? The papers would be in Zeke's room rather than here. "I'm going to check Zeke's room." He needed to see for himself. But already his mind was switching to which pawn to move to counter this upset.

He wasn't out yet, but he was a step behind.

He hated to be behind.

His mind ground out the possibilities and opportunities. There would be no sleep for him tonight.

Zeke and Moses made quick work of the rest of their trip across the sage fields and lava beds. They were hired on the spot. Camp 13 became their new home—for the foreseeable future. Zeke managed to leave a letter with Cookie before his first day passed in this massive lodge filled with all sorts of loggers.

They were outfitted and working before the first day was done. Now, a full week later both were so sore they could barely climb out of bed in the morning.

They'd unknowingly timed their job hunt with perfection. Harvey, the boss, called The Bull of the wood, was in camp inspecting his crews and his investments when they rode in.

And he put them to work right after he fired two other men— calling them lazy dogs.

Harvey stayed on. Eating his meals in the dining hall like all of them did.

That was where they were now.

Harvey sat by Zeke and Moses and asked, "You say you did survey work before you came here? I'd ask why you quit, but I'm sure I wouldn't get an answer." Leaning over his bowl, so close he had to turn the angle of his spoon to maneuver a scoop, he looked up with the greenest eyes Zeke had ever seen as he shoved a spoonful of food in his mouth. "I have survey work if you ever need it, but what I really need is someone who can read, write, and organize sums—and can count trees before the cutting begins. Most of these yahoos I wouldn't trust with my enemies' mother, let alone my books." He said the last part loud enough for the room to hear and laughed when several gave him grief back.

Zeke couldn't tell if Harvey really did trust him or if this was his normal routine with the new guy, but he could tell Harvey was a businessman through and through, but he also understood his workforce.

Harvey was square built and obviously the man in charge of everyone's paychecks. The entire logging camp of men seemed to keep their heads down around him as they shoveled chili bean breakfast into their mouths.

Zeke scooped a bite and ignored the pain in his flexed forearm. The others told him it would take a week to break in his body to the routine. It had been a week, and he still hurt in places he didn't know had muscle.

"You change your mind and decide counting would fit you better, let me know." Harvey turned away from Zeke before he hollered, "My ride ready, Jiggy?"

"Yes, m'lord. We wouldn't want your feet to be spoiled by the long walk." The room laughed at the fancy bow Jiggy presented Harvey with.

Harvey laughed himself and sallied, "It's a good thing the oxen like you so well."

"Indeed, sir. Shall we go."

The entire group of loggers seemed to push their bowls aside, slide their chairs back from the table, and pull their mackinaw coats off their drying hooks at the same time. Fifteen minutes later, they were down the road, rain soaked, and halfway to the place they would clear fir trees with girths as round as an oxen's belly or bigger.

Moses and Zeke walked in their usual silence, listening to the chatter of the men around them and watching the beautiful wet morning come to light and wake the forest.

Today, they wouldn't be up on springboards sawing like they'd been all week. Today, they'd learn to tie a log to a string of oxen and pull it from where it fell to the counting pile.

Harvey had explained the process to them the first day. Someone counted the trees and made a mark on the ones that would be felled, and the ones that weren't marked were left behind.

Then, after they were cut, the logs were dragged and piled, ready to be put on the large sled that would be pulled by Jiggy, bullwhacking on the backs of eight or ten pairs of oxen. Jiggy, balancing on the first pair of oxen's backsides, would drive the sled while he gave his barking commands, and down the skid road they would go until they came to the nearest mill.

A hard, yet efficient process.

An hour later, Albert, who everyone called Frenchie, had shown them both how to attach the log, then they were walking the eight oxen team and dragging that log. "A little to the left, Moses. Straighten out the back."

Moses had to grip the reins of the oxen in one hand and throw his arm up to tell Zeke what was needed to keep them running smoothly forward. The log they were moving thumped down the skid road until Moses directed them to a clearing that held many logs just like the one they were towing.

They pulled forward as if they'd done it a hundred times. This was the best work for Zeke. He fell into bed so tired every night that he could take a break from puzzling about David's lies.

Mud squished under the log moving forward in front of him. Moses marched the oxen parallel to the other logs. All they had to do was unhook it and roll it to the rest.

Loading Jiggy's sled was not done until later.

The opening with mostly flat ground looked like a small lake made of cut logs. Another logger was crossing the space by jumping from one trunk to the next as wood trunks lay there waiting to be processed.

"Pull up! We're about there! A little more!" Zeke stepped to inspect the space between their log and the one they were going to roll it alongside when Moses turned the head of the oxen.

The flat ground gave no resistance.

The log changed angles and rolled right into Zeke's leg. The weight of it pushed his knee backward at a wrong angle. "Stop! Stop! Hold up!" he yelled. Pain burst white-hot at the back of his leg and made little white sparks dance in his eyes. But the log was already done moving. Moses was done leading. And Zeke's knee was still bent the wrong way.

The other logger crossing the tops of the logs was at Zeke's side in a heartbeat. Zeke held his breath against the pain. Pinned between two logs was the last place he wanted to be.

"Here," a heavy accent said before the logger helping him, with bulging arms the size of Zeke's thighs, rolled the log until his leg was free.

He released his breath on a groan. The pain lessened, but not enough for his liking. He tested it for weight bearing, and it was no good. He limped in the mud, clutching just above his knee.

"Good, Bjorn. That was a good move. Way to respond so fast." Harvey was there, by Zeke, and supporting his weight before Zeke could catch his breath. Harvey went on. "Moses and Bjorn. Go on back. We need a full crew to be safe. I'll take him back to Cookie."

Harvey supported Zeke to the wagon that was set up for the boss just a couple hours ago. He helped Zeke navigate the skid road and the climb back into the wagon. Zeke's forehead was covered in sweat and rain by the time they were rolling back to camp, and the swelling in his knee was pulling his tin pants tight at the joint.

"You got lucky. I've seen so much worse. Turns out, you'll be my books guy after all, unless you aim to leave Camp 13. I'll show you the books tomorrow."

Zeke couldn't believe he was hurt already. It had only been a week. And now he had another worry to add to all those he brought with him from Auburn.

He needed to catch a break.

Chapter Seven

July turned to August and August to September. Heather and Riley found their routine. Most days, Riley was off with the oxen to pull stumps by the time Heather was ready to go outside and face her new garden. The sun warmed Heather's back as she bent over the nursery of green bean and tomato plants before her. She gingerly tended them and fended off bird and bug, even though there was a good chance they wouldn't get to eat the little green tomatoes. But it wouldn't be because she didn't keep the nasty slugs from eating them before the sun could ripen them.

Fall was in the air.

It dried and crinkled the leaves until they were all shades of orange in the trees around them. She worked her garden for a couple hours, letting the warm dirt squish between her bare toes.

A stick snapped and a horse whinnied. She looked up, barely concealing a start. A lone man sat on a dapple-gray horse. He chewed a blade of straw that poked out from the bushiest mustache she'd ever seen.

Heather took the few steps to the gate, closer to where she'd left the old shotgun Riley brought along from Meramec. She and Riley had learned to use it in the last month and keep it close—mostly thinking of wolves.

Realizing too late that she was giving the stranger a full view of her ankles, she plucked her skirts from her waistband where she'd tucked them to keep them out of the dirt and let them fall back around her ankles. She wished she'd put up her hair before she'd come out to tend her plants, it billowed around her on the breeze.

"Ma'am."

"Sir?" She didn't offer to help him in any way. Her skin told her to keep watch. "My husband is working in the back." Finally close enough to draw it up, she pulled the shotgun to a cradle position. The cold metal on her arm was the only thing that kept her nerves steady. "Would you like me to fetch him?"

He leaned over the pummel of his saddle and quirked his eyebrow, inspecting her more closely than she had the tomato plants. "Just passing through—admiring the scenery this beautiful morning. Don't need anything."

She wanted to shiver but made herself stand solid and tall as his gaze made a slow travel over all her form.

"We don't have anything to offer you. As you can see, we're just getting started." She waved at the garden but didn't keep her hand away from the gun for more than the merest second.

"No worries. We're neighbors. I own the land to the north and east of yours—I don't come out this way too often. Didn't know this plot was empty, or I'd have bought it up. The creek crosses into the tree line, real nice-like, way back against that hill."

"Yes, it does. Our oxen prefer to spend their days alongside it. It is beautiful country. The land will grow anything as those *Manifest Destiny* flyers told us they would."

He let his gaze slide over her a second time with the speed and slime of one of the slugs she'd plucked from her seedlings. "I won't keep you now. I'll be back by another time." His bottom lip pressed out in a flat line. His top lip was buried under his mustache.

"Sounds good. Then you can meet my husband, Riley."

His eyes were hard to read. He spat the blade of straw to the ground. "If you decide to move on, be sure to let me know. I'll pay a fair wage for the work you've put into the place."

The cowboy rode his horse forward, right up to the low fencing she'd used to surround the small garden to keep the wild rabbits out. As his horse stepped along, he craned his head back, milking every last drop out of his opportunity to stare at her.

She stayed where she was until he was well out of sight.

Was this how it was going to be? Moving all the way across the Trail to get away from Riley's miserable pa only to settle next to a possible land tyrant? His eyes said he would be just as happy to stake a claim on her as he would their land. She did shiver then.

Ten minutes later she was still standing there, clutching the shotgun, trying to figure out what she was going to do about the creepy neighbor and how or what she would tell Riley, when all four of their oxen came plodding back to the barn with the leathers and chain dragging behind them. "What in tarnation?" *Forgive me, Mama.*

She propped the shotgun back in the corner of the fence and gave one last glance in the direction the neighbor cowboy had left before she slipped to the head of the oxen, crooning the melodies she'd used on the Trail to put them at ease during storms. She led them to their rickety paddock and freed them of their pulling gear. "Where is Riley, boys? Why would he let you walk off?"

Soon after, with stockings on and boots laced tight, she was jogging through the tall grass toward the woods. She didn't know where he was working exactly that day. He'd been moving around all summer. She followed the oxen's most recent beaten down path.

Riley said he was going to unearth one root ball at a time. Hard, dirty work that left him nearly falling asleep in his supper each evening. But he always had a smile for her and kiss for her temple.

"Riley!" She checked her jog into a fast walk, so she could listen for a reply. When none came, she fought back the desire to slow her steps and turn around and go back to the cabin. What she didn't know couldn't hurt her, right?

Something's wrong. Dread spun a web in her belly. If he was hurt, she needed to hurry, not turn back. She called again. Nothing but silence.

A massive stump with roots sprawling up to the sky and covered in fresh brown dirt, gouging a path in its wake, had come to a stop and blocked her view of Riley's workspace. A robin fluttered down, grabbed an earthworm from the fresh turned soil, and flew off.

The tangle of wooden roots was pulled well past the others—farther across the field than it should be, tugged in the wrong direction. Presumably by unguided oxen.

"Riley!" *Answer. Answer. You're scaring me.*

Nothing but the wind in the grass and the chitchat of happy birds could be heard.

She walked into the sun, squinting into its brilliance, wishing the brightness would blind her—take away the need to go forward and see whatever was there.

She came around the stump. Riley was pressed into the dirt groves. Crushed. The root wad had clearly passed over the top of him, catching him in its tangles and dragging him along under its massive weight.

"*No!*" she shouted. "Riley. Not now." *Not when our life's beginning to blend, and we're finding our way.*

She dropped to his side and dusted the dirt from around his head. She knew the truth before she checked him for breath. His ashen skin and caved chest said it all, but she checked anyway.

His pa's words about dying by the end of the week, from the day they left Meramec, seemed to rain over her even as the sun heated her cheeks. He'd made it months not weeks, but this…

She pulled his cold hand into her lap and clutched it. Wishing she could press her warmth back into it. "You aren't supposed to die. What am I going to do now? What am I going to do without you?" There was no way she could run this land. There was nothing here. Nothing established. The shack was little more than a hovel on a great piece of land. She thought of the cowboy with his leering gaze and irritation about her and Riley claiming this plot.

He would be back.

She could try and sell to him, but going to his home would be like willfully walking up on a hungry wolf. He would snatch her up and take her along his path of life without a second thought—she would be consumed.

She would be powerless, voiceless, choiceless.

No.

She had to make a decision before that man found out Riley was—

She couldn't even say it to herself. She kept her eyes pressed shut, rubbing her sleeve across her dry cheeks. On her wedding day, she thought she would cry for Riley if he died, but she was wrong. Here she was. Her well was dry.

She would have to do something—go somewhere, but not until she sent word to his pa. It was the right thing even if his pa was terrible. Would Riley be grieved by his own parent? *If his pa didn't grieve him, the town would.* And she was the only one who could tell them.

She needed to write that letter. No one knew her here. They'd gone into town together a couple times, but mostly she stayed back to tend the garden and the ovens while Riley fetched what they needed. No one knew that the spark of married life that she and Riley had begun to forge out here in this small shack was snuffed out so small there wouldn't be any smoke to signal the loss.

She couldn't make herself let go of his hand. If she did, she would be truly and well enough alone. Ma was dead. Cora Mae and Rose where on the other side of the Trail. They might as well be on the other side of an ocean.

This could not be her life.

She wouldn't start over when it came to family.

Rebecca wasn't too far away. *That's it. I'll make my way to her, mile by mile, if I have to.* She would work and save and find Rebecca. She couldn't surrender to the solitude. She didn't have the strength to begin again—with nothing. She didn't have the strength to carve out a life and defend it here on this land. She wouldn't settle until she was by family. *I must get to her.*

Riley had kept her safe up until now. Riley made sure she was cared for across the Trail. Now, there was no one who could help. Could a person be smothered to death by death itself? Somehow, she hated her pa even more in this moment. If he hadn't left, would she even be here?

Still holding onto Riley, she screamed to the empty land around her. "Pa! Where are you?"

A pair of ravens made their way from the nearest treetop to land in the dirt only yards away. *Raa, raa,* squawking and mocking her loss.

She knew why they were here. How dare they come and steal from her. Each flap of their silken, ebony feathers bore the whispered phrase, "Riley's dead. You're alone. Whatcha gonna do?"

Releasing her husband's hand, she sprung from her place and charged the birds.

The birds only flushed a few feet back before landing again.

"Go! Leave! You can't have him! He loved me. I was going to love him." She cried out from the deepest parts of her soul, but drought staked its claim on her tears the day Mama had died. She'd cried them all out on her wedding day. Riley had watched then and he couldn't see her now—not anymore.

She darted and charged at the pair of black birds throwing dirt clods at them until they finally gave up their vigil and flew away. She collapsed—chest heaving—out of breath.

She tipped her head back until the sun blinded her. "What am I going to do?"

Could she even make her way to Rebecca? She had an address, but she didn't have any money—just the oxen, the wagon, and a few farm tools. She sucked in a deep breath against the vice in her chest.

The smell of fresh-turned soil filled her lungs. She had to send a letter to Meramec about Riley. His people needed to know. It was the next step—after she protected Riley from the birds. Without clearly making the decision, she found herself getting back up and walking to the place Riley had laid out his lunch and tools before his day's work began.

She found his shovel and walked back to his side. Did he know that today would be the last time touching his tools? *No. Of course he didn't.* Why didn't she feel surprised by his death?

She didn't know it was going to happen, and yet somehow this outcome wasn't a surprise.

"Sorry, Riley, for *ever* so much. I'm so sorry." She scooped her first shovel full of fresh, brown dirt that smelled of life and growth and poured it over his still-open eyes.

She scooped and scooped, apologized and scooped until the mound was nearly hip high and shaped perfectly against the root-wad headstone.

There was nothing more for her to do here.

She collected his tools and his lunch basket and carried them in her dirty, blistered hands back to the empty shack. The sun was beginning to settle behind the distant hills. Darkness would come swiftly, but she wouldn't let this day end until she walked back and placed Riley's mother's Bible on his grave and had the letter written and ready to be delivered back across the Trail when she went to Milford tomorrow.

How long before his father would know? How long before those she loved, and those who loved her, knew she was all alone?

Chapter Eight

The next morning, Heather was up in the dark. Sleep was nowhere to be found, buried with Riley. She loaded all their possessions. The months on the Trail were good for something. She knew how to pack everything in the wagon, how to hitch the oxen, and how to handle them.

By the time she would usually be fixing a midday meal for Riley, she was rocking and swaying on the wagon bench down the rutted road. The rhythm more familiar to her than the shack that had been their home for a couple months. She didn't know what would happen with her cabin yet. She'd wait to decide.

Could this really be happening? She didn't know where she'd end up or where she would make camp. *Maybe moving forward will bring me options*—prudent options that would eventually take her to Rebecca's. If Cora Mae was here, she'd have an idea—a gumption.

A basket filled with muffins she'd made when Riley was still alive sat on the bench next to her. They weren't very good muffins. How could they be when she didn't have enough eggs or butter to work with. When Mama was ailing, baking filled a regular part of her weekly routine. She'd used Mama's recipes to make all kinds of pastries and desserts to be sold at the town's mercantile, making just enough money to keep them in medicine for her.

Baking helped the time pass when Ma's pain was great.

Could baking turn into pay out here? In the wilds? Was there even enough people to appreciate it, or did they all live too spread out in lush landscape with its green and fertile hills and valleys around them. Did people have time to stop and eat pastries with all the digging and planting required to survive?

Heather looked under the canvas hoop into the back of her wagon, mentally listing all the baking goods she had left—a few portions of flour in the bottom of one barrel and the sourdough starter ever-prepared. But without eggs, milk, butter, and maybe honey, there wasn't any money coming out of this wagon.

The oxen carried her down the rough road back to the town of Milford. From what she could tell the first time she was there, Milford was a small town, if it could be called that. Mostly it was a group of people who built along the banks of Silver Creek and made a habit of helping each other.

They had their own people.

She didn't.

I don't belong here with them. Her people were back in Meramec, Missouri, and in Eagle Creek—wherever that was.

She pulled up her oxen next to the building she and Riley had entered the first day they'd rolled into town. This was where they'd found out about their empty shanty. This was the mercantile and the post office all in one. *Time to send my letters.*

She jumped down from the wagon, not caring who was watching or what they thought of her unladylike behavior. *"Being a lady is never the question, behaving like one is always the answer."*

"Thank you, Ma." She strode forward. "Now you have me talking to myself." *Suppose that's the way of the future with no one else left around to care what she had to say.*

"I talk to myself all the time. Nothing wrong there." The saucy voice startled Heather. "Get worried if more than one voice answers ya. Ask me how I know that?"

A wiry, trim-figured, dark-haired girl of at least sixteen beat her to the door of the outpost and pulled it open for them both to pass through. "I'm Liza, by the way, and only Liza's allowed to talk back to me."

An older man behind the counter, whose face bunched in a ripple of wrinkles, said, "Liza, you're back. What a surprise."

"Told you I clung as tight as the stink of ten miners, when

I decide. And I decided. Things got to change. I've mulled it over. I ain't marrying no sniveling, weasel-face man who only has enough work in him to feed a mouse, and only helps if he's helping himself to the cheese that ain't his." She muttered, "No good thief." She paced down the aisle of market goods as she said it.

"You been practicing that one." He folded a pair of crisp, new denims and set them on a stack of more denims that were crammed between every kind of menswear needed by farmers, loggers, miners, and herdsmen.

"Practiced all the way over here. I aim to move along as soon as I can. Charley is no good. He thinks he has me over a barrel—him feeding me and all—even though it's me that's cooking for him. He don't know I come here every day to find a new path for myself. Don't you tell him, neither. He already thinks I'm a hoyden and would probably slit my throat, if he found out."

"Won't tell him. Told you I wouldn't yesterday and the day before that and the one before that. You can keep coming and askin', but I don't have any way for you to escape him unless you figure on marrying up with someone else."

"By the bull barley, I'd be slitting my own throat if I did that. Something will give. It has too."

Heather watched the whole conversation unfold as she came into the mercantile. Liza, her clothes more worn and tattered than her own, walked about the aisles picking up items inspecting them and then carefully putting them back down in the exact position they were originally found.

Liza had a tin of beans in her hand when the proprietor spoke to Heather. "Can I do anything for you? Don't mind Miss Liza. We go way back."

Liza's snort-laugh made Heather smile. Was there anything about the girl that was normal and orthodox?

"Waaay back. Almost two weeks now. Feels like a lifetime," he teased.

Heather noted the spark of compassion that lit in the proprietor's eye. He was careful to keep it turned away from Liza.

She held out the two letters written on the paper her sister-friends had given her. "I need these mailed, if you please. They need to make it back across the Trail to Missouri. My husband died yesterday—farming accident." She ducked. Swallowing a lump, knowing the tears would stay checked. "His family is back there. They need to know."

"Are you planning on going with it?"

"You mean, am I going back across the Trail? No. I'm on my own and I don't know what I'd do back there any more than I do here. I have family over in Eagle Creek. Do you know where Eagle Creek is?" She thought about how Cora Mae and Rose would feel if she said those words in their hearing. Cora Mae would scoop her up in a blink, but it was the same dilemma as before. Cora Mae couldn't take her with her, into a new marriage, and Rose didn't have a place to offer.

"Eagle Creek. Ahh. I think that is out past the Quicksand River. Lewis and Clark named it. Most folks call it the Sandy River these days. Nice enough. Ten days…a couple of weeks travel maybe."

She heard his words. She would think about what they meant to her plans later.

Deciding not to go back to Meramec felt like a step toward gumption. She thought about her time with Riley in the tiny shack. She'd changed more than she realized. She wouldn't fit back in Meramec. *Even if Cora Mae was willing, I wouldn't want to go back with her. I would rather face the new and unknown than return to the old.* It seemed like it would be different to go and find Rebecca.

The proprietor was still looking at her, so she blurted, "I can cook. But I'm really good at baking. But I don't have the goods I'd need to do anything worth tasting." Heather pressed her lips closed. If she told this much of her personal business to the first person she came across, she would open herself up to all kinds of danger.

"Two of you now. Well, at least you can cook and bake. That's something at least. Any chance you'd be willing to marry the lazy, two-bit swindler, Charley, Miss Liza's refusing?"

Heather tried to swallow the lump in her throat that instantly choked her at his suggestion. Thoughts of her first wedding day and all she'd lost crashed in—not good memories.

Did anyone ever get married the day after they covered their husband with dirt? She'd buried her mother and married Riley on the same day. *Riley.* Maybe she should marry this new stranger and keep her pattern going. She reached up and rubbed the lump in her throat, trying to draw a full breath.

The proprietor must have sensed. "Sorry."

She blinked and stared at the man with owl-eyes. Not a single tear pooled, even as her soul cried. She shoved all things sad—all things loss—down, locking them away with an iron fist. She dipped her head to acknowledge his apology and then answered his question. "No, sir."

Being alone was the most overwhelming thing she'd ever faced. Up until Riley's accident, her darkest moments had been experienced surrounded by friends and familiar company at least.

"Minus the widowed part, she's like me." Liza came close. Close enough their shoulders brushed when Liza turned back to the proprietor. "You told me about a cook position last week—some logging outfit?" She turned and looked up to Heather. Heather wasn't exactly tall herself. Liza was a tiny thing with a slight hint of curves in the right places.

"I'm not sure the job will still be there. Camp 13 Logging Company's cook is looking for an assistant. He's getting on in years and his old body gives him fits. Hard to keep up with the relentless task of feeding anywhere from twenty to forty men several times a day. They eat more than a pack of grizzlies coming out of hibernation."

"She could do it. Or at least I could, if I could cook," Liza tossed out there.

"Settle down there, miss," he scolded.

Liza slumped, but her brown eyes locked on the man behind the counter, daring him to say more.

"I never said you couldn't do it. But they wouldn't take kindly to eating shoe leather which is what Charley says you cook him every night."

"I get no thanks and appreciation working for Charley. Shoe leather? I hunted that deer myself. The gun knocked me on my rump when it exploded by my ear, but I got him." She shoved her finger into her ear like it was still ringing then splayed both hands palm up. "I harvested his dinner with these two hands. See the thanks I get." She lifted her hands to Heather for inspection.

Liza's hands bore calluses, but they were clean. Heather understood this girl. From what she could gather, her experience was different from Liza's, up to this point, but, if nothing else, they really were in a kindred situation. They both needed to make a way for themselves, or they would be giving their freedom into the hands of strangers. It was time to speak up.

"I can cook. I've made enough baked goods to meet a town's needs before."

Did baking for the pastor's wife's sewing circle and stocking the mercantile with fresh goods count as the whole town? She may have stretched the truth, but she could bake for any number of folks if she had the right ingredients, equipment, and maybe a little help. Liza was watching her, hands on hips.

The proprietor sucked his teeth and studied them both before he said, "Tell you what. You pull that wagon of yours around to the back and tether the oxen. You make me a few samples of both your cooking and your baking and I'll pay you in dry goods and sundries. That way you can show up at this logging company with your hands full. Not that you won't have your hands full with a herd of grubby woodsmen."

"I can do that. Do you have apples?" Heather asked.

"I do. And I have a newfangled wood cookstove that I've never been able to make the same temperature twice in a row. You figure out the knack of it and share it with me and I'll throw something extra in the deal."

"He'll throw me in the deal." Liza nearly vibrated with a *pick-me, pick-me* look in her eyes.

"I can't do that," the proprietor growled.

Why was Liza looking at Heather like she could fix things? Heather had as few prospects as Liza—fewer if you counted Liza's employer who was apparently trying to be a slug-of-a-suitor, which was one possible opportunity more than her. She couldn't give the girl the answer she demanded when she had nothing to offer her.

But she could work in this man's kitchen. It would feel good to bake. She could think things through with familiar smells surrounding her. "Do you have any cinnamon?" When she didn't say a direct *no* to Liza, Liza's face lit as if she'd said yes.

The proprietor stopped folding and straightening items. He looked up at the low ceiling that had things hanging off hooks in every spare inch. "Might. You'll have to see. Might be some on the shelf over there too. I don't have cause to use it much. But you're making me hungry. Hope you can do what you say you can."

A burly man with a broom's worth of gray bristles across his upper lip came in.

The proprietor said, "I have to help him. Head around back. And help yourself. None of the goods are off limits back there. And sorry."

Why did he make that face at me? And why apologize?

"That was ominous," Liza said.

"Agreed."

Liza went with her as if Heather had invited her along and even held the door. The dark-haired pixie followed her out and to the wagon. "I'll help you."

Heather looked at her and smiled, unsure what to say. Things were changing, hopefully moving forward. She appreciated the distraction from all things Riley.

Without words, she and Liza both climbed onto the wagon, and Heather navigated the half-circle that brought them around to the back of the weather-beaten, wooden building. There was a lean-to of sorts beside it—shoddy and by no means weatherproof.

Liza jumped down and worked her way to the lead oxen. "I

don't know how to undo them. But show me once. I'm a fast learner, and I don't waste time."

Heather made short work of unhitching the animals. She hobbled them as she had a hundred times on the Trail.

Liza hovered over her shoulder and then tried hobbling one ox herself. Heather helped her. They walked to the back of the building, and both paused to consider. Looking at each other with wary eyebrows raised, they pulled the latch.

The door swung open easily and on first glance the owner's apology made sense. Dirty dishes were stacked on every surface. The only clear area was a wide, squat rocking chair with wood blocks under both legs to keep it from rocking.

"How many tin plates does one man need?" Liza snorted as she flicked a ragged fingernail across the edge of the nearest one.

"Apparently, one for each day of the month and a few to spare."

"He better give ya a fair shake. This is worse than cleaning up after hogs."

Everywhere Heather looked were empty tins, garbage, and the signs of a bachelor too busy to pick anything up behind himself or take his precious time to put anything in order.

How could this room smell so bad and the store itself smell warm and welcoming like leather, soap, and coffee beans all mixing their scents together.

While Heather took it all in, Liza found the man's washtub. The smaller circular type. She ran around throwing tin plates and dirty dishes into it. "Now, this is where I know how to shine. I can't cook a lick, but I can scrub until the cows come home. And I have a few times. I'll find a pump and start with the table and that surface. Once it's clear and clean, you can start on your part. We can do this."

Liza hoisted the tub of food-encrusted dishes until it perched on her hip. "Can you hold the door? I think I saw the pump out there. I'll bring you in some fresh water before too long."

Heather moved in a circle until she took in every detail. This tiny home was a hovel. Worse than the shanty she and Riley lived in. *Used to live in.* She sucked in a breath. Instead of remembering yesterday, she stepped forward and accidentally kicked a tin cup that held the dregs of dried coffee inside.

When she was at home, beside her mother's bed—even at the end when things were the hardest—she would pray. Her heart missed prayer. Since coming to Oregon, her prayers were as stuck as the coffee sludge was to the bottom of that mug—alongside her tears.

She couldn't muster a single one, prayer or tear, and that broke her heart almost as much as Riley's death. If she didn't pray, if she didn't hold fast to her Savior, what was she? Where would she end up and who would she become?

She wasn't trying to leave the Lord out. She wasn't mad or bitter toward Him. *No. I'm empty.* All hope had poured out of her.

She froze to the spot thinking, wishing she could pray for help, until Liza bustled past, scrubbed the tabletop until her hands were pink, then blasted by her again, presumably back to the pile of pots and pans.

With a clean table before her, Heather turned to the shelf of dry storage, the most orderly part of the space, if you ignored the thick dust layering each container. The proprietor obviously didn't cook for himself much. His meals seemed to be a conglomeration of dry tack, jerky, and whatever came in a tin.

She began to pull the supplies she would need, quietly letting her mind wander. Hands busy while her insides were sifting and sieving everything and anything from the time she left her mother's graveside until she stood here in this kitchen.

With sharp keenness, Liza anticipated her needs. First an hour passed, and then a second. Apple fritters with cinnamon sat cooling on the clean table, a hearty stew bubbled on the stovetop. Fresh biscuits baked in the oven.

"That's the last batch of dishes," Liza announced. "Smells good in here. Think he'll let us eat with him?"

"Here, eat some now, before he comes," Heather offered. "I've been nibbling and tasting all along."

"Don't have to ask me twice." And she didn't. Liza snitched a plump apple fritter and took a big bite. "Oh. Yum. Been wanting to do that since the first batch came out." She talked with her mouth full. "Never had one of these before. Little piece of heaven right here on this earth. *Mmm.*" She made a show of shoving a second, even bigger piece into her mouth. "This body needs a little of that more often."

"Knock, knock," the proprietor called out and rapped on his own back door. "You two've tortured me with those delicious smells for long enough. I closed up shop early so I could see what you were about."

He stepped over the hearth and came right in. The small space shrunk considerably. Heather dried her hands on the cleanest piece of toweling she could find in the cabin. Liza had the rest of towels scraped, scrubbed, wrung, and hung in a tidy row above the cookstove.

They would be dry by the time they had to do the dishes again. "You two make a fine pair. There was enough work here to keep five women bellyaching for a week, but you have it in hand."

He sunk into his non-rocking, rocking chair. "Smells good in here too. And I don't mean the cooking." He grinned at them both like he was a little boy on Christmas morning. "Speaking of cooking."

Heather dished him a large helping. She placed a bowl of hot stew beside the fresh sourdough biscuit she'd just pulled from the oven and slathered in butter. And then picked the biggest fritter to go beside it. *Would he like it?*

She was better for making it—soothed somehow. Still unable to pray, like a loaf of bread when the yeast doesn't take.

But she was settled.

She would go to this logging camp with a mountain of fritters. She would meet this Camp 13 cook. There, she would do her best to be useful until she could make enough money to head past the Sandy River to Eagle Creek.

Eagle Creek was possible.

Rebecca was her goal.

She would write a letter to Rebecca, telling her she was coming, eventually. But it didn't make sense to send a letter now. She couldn't go straight there with the slight provisions she had. Camp 13 needed to work out.

If Rebecca was ready and waiting for her on the other side of all these unknowns, she could make it. She could weather it all without crumbling or falling apart.

The proprietor tucked the last bite of the fritter into his cheek and talked with his mouth full. "Cookie would tan my hide if I kept you to myself. Boy, am I tempted. I haven't eaten like this in a month of Sundays."

Liza spouted, "And you have a month of Sundays worth of dishes you don't have to clean for yourself in the bargain. I think that was the whole reason you offered."

He guffawed and looked sheepish at the same time. "Might be." He patted his full stomach. "But I'm a man of my word. I'll bring you directions to Camp 13, and here is a letter from me, if it will help you." He pulled a folded piece of paper from his shirt pocket and handed it to Heather.

Heather took the paper and showed the man how to use his own cookstove.

"I should be able to remember that. Not sure anything I make will taste good." He patted his stomach. "Cookie is the grumpy sort, but he will trust my word, I think—and as to the dry goods—I filled your wagon with several items. You should check it over before it gets dark."

Heather grinned at Liza.

The tiny, feisty woman grinned back at her. Cora Mae would love her.

Heather and Liza were a good pair. How nice had it been to keep baking and not have to think about cleaning out this bowl or that pan. If they were working to feed a whole crew, meal-after-meal, that could come in handy.

She tried not to think too much about what that would be like. Better to think about making enough money to travel to dear Rebecca.

"I'll open the shop early tomorrow and I'll clear out of here. That way you two can use this place to bake up a sampling of your finest. Just be sure to make a few to leave behind." He grinned.

"I can do that. Are there any more eggs to be had? If you have some, I can make you another supper that will last you a few meals."

"I'll do you one better. You leave me enough of those"—he pointed to the fritters—"so I can have one a day for a whole week, and I'll give you three of my best layers. I have more chickens than I can keep up with. I'll work on making a cage and tying them to your wagon in the morning. And I'll make sure there are enough eggs for your fixings." He licked his lips as he left the small space to them.

"Thank you." Heather almost smiled. She'd done it. They'd done it. The first round was a success. She wished she could tell someone. Liza, looking pleased too, obviously already knew, and they had no one else to share it with either.

Before she could undo all the good the day had brought by remembering what had happened the day before all over again, she blurted, "Liza, you want to stay with me in the wagon? There will be plenty of work for you tomorrow, and it sounds like *we* will be off from there."

Liza bounced in place and bobbed her head.

The proprietor ducked back in. "Here are those directions to Camp 13, ladies. And do you want this?" He handed Heather a black crepe armband to mark her grief. "It was my wife's once upon a time. She doesn't need it anymore. She passed and is spending all her days with our boys now." He didn't wait for her to answer as he shoved them both at her.

"Thank you." Heather took the directions and the armband, more grateful than she could show. She was the only one who would be remembering Riley. No one else could because no one else knew.

"Best of luck to you both," he said as he made his way out the back door.

Liza came close and led Heather out of the room by the elbow as she read over the directions they would take the next day.

Once Heather had read it, Liza said, "I'll gladly stay with you. Can we check the goods over fast and then walk back to my place in the woods? Help me gather my stuff? I don't have much, but I'd rather have it than leave it behind. Maybe leave a message for my family."

Liza has family she's willing to leave behind?

"Sure. Let's do that. I'm bone tired, but the walk will do me good. Tomorrow will come fast, and we have more fritters to make." Heather looked over the goods. "Looks more than good. I'll know better tomorrow if we need to ask for anything more. It would be wise to not use everything up on this first gig, in case we need to have a repeat performance, if Cookie doesn't happen to like us."

"Can you do anything other than fritters? Might get tired of them after a few helpings."

"Ma gave me all her recipes. I brought them with me but haven't used them since I got here. We won't run out of ideas. It's always the ingredients that leave you wanting."

Liza turned them both to the path between the two buildings and across the one dusty street. That was all that made up Milford. They were headed down a deer trail cross-country to the tall stand of trees farther down Silver Creek. Dry leaves crunched under each step they took.

"If we need more ingredients, I'll take to begging. I've done my share of that. Ma and Pa are poor. Always have been, always will be. They ain't doing nothing wrong, mind you, but they're content to live out their life not knowing when or where their next meal is coming from. I think they would be better farmers than townsfolk, but they've never had a chance—never made a chance. My folks love me, but I want different. And I aim to have it too."

Liza's flow of words triggered her own. They sprang from Heather like she'd hit the trigger of a shotgun. "My mother died this spring. Pa ran off a long time ago. He's a good man. He loved

Mother more than he loved anything. She died slow and hard. He couldn't—" She swallowed. How would she explain Pa?

"No need to tell me the ways of the world. I've been around awhile. Pa is gentle as a June bug and just as annoying. He's kind and nice and soft-spoken, but he's never done anything that lasts in his whole life. I love him—gosh, I love Ma too, but I don't want to end up like them. I'm the oldest at eighteen, but my brothers and sister don't seem to mind how my folks do things. I'll have to show them how to do it different. Once I do, then they might see the way of it."

Heather asked, "Are you afraid to go to the logging outfit? I mean, it will be a bunch of men—we could be two lone chickens walking into a den of foxes."

"I had to face all that when I moved away from my folks." She walked on. "The loggers could be as big and solid as a bull buffalo, and I'd know how to give 'em what for. Pa taught me how to protect myself before he let me be a housekeeper for other folks. But that's part of the reason I've got to go. Charley ain't much of a boss. He is lazy as a lapdog, but he's starting to touch and feel where he ain't got no business touchin' and feelin' when all I am trying to do is keep house for him. Why do you think I'm staying away? Why do you think I made my camp tucked away and hidden like this? He needs to cool off and forget about it, before I have to break his fingers." Liza came to a stop. "This is it. Welcome to my humble abode. It shouldn't take us long to gather everything. I may leave some things behind. Not sure."

In the fading light, Heather could see a makeshift campsite. Not a cabin or shack in sight. Just some wool blankets tossed over branches to tent over the bedding. Liza went right over and rolled a collection of old rag quilts up. She tied a leather thong around them and then turned to a box that was holding a bunch of her smaller things.

Heather took the bedroll, leaving the thin girl to pick and choose what she brought along.

"I'll take this and this. I can leave this." Liza flopped a Bible down in the dust.

"Why leave that? It's a Bible."

"Supposed to be my family's Bible. But we just got it. Doesn't even have our names in the front. Pa got it from a dying man." She shrugged. "Ma and Pa don't know how to read or write. I do. Barely. But I don't aim to claim a husband and that means I won't have babies of my own. What's the point? There will be nothing to write in there. 'Sides, it's heavy."

"True. But it's a Bible. Don't you read it for yourself?" Heather felt a guilty wobble in her belly. She'd left off reading hers on the Trail—or was it before that? It wasn't like she meant too. There'd been so much. She missed it. She missed the quiet peace that covered her when she settled with it.

She waited for a quote from her mother to float through her mind, but either her mother understood or Heather was too tired to hear it. It had been a long, couple days. Liza's Bible felt like a long-lost friend come home in her hand—she wished she could walk back and find hers and sit awhile with it.

"Read it? Who has time for that?"

Heather almost laughed. *Almost.* Could Liza read her thoughts? *Ma, you'll be happy. Here I am giving Liza advice that I need to hear myself.* "I usually do. But it's been awhile. I like it. The words settle me—fill me with peace—and they make me remember that God has a plan and it's a lot bigger than the parts I can see today. I'll carry this. It's not too heavy."

"Suit yourself. I can always get rid of it or give it away later, or you can have it." Liza shook her head and went on. "I had this one friend. Hazel was her name. She would always go on and on about the Good Book and Jesus." Liza rolled her eyes and collected more of her things. "Never rode straight for me. No offense. I'm the only one looking out for myself. If I don't figure out what tomorrow holds, I might as well lay down right here and wait for a winter freeze to claim me. Nope. I gotta take care of me." Liza tapped on her chest with one finger, nodding her head.

Her black hair barely moved from its heavy pins. "I need to fend for myself. To trust anything besides *me* to take care of *me* is insanity and only leads to pain." She turned to look Heather in the eyes. "Ask me how I know that."

Heather hugged the Bible, trying not to think of Riley's family Bible that she'd left on his grave. It felt right leaving something Riley valued so much. "There's more to it than that. I'll tell you sometime." After noting the stubborn tilt to Liza's chin, Heather changed the topic. "Anything else I can carry? I have room for one more thing."

"You think we can bake up the fritters fast enough to leave Milford tomorrow?"

"Sure. I need to write another letter before we go." She sent the letter about Riley this morning and now she'd need to update Rose and Cora Mae of where she was headed.

"Let's get back then. This is all I need to take. Let's get that letter written early like." She scanned the sky and kept on talking. "I'll wake you as soon as my peepers open. You do the same if you wake first. I want to get gone before old Charley decides to put forth his thimbleful of effort and come after me. I can't have him touching and squeezing again. It ain't right."

"No, it isn't. I'll wake you. I'll even write my letter tonight while you're giving your stuff a new home in my wagon. I have a few candles left. Do you want me to write a letter to your parents? Are they close?"

"No letter. Can't read, remember? They live in Oregon City. They haven't heard from me since last Christmas when I left. The place we was staying was packed tighter than a pregnant dog's belly. I aim to ask the proprietor to send on a message, if someone comes through heading that way. It would be a lot easier than getting a letter clear back where you came from."

Liza sped them along the path. She obviously had the trail memorized in the growing darkness.

Heather followed her as an idea came to mind. Maybe she could help someone else, as Riley helped her.

"Cast your bread upon the water, you never know when it will come back to you." This time her mother's words blessed more than they hurt. "Liza, do you really think your family would like

to farm? That it would help them? The place I left behind yesterday has a garden started and a small shack. It's bigger than the one we cleaned today, but not by much."

She thought of the man with a bushy mustache that looked her over like a prized hog. He would be angry, but it was hers to give and having people she sort of knew there to watch over Riley felt like a nice idea. "They can have it. I can't tend it. It's too much for me. Do you think they'd mind seeing to my husband's"—she swallowed—"grave?"

"They'd probably love it. Assuming nothing better has come along since I left. Yes."

It felt good to give—made the pressure in her chest loosen a mite and Heather could tell the girl in front of her was happy. Their brisk walk from Liza's makeshift camp turned to a near skip—high with energy.

How did she do it after cleaning all day? Heather felt tired all the way to her toes. And knowing she would spend all day tomorrow working nearly made her groan.

"Thank you for thinking of my family for the farm. It will be good for them."

"Will you want to move back to be with them?"

"No. I'm glad I'm going to that logging camp with you. But I wish that the tadpoles would quit sloshing around in my belly. They're stealing from the happy fritter I put there."

"I know what you mean. I know just what you mean."

What would Camp 13 be like?

Chapter Nine

Auburn, Oregon Territory

David lifted his hand, rapped three times, before Jasmine answered the door. More than a month had passed since he'd claimed his gold from the dead man. He still needed to learn more about Zeke and the deed.

Jasmine opened the door to him. Her soft, golden hair pinned on top of her head. He'd urged her to continue cooking and cleaning Price Mansion after Price died and Zeke left. They didn't need the money she earned since he had the gold, but they needed a reason to have access to the place.

The fat lawyer and Patrick sat with their meals, out of sight from the entrance, as they'd planned for and expected—to catch the two men together with a meal in front of them gave David the most opportunity to glean new information.

Jasmine prepared the meal and had already been invited to dine with the men—as she'd done with Mr. Price and the boarders.

David stepped into the mansion, ignoring the high ceilings, twelve-inch crown molding, and all the other rich wood details that would soon be his, and focused on Jasmine. Seeing wet eyelashes—false grief—on the woman who already proved she would follow him anywhere filled him with courage and desire. He moved close to her, out of the other men's sight, and ran his hand down her arm. He let the side of his thumb trace her curves.

She shivered at his touch.

Covering her response with a coy smile, she said, "Welcome,

Mr. Vickner, Patrick is dining with the lawyer. I'll show you in."
She let her voice carry to the dining room but pressed herself
flush against him for a half-second before turning to play her part
better than any actress he'd ever met.

He watched the sway of her curves, in her black widow's
weeds, as she led the way to the other two men. The town still
didn't suspect they were a couple. This night was off to a great
start. He held all the pieces, knew all their possible arguments.
I'm prepared for every outcome. He would win this round of chess.
No mistakes.

David pulled his hat off and greeted both men—the lawyer
second. "Hello, sir. I didn't expect to see you here. I came express-
ly to see you, Patrick."

Just as David hoped, Patrick turned to Jasmine. "Well, you
found me, I'm here. Shall we ask Mr. Vickner to dine with us,
Miss Jasmine? Would it be too much of an inconvenience?"

David was careful not to show Jasmine any partiality in the
presence of either of these two men. The lawyer had the best
of reputations, even if he looked like a stuffed pig. David knew
better than to underestimate him as a potential opponent. And
Patrick's gaze—as if he could see right through him—made him
wary. David wanted to check over his shoulder.

"I made plenty. I'm still used to cooking for three men, you,
Mr. Price, and for Mr. Zeke." She timed a sob to perfection,
grieving right in front of them all—making it nothing but natural for him to comfort her and still ask about Zeke and the will.

He patted her on the back like it was the first time he'd
touched her.

She turned into David's chest and buried her face. "They're
both gone," she sobbed.

After a wary pause, "Both?" Patrick asked. "Price and Zeke? Is
that true? You have had word of Zeke leaving. But of his demise?"
Patrick waited for the lawyer's answer.

The lawyer took a bite of the green beans swimming in a de-
licious-smelling gravy from his plate. David almost forgot what

Jasmine's cooking tasted like. He wanted to punch the lawyer for taking even one bite of what was his.

The lawyer licked his lips. "No word." He then scooped another mouthful.

Patrick looked at David with an eye that could only be described as smug.

Does that buffoon know something? He was holding out on him. *I'll find out and I'll show him who he's messing with.*

He squeezed Jasmine's arm and led her to her chair. "Poor Miss Jasmine, you've been through enough. It hasn't even been that long since you nearly witnessed a murder—and the loss of your husband so fresh." He turned to the lawyer. "We should have a wanted poster drawn up. I've a man in the next town over who said he's willing." He helped her sit, pushing the chair in behind her. "I could spend some of the manhunt offerings on it."

The lawyer spoke with his mouth full. "There now. I don't think that's necessary. Zeke, *if* he did it, won't be allowed to get away with his awful deed. Not in our town."

My town.

Jasmine shuddered.

Patrick spoke, facing Jasmine. "We'll find the culprits to the tragic death of the man—God rest his soul—you are safe in Zeke's house. Nothing should make you feel differently than when you took your meals with Price, Zeke, and me. I'm sure he has an explanation for his whereabouts, or he's simply off on a survey job." He turned to include David. "Like you said, David, it hasn't been all that long."

"Survey job? I think not. I think he's taken the coward's way and run." David stood behind Jasmine to offer her comfort and pressed her to eat. He watched irritation cloud Patrick's eyes. He pulled in a slow breath and unclenched his belly and fists before he went to his chair.

He needed to collect himself. He took his time pulling a napkin across his lap—always the businessman—always the professional. *Always in charge.* "Still, a wanted poster is a good idea. I'm surprised we haven't thought about it before now. I'll send word to the artist in the morning. As good citizens, it's our job to actively pursue justice."

He looked around the room, imagining himself at the head of his own table. This table. Tall walls, long windows, and thick carpets, the perfect backdrop for a man of his talents. He caught Patrick studying his perusal.

"Lovely home, isn't it," Patrick said, without looking around.

"It never ceases to impress me." Jasmine passed Patrick the creamed green beans.

"Wasted on that murderer," David murmured and ignored the lawyer who stopped eating and glared at him.

Patrick plowed his way through the tension. "Zeke is a family man underneath all his bachelorhood. I'm sure he'll fill every room of this big old place with his brood. Miss Jasmine, *when* Zeke comes back and settles in, you'll have to stand with him at the christening of his firstborn since you've been such a faithful friend—knowing him since he first moved to town and all."

Under the table, David wrapped his ankle around Jasmine's.

She took a small bite she'd cut to a perfect shape before spearing it with her fork. She kept her head down and made as if her food was the most interesting thing in the room, moving her foot closer to David under the table to make his affections easier.

The lawyer made use of his linen napkin. "A fine meal, Miss Jasmine. One of the best I've ever had. No wonder Price kept you coming in to care for him. He always was a wise, old codger."

"Thank you, sir." The close moment passed.

David watched Patrick shoveling his food into his mouth— no longer paying attention to anything. The man was only a few ladder rungs up from idiot. No contest in that corner—even if he did know something.

The lawyer added, "I think it is a waste of time and money, but when you get the wanted poster made, you should give me one. I'll take it around and show the hill folk. They don't come into town often and might know something we don't."

"Maybe Zeke is hiding close by—with one of them," David said, but he watched Patrick closely as he spoke.

There it was again. The smug smirk. "Sure thing."

"You think Zeke could be close?" This man knew something. *I'll have to search the house again.* This time with a focus on Patrick's living quarters. What was he hiding?

Chapter Ten

*H*eather and Liza rolled out before first light. A sprinkling rain turned to a downpour around them. "Think the canvas will keep our goods dry?" Heather asked.

Liza pulled a quilt around both their shoulders. "Did it on the Trail?"

"Yes, but Trail goods were packed in different containers." They rolled along slow and steady until late afternoon. They rested and fed the animals but didn't bother building a fire. They snuggled back-to-back under their quilts, woke early, and set off again, slow and steady. The road, that could barely be called a road, winded its way amongst the massive fir trees, running alongside a creek that had plenty of flow. Deer, rabbits, and red-tailed hawks dotted the way. Liza insisted she learned to drive the wagon. Heather enjoyed the distraction of teaching her. It settled the flip-flopping of her stomach.

The closer they got, the rain clouds cleared off and the road began to change. The track before their wagon grew smoother and wider and in places that would bog down in mud when the fall rains poured. Skid-poles had been cut and laid horizontally across the road. The wagon bumped along the skids. They could arrive at Camp 13 around the next bend or the one after that. Heather read and folded the paper in her hands so many times the edges were frayed and the ink was wearing off.

This is it.

They were on the last strip of land before the directions the proprietor gave them ran out.

Who or what could be next? Was this even smart? Would they be safe? Those and many more thoughts wore the grass down to dirt in her mind. She squirmed on the bench seat.

The oxen bellowed at Liza pulling the lead too tight. Her new friend must be as nervous as her. She reached over and rested her hand on Liza's leg. Riley had done that to settle her on their wedding day. It helped then, maybe it would help them both now.

Liza relaxed, and Heather chose to settle with her. They were a matched pair. She wished she could pour her heart out to her sister-friends. *They would love Liza.*

Why was everything so hard?

Why was she here—in Oregon Territory—in the middle of nowhere when she wanted to be with Cora Mae, Rose, and Rebecca?

Why did things have to get so messed up?

Self-pity washed over her, less forgiving than the bench under her. If she counted her woes and fears she would be tempted to run from life, like Pa.

No. She rallied, "Tell you what, Liza, if this logging gig doesn't work out. Let's turn around and go back to town and cook up another batch of those fritters and maybe some bread. Let's start a traveling restaurant. I have a friend that lives away off—but not too far—if we can turn a small profit with cooking, we can earn our way there. I'd have to learn how to cook over a campfire. It could work."

Liza let the team have their head. "I'm stickin' with you. Like it or not. Closer than a wart. I can't be alone, again. And there's no room for me back with my folks." She shuddered. Heather could feel it in the wagon seat.

Liza added, "Anyone tries to mess with you, I'll scratch their eyes out. You do the same for me?"

Heather chuckled. "Yes. Scratch their eyes out."

Liza was ramrod stiff beside Heather and her words were as serious as influenza.

Heather's worries didn't bother her half so much when she knew Liza shared them. Where would she be if she didn't have

Liza with her. If she was facing this alone? Now, it was her turn to shudder.

"Don't go soft on me. Here's what I learnt. The eyes are the softest part of the body. Scratch 'em. Then you kick 'em in the knackers. Always works. Always!"

Heather did laugh then. Liza's shoulders settled a fraction of an inch lower than her petite ears and she breathed out what could only be a grateful sigh. But none of that mattered now. The building was coming into view.

They were here.

The rutted road with skid-poles for traction in the mud led them straight to the largest log home she'd ever seen. A couple other regular-sized log cabins looked like infant children next to the massive building with CAMP 13 burned on a giant wooden sign.

They pulled the wagon to a stop and took it all in. There was no one in sight. And, for as many logs that must've been used to build the lodge, there were still plenty of old growth firs with girths bigger than her oxen's bellies standing like tall sentries around the place. She swallowed.

This wasn't a home. *It doesn't have to be my home.*

But home was next, if she could earn her keep here.

They finished pulling forward, climbed down, and tied the wagon to a rail. The few steps to the oversized front door had no porch to surround them, and there wasn't a window in sight. Hopefully, there were windows on the back side, or this place would be nothing better than a giant cave.

The wagon wheels settled six inches deep in the muck from many oxen.

By the time she had the animals tethered, Liza had the bundle of fritters secured in her arms. She was holding them like they were a king's ransom, and she was their lone guard. She tiptoed on the rutted patches of driest mud she could find.

Heather understood. If those fritters were dropped, stolen, or ruined, they might not get this job. A traveling restaurant was an idea, but not a very smart or safe one. They would probably survive but possibly not the way they wanted.

Both women knew what was at stake.

Liza's description of Charley's roving fingers came to mind at the same time as the image of the creepy neighbor that watched her in her garden. Hopefully, this would be a better option.

How long would it be before she felt safe—before she felt like her life was her own choice and not blown about by the wind?

She rushed up the steps, avoiding the worst of the muck, Liza beside her when she knocked. The log door was so rough and heavy it hurt her hand to pound. She waited after the first knock, but when no one came, she pounded again with the heel of her hand.

Still no answer.

She shrugged, as Liza balanced the fritters and pulled the bar up from its latch, loosening the heavy wooden door to swing in. They walked in together letting their eyes adjust to the dim lighting of the room.

The wide-open space smelled like cooking meat, sweaty men, and fresh-split wood. Massive wooden tables lined the room with split-log benches and log-rounds at each end. The exposed timber beams that ran the length of the ceiling were bigger than any one man could hug—higher above their heads than a second story.

As she stepped in, Heather felt waffling lumps under her feet. She looked down at the wood-plank flooring. Pockmarks riddled evenly across every square inch, creating their own finish pattern. Two overlarge windows ran the back wall. Each with a couple wooden rails across the center which blocked some of the light but protected the glass. Several flicks of light came from tin pails on the tables filled with some sort of wax candles, softening the roughness of the space.

The largest stone fireplace Heather ever saw sat smack in the middle of the back wall and hooks never more than a foot apart covered the sides of its chimney in its entirety. Shirts, heavy mackinaw coats, and trousers of all sizes hung to dry both there and all over the wall behind it. Socks hung from a couple bars for the same purpose.

It was all so masculine, rough, and massive. It was a safe shelter, but a little daunting, but what did she expect. This place fed and housed a crew of hardworking men. Was there any harder work to be had than felling trees? Maybe pulling roots?

Riley. A rod of grief ran her through, freezing her in place until Liza bumped into her.

Heather took the next step into the room ahead of Liza. She had to do this. She had to succeed here, so she could make it to Rebecca.

The echo of pots and pans clattered from behind the long, split-log high counter that blocked her view of the kitchen. She stood on tiptoe to see over some shelving and spied the top of an enormous baking oven. It was the twin of the fireplace in its massiveness. She didn't even know they made them that big.

She could make dozens of things at the same time on it and in it. She glanced around at all the tables.

I might have to.

After a last quick glance at Liza for confidence, she called, "Hello?"

A pile of tin plates clattered, and a gruff voice bellowed without coming to greet them, "You young, pie-biters can't be hungry yet. I fed you a belly full of fried taters only a few hours ago."

Heather and Liza crept closer to the source of the voice.

A squat, gray-headed man grunted as he stood from the place on the floor where he was bent over trying to reach the right pan amongst many. His hips and knees popped, and he groaned.

"And I fixed ya enough eggs to make the chickens riot—saved them eggs for four days to get enough for you yahoos. Get back to work so I—Women?" He stood so fast the clattering tins fell all the way to the floor, making a ruckus that rattled the windows.

The dumbfounded look on the cook's face was probably the only invitation she was going to get. "My name is Heather, and this is Liza. The proprietor at the mercantile in Milford sent us a letter of recommendation. We are here to help you cook."

Liza already had the basket of pastries up on the counter and was trying to untie the sheet bundling them together.

"We needed another cook, but who said we needed women?"

"He said there was a flyer posting such in town. Was he mistaken? I can cook all manner of sorts and bake anything. I'm used to baking for a town. Suppose this could count as a town."

"I don't need no help. I've filled these boys with sow belly and beans for probably longer than you've been alive." He kicked a pan. It rattled against the shelving. "I'd rather have scorpions in my coffee grounds than a pair of lookers, like you, in this kitchen."

"But haven't you been complaining about your achin' bones—" a male voice said from behind them.

"*Yeeep*." Heather squeaked, and Liza jumped between her and the man coming down a set of stairs that led to a loft office—she could see the top of a big oak desk behind him.

"—the heavy lifting, and your sciatica?" the very male voice continued to ask.

Heather started and pressed her lips tight to keep back another squeak as he came close. Liza wasn't so gracious. She darted forward to stand in front of her like a banty rooster protecting his coop—between her and the man coming toward them. Heather's chest heaved. She glared at the newcomer.

Hard to glare at someone whose kind, dark eyes weren't even paying attention to you, but instead, were focused on the old man, sparring with him. Especially hard to ignore when he came toward them with a limping swagger and a dark, cowboy hat.

"Cookie, you should at least see what she has in there. Smells better than anything that's been inside this building since Mrs. Hershaw brought round a dozen of her blackberry pies."

"I don't cater to no city folk soft-grub, and I'll never warm up to that calf-slobber meringue. You boys have been good with turnovers, airtights, and whistle-berries up until now. No need to change. You're as healthy as the oxen and stronger yet. Don't tell me I let any one of ya starve. Nooo siree. No lean belly ever fed a fat brain. I feed you all like spring porkers."

"I put no slur on your cookin', Cookie, even if you have buried us in beans and bacon. This place would go to pieces without you."

Cookie was about to interrupt, but the tall man put his hands out to stop him. "But yesterday, you were complaining that you hadn't been able to make the ride to town since long before my knee got hurt three weeks ago. They could help with that. If they really can cook, that is?"

Liza had returned to the fritters and finished untying the sheet with her teeth. She had secured it too tight, or her fingers were too nervous for any other effective entrance. The cloth opened and the small mountain of fritters came into view.

Cookie leaned over for a closer look...and smell.

Liza darted behind them all and found the closest tub that was obviously used to carry dirty dishes because a few were inside it. Dirty tins, forks, and coffee cups littered the long tables. She talked the whole time she cleared. "I don't cook, but I can scrub and fetch and carry all day long. That's what Heather uses me for. I keep things clean and coming, so she can watch her oven." Liza pretended to ignore them as she continued to collect the dirties, like she did it every day. "Heather has a whole box of recipes from her ma too. She can cook lots of tasty vittles."

Cookie held a fritter and bit off almost half of one in one bite. The dark-haired man leaned over beside Heather to choose his own. "Good?" he asked Cookie.

Cookie shoved the second half in his mouth, and without chewing said, "Need to test another."

A warm chuckle rumbled from the man beside her. Heather was too intimidated to join in. She could feel the heat emanating from him, and it didn't help the skittering in her stomach any. She turned her shoulder so she couldn't see his face—and he couldn't see hers.

A second fritter had to be a good sign, didn't it? If they turned her away...

The man with the limp claimed his fritter, and she couldn't help but watch both men chew, wishing she was as brave as Liza who strutted right past them all and went behind the counter and made small work of straightening the pots and pans Cookie had been wrestling with.

"I could eat these every day and be a lot happier than with your never-ending pot of beans."

"Yah. So you say, Zeke. But what are we gonna do when the crew gets back? Can you imagine? Two pretty lil' women here? That would be like laying out a rasher of chuckwagon chicken and asking them not to touch."

Zeke.

His name was Zeke.

Did he know that he had a piece of fritter on his dark beard? She nearly growled at herself for noticing. When had she turned herself to include him in the conversation again? She didn't need his dark-eyed, dark-haired, distraction at the moment.

Getting this job was her future.

She locked her eyes on Cookie. It was smarter than craning her neck and blinking up at Zeke's handsome chin like the damsel in distress she was. She dug her nails into her palms. Besides, how could she know his chin was handsome? It was covered in a thick, black beard.

Maybe Liza needed to claw Heather's eyes out in order to keep her focused.

Cookie looked at Heather. Really looked at her. Then he looked back at Zeke. "They'd be mauled like bacon. I won't take responsibility for 'em. No matter if they can cook better'n my ma. And that's a mean compliment, young lady."

Liza popped up on the other side of the counter right beside Cookie. "Don't have to worry about us being carnally tempted. She's a widow for less than a week." She pointed to the black armband that the mercantile owner gave Heather. It was tied above her right elbow. Liza went on, "And I'd rather drink poison than get hitched with a feller. If anyone tries to touch me, I'll skin 'em with this." She pulled out one of the dirty butter knives. Not much of a threat unless you reckoned with the glint in Liza's eyes.

"Liza's right. We aren't looking for attention. We have plans away from here, but we need to build up some money before we go. We are hoping for a short stay."

Cookie turned from Heather to Liza. "You might hafta use that blade, missy. You haven't met Jigger Jones or Frenchie yet."

Zeke tapped his cane on the ground, accentuating his injured leg, which was buried under some sort of bracing and wrap. "You let them try their hand for a week. I'll take on the boys—even Jigger Jones and Frenchie. Even with this." He lifted his favored leg. "I can knock heads if I have to."

"You trying to soften me like butter?" Cookie growled his insult between clenched teeth, even as he wiped the stickiness from his pastry on his voluminous flour sack apron.

Zeke gave one brief nod.

"I'll give in, on one condition. You do take on the boys *and* you let these gals have your cushy digs. I won't sleep unless I know they are locked down tighter than stolen pirate's booty, every night. Your room has a dropping bar that no one could break through. And if you want me to agree, you *can't* go back into the field while they are here, even if your bum leg heals up. You hafta keep the job Harvey gave you in the office. You play foreman, as long as they're here. I want you pushing those papers right up there where you can see and hear everything."

Cookie stabbed a chubby finger at the large log loft that spanned the length of the wall on the opposite side of the kitchen. The loft that Zeke came down from to begin with.

"I'll do it, if I can make my bunk up there too. And not be in the bunkhouse."

"Deal."

"Deal." Zeke picked up another fritter.

"Deal." Liza butted into the men's conversation.

"See you at supper, ladies." Zeke left them standing before Cookie.

Finally. A break. Heather had to turn her back on him before she turned into a puddle of gratitude and tried to hug him. If she didn't feel so tired and empty, she would thank the Lord for His provision.

She ignored the sound of Zeke's cane thumping the timber as he walked away, asking Cookie, "What's the plan for supper?" They needed to know what to do next.

"Wait, Zeke." Cookie waved him back. "My plan is to have you two settled and ready to be locked in for the night, before the boys get back here. Hang onto your bonnets. This evening could be a wilder ride than the time Jigger Jones sluiced his team of oxen, running them down the hillside so fast they nearly tripped themselves." Cookie paused and turned toward Heather. "Let's bring your things in and find a place for them. Zeke will help. And then we'll talk supper."

Why did her heartbeat seem to match the thud of the cane coming closer behind her? She barely knew the guy. She really needed to get through this day and get a good night's sleep.

Liza's whisper was heavy enough for all four of them to hear. "You can grab my stuff, Heather. I'll stay here and make sure he has no reason to change his mind." The grin it left on Cookie's face allowed Heather to follow behind Zeke alone, with no worries on Liza's behalf.

Chapter Eleven

Qeke led the pretty blond out the door. Why had he stood up for her and her friend? Was he hungry for lunch or what? Did he really want to be trapped indoors doing paperwork instead of felling trees in the field? His leg was almost better already. The swelling was improving every day. Did he really want their feminine presence around to remind him of all he was missing with Jasmine? He spoke up, "Carrying things back and forth through this muck will only make a mess. Let's bring your wagon and animals over to the cabin."

He waited for her to come down the steps and stand beside him.

He saw her nod before he went on. "See that building between those trees. That's my place. Now your place. I'll gather my things and move them out while you move yours in. It won't take long. I don't have much."

She still looked a little frightened but matched his pace. "Are you sure you're fine with us putting you out of your lodgings?"

Her soft, sweet voice made him angle his shoulder closer to hers as they stepped around the worst of the muddy path. "I've only been here in this cabin a few weeks. I stayed in the bunkhouse before I hurt my knee. I'm not attached to this place yet, and once my leg heals, I'll be back in the bunkhouse." *Unless you're still here.* He left the last words unsaid.

Her cool-blue eyes were staring up at him like he was a coyote hunting a mouse, ready to pounce on her at any second. He untied the reins from the rails. "Here. Let me help you circle this around." He gripped her thin arm while she climbed into her wagon as if they were at Sunday church. "Miss Heather. Right?" He went to the head of the wagon and pulled the lead to follow him.

"Yes."

Her soft voice ran over him like a clean, misty rain as the wagon rolled forward. She was such a contrast to her spitfire friend. He tried to think of something to ask her, so he might hear her speak again, but nothing came to mind.

"Cookie called you Zeke, right?"

He grinned. "At your service." He turned so she could see his smile before he offered a mock bow. He tried to make the use of his cane look regal as he walked alongside the wagon and oxen the thirty yards that made the distance to where he'd been bunking since he was hurt.

Moses was still out cutting trees with the rest of the men, but there was no way Zeke could keep the pace with a gimpy step. Such a shame he twisted his knee at all. Everyone said he should count himself lucky he wasn't crushed—that he wasn't down permanently. They were right. But he hated to be so confined—especially since he could get news from Patrick to come back home any day.

His leg was on the mend. Getting stronger every day. Surveying for the boss was something he could do at his own speed, with his cane. He went ahead of the crew and scouted, counted, and tagged the trees that would be brought in. He could do that with a limp.

The job was a good enough fit. He was still out in the field when he wasn't copying his findings into the log books in the loft office.

He swallowed the part of his pride that couldn't deny that he was here, helping the soft-spoken blond, because he was a little removed from the main group, *again*. Even here at Camp 13 there were no roots or family for him. His chest pressed.

Unless he counted Moses. Could Moses even be counted as family?

"We can leave the dry goods in the wagon." Heather climbed

down from her wagon seat and filled her arms. "I'm sure Cookie will have to move things around to accommodate them."

He stayed ahead of her and began to head into the small log cabin, but hesitated. "Let's start with personal things. I'll bring my stuff out and put them there." He pointed to the spare corner of the wagon bed. "And you can start bringing yours in as soon as I make space."

"I'll bring Liza's in too. None of our things are very heavy." She curled her arms around a bundle of quilts.

They took turns being outside and inside like some sort of unplanned dance. Zeke was on his last trip out when he met her at the doorway. He lifted his things high, and she ducked. Sliding past him, she grazed his chest with her shoulder. All his senses lit. And then guilt poured cold.

Cookie would have killed him on the spot. *She may be pretty—beautiful in fact—but Cookie said hands off, and she's not Jasmine.* He studied her as she went about the cabin.

He really needed to hear from home—from Patrick. He rubbed his sore knee. How long had his letter taken to return to the barkeep for Patrick. "It's been long enough."

"What was that?" she asked from around the corner.

"Sorry. I was talking to myself. If I'm not careful I might turn into one of those old codgers who plays both sides of a chess match. I could blame it on too much time out here in the woods, but I'm afraid that would be a falsehood. I'll probably talk to myself at the next place I work too."

"I've been doing that recently as well. You don't plan to stay on here either?" She came back to the wagon for another load.

He paused before her. *What had her thoughts churning so much she talked to herself.* "No. I'm passing through, but I'll be staying for a while. Until this knee heals at the least." *Come on, Patrick, send me word. I'm turning into a loon.* He reached into the back of the wagon and gathered an armful of the ladies' things. Heather right behind him. He felt more than saw her stiffen when he turned to fill her arms. She stood as straight as an axe handle now that he was so close and facing her.

CARA GRANDLE

He held the bundle of clothes a space longer before he released them into her hands. "I'm sorry for your loss. My folks both passed a couple years ago. It's never easy to say good-bye."

He didn't stay by her side to see her reaction. He left her arms full and turned back and plucked a small wooden crate of their things and headed toward his old cabin.

She might not appreciate a stranger poking at her wounds, but he felt compelled to thaw the frost haloing her anyway. It would give him something to focus on while he waited—while his knee healed. It would've been nice if there had been someone to reach out to him those first months after his folks passed.

Camp 13 was big enough to house a horde of men, but two defenseless females, one with eyes that swam with pain, he wasn't sure it would hold up. *Don't grow too attached.* He set the crate on the floor at the foot of his bed—her bed. His neck grew warm.

Zeke stripped his quilt and wool blanket off the mattress, before he went out for another armload. He left the sheeting. It wasn't clean, but he couldn't do anything about that and figured the ladies would want to have it anyway. On his way out, he was going to pass her in the doorway again.

He hoped.

The feathery curls that danced around her forehead played in the breeze as she stopped and waited for him to come out instead of passing him like he'd done before. Why did it feel like someone took something from him?

The dance continued. He came out. She went in. "Only one more load to go. Liza and I will settle in later. I think it's best if I head back to the kitchen and help work on supper."

He lifted the last of their things. "By all means. If you impress the crew, then Cookie won't be able to send you away even if he uses a whole keg of gunpowder to blast you out. The boys are partial to their food. What goes in their belly is usually the highlight of their day. You feed them good, and they will champion you fearlessly."

After her stuff was settled, he climbed into her wagon. "I'll settle your stock and add your chickens to our coop." He gathered the reins. "And I'll have some fellas carry your dry goods in later."

She gave him an agreeable smile and then turned away as if she was shielding herself from him. Coming to the logging camp full of strange men would feel like Daniel walking into the lion's den on purpose. He spoke to her back. "My girl back home is a widow. Not an easy thing."

She was holding her skirts out of the mud when she turned and gave him a nod.

There was no understanding between him and Jasmine, but this shy creature didn't need to know that. Especially, since it was his chief desire to get back to Jasmine and make her his girl. Stepping out with Jasmine was the first thing on his to-do list when he made it back to Auburn with a cleared reputation. He needed some truth in his life. Not all the hiding and holding back. He wasn't good at it.

She adjusted the black band on her arm and said, "I'm sorry for her."

"It's not right when loved ones die young." He considered his parents young.

"It seems love creates more pain than it's worth." The sorrow in her blue eyes sucked him down a deep well. It would take time and patience to draw up anything other than grief for her. How long would it take? And what would it be like to glimpse joy and peace in those same pale-blue eyes?

While he stood there trying to fathom her pain, she left him staring at her back as she picked her way across the path to the lodge. Her sleek figure compact and curvy in a subtle way—a trim ankle barely visible.

She would've made Jasmine seem tall and gangly—and Jasmine would seem happy by comparison. And yet he couldn't remember Jasmine ever laughing or spontaneously sharing anything of her life. She was always such a good listener. But what did he actually know of Jasmine herself? Maybe he should have taken a lesson from Jasmine and been better at listening, slower to speak of his own life. He couldn't grow attached to this sad beauty before him, but he could practice lending an ear.

He had to do something, or he would go mad. *If the letter would just come and release me from the waiting and wondering.* Then he could go to Jasmine and sit at her feet until he understood what brought a smile to her face. He could still learn to draw Jasmine out.

He went back into his old cabin, standing there looking around, he was oddly displaced with feminine things settled on the dresser top and nightstand where his shaving tack had been. He wondered what the next few weeks would bring. He couldn't be a mover and a changer. Even if he wanted to be. He just had to let time pass.

Switching from the cabin to the loft reminded him of all the things he hated about being gone from Auburn.

He was a cleaver, not a leaver.

He wanted a family and a home three generations deep with a family plot out back to hold the fourth. He was built to grow old surrounded by community and folks with quirks and oddities that he overlooked because they were blood and precious. He didn't like living with only enough to meet his needs and uncomfortably at that.

He lifted his hat and ran a hand through his hair. He wanted to return to Auburn and make a home. All he needed was a chance to be his true self. He couldn't get that here—hiding—looking over his shoulder. No matter how fond he was of the silent Moses or Cookie, no matter how much friendly rivalry, banter, and competition came with Camp 13.

This wasn't home.

This was an escape.

Even Heather was simply passing through. If he stayed here, his life was stuck, like a rope swing always drawn back waiting to be released.

He had no control over what was happening back in Auburn or anything here at Camp 13 until Patrick sent a dratted letter.

He was right when he told Heather the men would match

their loyalty to her cooking skills. But because he could—while he was here—he would be the first in line to be her champion—their champion. *There's two of them.* At least that would give him something to do.

He'd be a caring uncle or loving brother to them both.

Didn't he wish someone—someone besides David—would be doing that with Jasmine? *Yes.* He would take the sad widow and her firebrand friend under his wing until they could navigate this place and these men on their own.

They need me.

For Jasmine, he would care for these ladies. And making the cabin and their few belongings feel like a home was the first step. Changing his mind about the dirty sheets, he gathered the bedding and headed to the wash barrel after putting their oxen in the big barn with Jigger Jones's stock.

A fresh bed, clean wash water, and the drop lock on the door needed to be double-checked for security. He would tend it all before he went back to the lodge.

He clenched his jaw and banged his knuckles across the washboard as he worked his frustrations out on the sheets—ignoring the pain of lye water burning the raw spots. If anyone tried to hurt them, they would answer to him.

Just like, someday, David would answer to him.

Chapter Twelve

The warmth from the massive pot of simmering stew steamed into Heather's hair as she dropped the dumpling in at the precise time Cookie had suggested. She knew how to do it herself, but pleasing Cookie was as important as making lots of good food this first night. The large kitchen warmed around her, and the smells of good food cooking relaxed her raw nerves. With her things tucked safely into the cabin next door, with a safe place to sleep, and with this abundance cooking around her, she could let the raw nerves relax.

As she worked, Cookie huffed and puffed and murmured to himself as he bent to pull the last batch of her fritters out of the oven.

He hovered and protected the sweets like they were fancy china. "These look fine. Fine I tell you. I'm planning on helping myself before the crew descends upon us. Don't you worry none. I have these beggars trained. They won't come in until they're washed. And they'll get a fine blistering from me if they get out of control."

Cookie murmured his approval as he savored his first bite of too-hot fritter.

"Will they be upset to find Liza and me here?" She looked for her friend in vain. Liza was running around cleaning and scrubbing all the tables and setting things to rights for their first meal.

"Upset ain't the right word. Most of them will drool over you as much as the desserts you've baked. But they won't touch nothing, or they won't have a job."

"Or a hand." Liza came in. Feet tripping across the ground

one tick shy of a jog. "I'll take any one of the brutes on myself with my meat cleaver iffen they even look like they're gonna take advantage. They'll be afraid of me, and I aim to keep it that way." Liza reached across Heather's workspace and held up the dirty cleaver Heather had used to chop the meat and potatoes. She plunked the knife into her dish water.

Cookie grunted, chewed, and bobbed his head—approval in the lift of his eyebrows.

Heather was so grateful to have Liza with her. "I'm sure we'll be fine." She didn't know any such thing, but she hoped for it. She would probably have fainted dead away if she was facing this situation all by herself. She could hardly believe she was here. What kind of things would she be writing home to Cora Mae and Rose about at the end of the night? What would she tell Rebecca?

Would the men drive them out or keep them around? She hoped to stay. Starting all over was even more daunting than taking on all the strange men.

Cookie went on about how he would crucify any man who tried to put his hand in his cookie jar. Would someone like that defend her one minute and ask her to leave in the next? She hoped not. Swirls of nerves flitted in her belly and made her breath come short. She'd done all she could. She'd taken Zeke's advice, putting her touch on every aspect of this meal even with the short preparation time. And she already had bread setting and cinnamon rolls rising for the morning.

She felt safer in the kitchen than in the huge open space of the lodge that served as dining hall to the men. But it was getting easier each time Liza set things to rights. By the time her friend was done, every inch of it would be homey and ready to be filled with good memories.

Boots, drying clothes, and logging tools had gone from helter-skelter disarray to order and care. Liza brought her sense of home to the cookstove space. If Heather could make the roiling in her stomach settle this might not be so miserable.

At least the large kitchen and oven space was easier to work than the one in her and Riley's tiny shanty. She sighed. Riley was only a few days gone, and it felt like she'd lived a continuous month since then—time passed simultaneously fast and slow.

She heard voices and clomping boots before the door opened and men poured into the room. One at a time and then in pairs they came. All shapes and sizes, they filed through the door. The scent of working men, fresh-cut wood, and wet earth mixed with the cinnamon. She pulled the towel from her apron pocket and pretended to dry water from her hands to cover their shaking.

Some headed to what must be their favorite spots on the split-log benches, others pulled off their boots, and a few hung their mackinaw coats on the pegs by the fire. One called out, "Smells like you worked up more of a sweat than we did, Cookie." The one who spoke, a very short, lean man with black hair slicked back off his head, stepped forward with a smile.

"Ain't no stinking or sweating going on in here. You fellas take a care now. We have guests. Guests of *mine* that plan on sticking around. And if you want any part of that heavenly smell, then you better put on your preacher-Sunday manners."

Heather watched the one who made the comment stop in his path to the wall pegs with his coat raised and take a look in her direction. Liza tucked the broom and bucket in the corner behind Heather. Liza was close enough her slim hip pressed into Heather's.

The largest man in the room elbowed past the speaker and came to the counter, towering over them both. *What was I thinking?* These men would eat them alive. There would be no escape. They couldn't outrun a single one. Heather darted a glance at the door.

Then the man spoke. "Smells goot. Vittles. Ummm."

Cookie jabbed a pudgy finger at the large man. "Grab your plate and file past, Bjorn, same as always, only save room on your plate for one of Miss Heather's fritters. And yes, I said *one* fritter, Bjorn."

Bjorn gave Cookie a toothy grin and was holding his tin out

so Cookie could use his oversized ladle to dish the dumpling stew straight from the pot on the stove where it bubbled.

A man with the fullest beard of them all spoke next. "What's the matter, Jiggy? Kinda quiet? I've never seen you speechless before."

All the men craned their necks to see Jiggy. He said, "One should never speak in the presence of fine beauty. Do you not see them? One soft and fair as a pearl freshly found, and the other a miniature goddess that would make Diana envious." He moved to his place in line with eyes only for Liza.

Heather felt Liza stiffen beside her. When Liza set her chin in the same way she had when she'd delivered her well-practiced snub of Charley, Heather reached out and tugged her friend's skirt to help her stay under control. She didn't want to jeopardize their job on the first day.

She rushed to speak before Liza could. "Welcome. There is stew and dumplings for you all, and I made four dozen fritters. I'm not sure how many of you there are, but we don't have to save any. There will be fresh cinnamon rolls in the morning to accompany the bacon and fried mush Cookie prepared."

The grunts and cheers spread around the room and the men moved to form the line before them. She was glad she was behind the counter because the great room began to feel smaller and smaller.

"There's forty of us on a good day. Where did you find them, Cookie?" one man answered her question and asked.

"You are the answer to my prayers. I've had enough beans in the last few months to—"

"Don't!" Cookie bellowed. "Don't even think about going on and on about eatin' whistle-berries around these careful ears. That goes for all of you." He flicked the ladle at the group, stew glopped on the wood counter. "I'll pack them up in the wagon and take them back to town myself, if you boys carry on and ruin them with your bachelor's jaw."

"I wasn't gonna say nothin' bad, Cookie. I'll be as silent as

Moses, if he would hurry through the line and let me sink my teeth into one of those tasty pastries."

A few men laughed.

"You gonna stand there and stare?" Liza's words made Heather jump. She looked around and saw the black-haired, smooth-talking man standing to the side of the line with his plate in hand.

He swept the dish in front of him like it was a fancy beaver hat and bowed. "I'll stand here like a gentleman should and wait until your fair friend gives us a proper introduction."

The front door behind the man opened to a few more loggers including Zeke. Zeke was a head taller than most men in the group, making it easy for Heather to meet his eyes across the room. Once she saw him, she felt more settled than the day she'd finished walking the Oregon Trail, maybe before then.

Why would that be?

Possibly because he knew more about her than anyone in the room besides maybe Liza, and he knew this place.

And he's lost his folks, too. She was sad about that, of course, but he understood. And he had a widowed girl back home to think of. She never took her gaze off his face until the man focused on Liza spoke again.

"Jigger Jones. At your service, my fair maidens."

Liza snorted. Heather smiled.

One of the men from across the room boomed. "You'll see why we all call him Jiggy when Tupper lays down his bandages long enough to pick up his fiddle."

The man who must be Tupper stepped forward. He had a roll of bandaging tucked under his arm. "Scott, I'll get to that shin of yours after we both eat. We don't want to miss this." He turned to Jigger "Jiggy" Jones. "While you're still play-acting like a fine gentleman, the rest of us are hungry. Keep the line moving." He gave Liza a comfortable smile and then he gave Heather one before he mouthed a how-do-you-do as Cookie scooped his plate full. Heather took in the whole room and tried to swallow back her nerves.

Jigger Jones was still waiting patiently. Eyes twinkling with devilment.

Liza was still smoldering and stiff as a poker next to Heather. If he kept this up Liza might burst into flames beside her and burn him. He would probably stand there and smile like he was selling secrets until he starved to death, if she didn't finish the introduction.

By the look of the satisfied smile on Zeke's face. He was obviously enjoying the sensation of her and Liza's first impression on the all-male camp. Heather spoke up loud enough to include the whole room. "Mr. Jigger Jones, this is my friend Liza. It's a pleasure to meet you. To meet you all."

Liza added, "And if you don't knock that silly grin off your face, then I'll take a rolling pin to it." The room rumbled with laughter and several men smacked Jiggy on the back as they got in line.

"A rolling pin?" one said.

"Any more stuff and nonsense out of you, Jiggy, and I'm gonna put you on kitchen duty for a week." Cookie must've seen the look of delight and the slight rise of the eyebrow that Jiggy gave to Liza because he added, "And your duties would happen after the ladies are locked in for the night. And I'm sure The Bull won't take none of your sass on payday when you haven't been out in the trees the whole week. He might get the itch to send you packin'."

Bull? What did that mean.

Zeke was suddenly right next to Heather. The counter between them, he managed to lean close enough she could feel the heat of him. "Bull means boss. Harvey is the big boss. He has logging camps all over between here and the coast. He comes around from time to time to keep us motivated to bring in the trees. He doesn't tolerate laziness. Ten men are lined up to take any one of these men's job."

Liza was apparently all ears too. "Hear that? You sass me, and you'll get canned. So just try it."

"If that's how you want to play it." Jiggy spoke his words slow and sure.

"I don't play. There's much too much work to be done." Liza picked up an oversized wooden spoon that somehow managed to make her look tinier. She snatched up the empty crate she'd used at the mercantile to collect the dishes. Even Heather's back straightened when she announced the new rules. "When you boys are done, drop your tins in here after you scrape them into this." She pulled out a big porcelain crock. "This is pig slop."

"We got pigs now too?" someone called from the back.

"Not yet, but you'd surely want to raise some, if you saw the recipes in Miss Heather's mama's recipe box. She needs a sight more 'n what's in the kitchen: more chickens, more eggs, a garden the size of Eden, and meat of all kinds."

"Venison?"

"Yes, sir."

"Lye too," Heather added.

"Lye?" Jigger Jones asked.

"Yes. I'd like to make up different soaps for kitchen use, laundry use, and bathing use."

"She's too nice to say it, but your stink is burning our noses. Some of you boys is dirtier than Matthew, Mark, Luke, and John's britches combined," Liza went on. Her voice gained confidence with each word.

"She talkin' about you, Jiggy. Even after you fixed your hair so nice." More guffaws echoed.

Jiggy didn't miss a beat. "Cookie never warned us that we'd be in the presence of such loveliness, Miss Liza."

Liza wouldn't answer him. She was standing starched straight and looked away like a grumpy cat.

"Thank you kindly for what smells like the best meal we've had in a month of Sundays." Jiggy was pouring his words over Liza real slow.

"Hey!" Cookie barked.

Liza cut Cookie off. "Don't thank me. I promise, you'd rather chew on one of your spikey boots than eat my cookin'. I keep the supplies coming and the dishes clean, and we need more of everything."

Jiggy leaned forward. "Those are the most fortunate dishes this side of the Blue Mountains."

"How would you know? You seen *all* the dishes this side of them mountains? Is everything you say salted with 'zaggeration? I only take a liking to truth-telling folks."

"You tell him, Miss Liza—way to comb his hair," one of the other men hollered.

Had Liza gone too far? Heather was nervous for all this work and plans to come crashing down.

Jigger looked a little miffed. He turned and spoke to the man. "You! Frenchie. Front and center after we eat."

She looked at Zeke. Were they going to fight after dinner? She needed to soothe their ruffled feathers. "If you don't fill your plate quick, Mr. Jones, then I can't guarantee that there'll be a fritter waiting for you at the end." All the other men had followed each other through the line ahead of him—happy to have a steaming hot meal.

He walked down the serving line as if he was wearing a duke's well-fitted coat, knee pants, and Hessian boots instead of rumpled work pants thickly treated with something to shed water, boots, and a bright vermillion undershirt that seemed to be the loggers' uniform of choice on this cool September evening.

Zeke was at the end of the line moving as slowly as Jiggy, only without the strut, toward his own helping of food. He cast his voice low. "The men did well. No harm done. They will be on their best *show-off* behavior for the next couple days. I suppose tonight will be extra-outlandish. They will fight for your benefit—nothing to worry about."

He held out his plate to Heather. She ladled a hearty scoop of steaming dumpling stew. He continued to talk to her quietly, "They're good men on the outside. But all came from somewhere. And most are running from something. I double-checked the drop lock on your door before I came in, and I placed a cowbell on your nightstand. Make a ruckus if anyone fusses with the door. I can teach you ladies to shoot a gun, if you don't already know how. Important skill in this life."

"I know how to shoot. I dare any of these blokes to come sneaking around. I'd love to take a chunk out of their hide."

"Liza." Did the girl even know how to speak in a quiet voice? Heather thought that lightning would strike them any second, or at least Cookie would reprimand them or ask them to leave. But the older man seemed to grow an inch taller when he heard Liza's threats. But there was still tension in the air.

Liza went on. "What?" She scanned the room stopping when she spotted Jiggy. "Don't be starry-eyed, I know what I'm about. And I mean what I say. Now, I got me some scrubbing to do. It's been *mostly* a pleasure to meet you all." She gave Jigger Jones the cut direct and pulled the already full crate of dishes to her chest to head back to the sink.

Three men moved to help her carry it. "I got it. It's my job now. If you want to help, then leave me with a full water bucket and full rain barrels outside whenever possible. I'd rather work in here than haul water all day long." Two of the three men moved to get water right then. Liza was delighted to snub Jiggy a second time on her way back past. She strutted past him like she was the queen herself. Heather didn't think Liza would have liked the look of appreciation Jigger was giving her backside.

Zeke was still standing there with his meal in hand. He whispered, "Things could get interesting. Jiggy will need to prove himself, and if she won't let him, then he is going to tangle with everyone else until she does."

"Will they hurt each other?"

"Nah. Nothing serious anyway. They'll knock each other around, bite, and stomp each other. The normal stuff. Look. Tupper is already preparing his kit."

She saw Tupper sorting his bandages and something else in a leather bag. Then she looked at Zeke while he was watching Tupper. She was quiet as she took in his eyes as warm and brown as homemade chocolate and just as dark. She saw kindness there under a black cowboy hat that looked like it had been stitched and molded specifically for his head.

She was glad he was trying to make her feel welcome and safe, and that he was willing to teach her the ropes. *Will he keep doing so in the days to come?* She wanted him too.

When he settled his tin of food next to her at the counter, she saw the cords of muscle bunch under his bold red sleeve.

Two men came back with buckets brimming with water. Liza moved to where she wanted them deposited. Neither sloshed as they balanced their way back to her.

When they disappeared, Jiggy made a show of stuffing the last of his fritter into his mouth and crossing the room, slipping through the counter opening and around the wall that separated the kitchen from the rest of the large room.

Heather couldn't help but notice that Jiggy barely cleared Zeke's shoulder—the smallest man in the room.

"Not very big, is he?" he whispered.

How did he know her thoughts?

"I thought the same thing when I first came here a month ago. You should've seen the show he put on for me. This is going to be something with Miss Liza involved."

He'd only been there a little longer than she, and he was already helping the boss, or rather The Bull. That impressed her. Heather looked down at his leg and the cane he was using.

"I'll heal fine. Need more time is all. I'm almost ready to go back in the field as it is, but I'm kind of glad to hide behind it tonight." He tapped his wrapped knee. "Don't get me wrong. I'm no chicken. I've had my turn. But Jiggy is in rare form."

Had Zeke really read her so well a second time? She looked at him strangely and he quirked an eyebrow, so she confessed. "I might need more than a drop lock on my door if you anticipate my thoughts like that. Does your sweetheart back home complain about that?"

He tipped his head to think.

Heather watched something change. His face bore a wisp of sorrow. Unless she was imprinting her own sadness on him. He was sorting his thoughts for an answer that she could see by the furrow between those dark eyes was going to cause him heartache.

She reached to touch his arm and thought better of it. "Pardon me."

She turned away from him to make it easier for Zeke to let go of whatever she'd caused him to remember and tried to be friendly with another logger. The fatigue of the day was beginning to rest on her eyelids. Had they left the mercantile just this morning? Had Riley been killed just days before that? It felt like years to her bones.

She was surprised Zeke answered, "I suppose Jasmine spends more time reading my thoughts than I did hers. *If* I have it right at all?"

"You doubt?" Heather wasn't trying to garner his attention. The opposite in fact. She was trying to deflect his attention. Her emotions were growing as weary as her limbs and she was sure to embarrass them both by bursting into tired tears, if he kept reading her thoughts. She almost longed for it—tears would be welcome rather than the knot lodged in her gut where nervous flutters had been all day.

Just a little more work and she would be able to lie down and stretch out in her new bed. She could gather herself then—and hopefully sleep.

Zeke still seemed to be lost in thought.

She said, "I think every man doubts, when it comes to knowing a lady's mind. At least, that's how I understand it to be."

He looked at her like he was trying to solve a puzzle. Every tingle in her body came out to play at the same time. He kept studying her. She added, "That confounding—eh?" She hated that her words came out a little breathy. The last thing she needed was for him to think she was flirting. He had a lady. End of story. His sweetheart, Jasmine, wouldn't be happy in the slightest if she knew Heather was wishing she could get a closer look at his lips than the view his thick, black, beard provided.

And what would Riley have thought? She'd had to make herself love him and now this, whatever it was—so fast?

"Yes, confounding, with you and with Jasmine." He shook his head as if to clear it.

Another round of tingles tripped over her at his raw words. She hardly recognized her reactions. Heather mentally chastised herself. *Liza isn't the only one ruffled by our new home.* She still had dirt on her clothes from burying Riley. Who was she? She needed time to figure herself out.

Jiggy interrupted her falling thoughts by strutting out of the kitchen hollering. "Your time is up, Albert! You and me, Frenchie! Time to dance." He said Albert without the *t* on the end like the French would.

Zeke savored his first fork full and then said, "This is wonderful, by the way. I'll be eating it here. Out of the way. I'll protect you if anything comes flying."

"Flying?" Heather didn't even try to keep her mouth closed when Jiggy and Frenchie stripped out of the top of their winter underwear and tied the long, red sleeves around their waists— chests bare. Shocked to see a man's bare chest and from the sounds coming from beside her, Liza was too.

Jiggy was much smaller than Frenchie, but every last nook and cranny of him was tight and firm—each muscle in clear rippled outline—not a speck of spare flesh on him. Frenchie was the same only much bigger and whiter. The two men squared off and paced in a circle to take the other's measure—one the color of buttermilk, the other the tint of light leather.

Zeke finished his meal and took his tin to Liza's tubs—obeying her scraping instructions before he came back to Heather's side. Liza was moving back and forth between tubs of warm water and suds and the counter. Zeke said, "She almost has all the supper dishes done even with all this going on."

"Liza's like a small tornado when it comes to cleaning."

"And Jiggy is like a twister in a fight."

She was still trying not to be shocked at seeing men with their shirts off in front of her. "I'm not sure I can watch this. Should we stop 'em?" The few times Riley's chest had been bared it was in the dark of night. And she couldn't remember ever seeing Pa without his shirt on.

Cookie came out of the large supply room at the back of the kitchen, tossing his toweling over his shoulder and folding his hands across his chest to watch. "I ain't gonna stop it. They need to blow off some steam. If they don't, we could have our hands full with you lovelies around. Let them take a lick at each other. They'll sleep like the dead after. It won't take 'em long to wear each other down. Never does. Whopping on each other is hard work after a day in the woods.

"I'll bring the dough for the cinnamon rolls over here in a minute. Let's get them put together tonight, Miss Heather. I'm gonna let you and Miss Liza have the morning off to rest and settle. Breakfast comes mighty early in these hills, and you two have had a day of it. They'll be back in, soon enough, for noon meal since I can't convince a single one of them to pack a nose bag and eat out in the field. I'll use you and Liza well at that meal tomorrow—if it suits."

"It suits." Heather shielded her face when Frenchie swung and connected with Jiggy's jaw and landed another to his stomach. "He's gonna break him."

Zeke leaned his weight onto his elbow on the wood counter. How could he be so relaxed? The thud of fist hitting solid muscle was repeated. The men came apart and circled. Jiggy's back was to her—and it was covered with dimpled patches of scars she'd never seen before.

Liza asked, "Did Jiggy have the pox? My sister had the pox. She had scars, but not like those."

"No. Most of the men have those. Frenchie too. See." Zeke pointed to the pale man's shoulder. "Most loggers have matching scars. From being stomped by Caulk boots. It's how the winner is declared. Once you win, you get to stomp your opponent. Each scar has a story behind it. Loggers are proud of them. Have a few myself."

She looked at Zeke. Were his on his back or shoulder or...she flushed as she thought about it.

"Here." He touched the back of his shoulder.

Heather bit back a gasp but it was already too late. He'd heard it. He'd guessed her thoughts. *Again.* The warm rumble of his laugh appeased her mind and set the tingles in her belly dancing. She found herself wanting to see him fight, so she could see how the pucker-scars would dot *his* skin—*his* muscle.

Who am I? She flushed scarlet. She was glad everyone was watching the two men.

She had to get a grip. She fussed around the kitchen, cleaning up behind the fritters. She broke so many personal boundaries with one simple thought. Boundaries she put in place because of what pain and abandonment did to a body. She went back to watching the fight so Liza wouldn't get after her.

Liza watched with lips puckered in disapproval. That made Heather think of the rolling pin she threatened Jiggy with. And that made her think of the cinnamon dough. She pulled one of two rolling pins off the shelf and moved to the section of counter that Cookie used to lay out the dough, making herself feel at home in this big new space. She would put herself to work. If she was busy trying to feed all these men then she wouldn't have time, or energy, to imagine the back and chest of the dark-eyed man who'd stepped in and made sure she and Liza had a chance at this job. The faster she rolled out the dough, the faster she could go to bed and sleep off all the pain and changes of the last several days.

Her fingers found the small bowl of flour and dribbled a handful over the surface before she went to work rolling. Her arms worked as she watched Zeke as he watched the fight.

He'd said each man came to work here because they had secrets.

What was his?

Cookie offered from close beside her, "I got raisins." Interrupting her thoughts, "You think they'd like that?" She nearly squealed when he offered a crock filled with the wrinkled delights. How long had it been since she'd had such a treat to work with?

"Yes, we would," Zeke answered Cookie.

Heather focused as much of her attention as she could onto the task in front of her.

Frenchie had a bloody nose, which didn't bother him, it seemed. He laughed. "You about out of goods, Jiggy?" He taunted with a smile, exposing a missing front tooth which he probably lost in one of these face-offs. All the men called out heckles, jeers, and cheers. The whole room filled with a deep, male rumble.

Zeke said, "Tupper knocked out his tooth. Frenchie deserved it. He was going in with his teeth."

He'd pegged her thoughts again. This time it was more familiar, and she was too tired to be startled or worry about what her face gave away. "He was going to bite him?"

"Biting is allowed. Though, I never try. I'd rather have a scarred ear than missing teeth. See?" He tugged one ear forward out from under his hat. It bore crinkling scar lines in the shape of teeth marks across the top. Easy to spy on several men in the room, now that she knew what to look for.

Liza came up beside her and snatched the second rolling pin and scooted her over with a nudge of her hip. Heather brushed into Zeke's arms where he leaned on the counter, forcing him to make way.

"Sorry." He beat her to the apology.

She should have said it. She was the one that bumped into him. She was the one still gazing up at him.

"Seems crazy, I know. But they're playing. So much is settled here in this lighthearted pounding—the logger's way."

"Lighthearted?" She almost said light-headed. That's what she felt standing so close to Zeke, with him bent over her to make sure she could hear him with all the cheering and jeering echoing off the log walls.

Jiggy did a fancy flip move that involved Frenchie's shoulder. He ended up swinging around onto his back. When he opened his mouth to chomp Frenchie's ear, she almost screamed, but Liza beat her too it.

Frenchie did a swift zig, zag, and dip. Jiggy came over the top of Frenchie, and Frenchie lifted his boot to leave another pattern of pock scars on Jiggy's tan skin before the wiry man fully hit the floor. Heather was surprised and a little impressed when Jiggy grabbed Frenchie's booted foot and gave it a twist and a yank. Frenchie fell like a tree. He banged to the wooden floor. The lodge shook. Men pumped their fists, howled, and stomped.

The four men who'd moved the bench in front of the barrel stove, to keep the fighters from falling into it, clapped their approval.

Jiggy was up in a bolt, and he planted a half-a-boot stamp on the back of Frenchie's shoulder.

"See. That wasn't too bad. He played nice. I wasn't so sure he was gonna."

"Nice?" Heather could feel Liza's contempt in that one word. The poor girl didn't have any warning.

When Jiggy stood and took the praise of the surrounding men with a flamboyant bow, Heather almost laughed.

Liza was most definitely not finding the humor in it, if the manner of her rolling the dough was any giveaway.

"They'll head in their own directions now—most to bed. Some will wash clothes or repair tools. The only thing on their mind now is sleep. Except maybe…"

Jiggy was coming toward them. His bare chest heaved for breath and glistened with sweat. But he never wavered. He was locked on Liza. Heather took a step to her friend's side, and Cookie matched her move from the other.

Liza pretended not to see Jiggy's display of maleness and kept rolling the cinnamon roll dough.

"You making that treat for me, my sweet. I fought for you, and now you're caring for me? What big heart beats beneath that fine chest of yours?" He looked at her chest for a brief moment and then locked eyes with her. Jiggy reached to sneak a pinch of the sweet dough.

Liza slammed the rolling pin across the back of his hand, and before he had enough time to find out how bad his finger hurt, she clonked him on the head with the wooden tool hard enough that Jiggy's eyes rolled white before he slumped to the ground.

The whole room stopped dead quiet for a pinpoint second before the room exploded in whoops and catcalls.

Cookie clapped his hands louder than any of them. "If you wasn't so pretty, I'd wonder if you weren't my own long-lost daughter—after my own heart you are. Best thing I've seen in months. For that, boys, I'm opening the box before breakfast. Come clean or don't come. Off with you now." Cookie took over the filling of the sweet bread rolled out in front of both ladies.

Cheers filled the space all the way up to the massive log beam that spanned the length of the lodge.

"The box?" Heather asked.

"I'll explain."

Zeke was about to do so when Cookie added, "Zeke, you should walk the ladies home for the night and make sure they're settled."

"I warned him to stay clear of me," Liza muttered, looking like a riled bobcat still ready to scratch.

"I heard you. We all heard you," Zeke said on the edges of a laugh. "His fault all around. And he'll own it. He's a good one that way."

Jiggy was coming to on the floor. He turned his head from one side to the other.

She went on, "Good or not. No one teases and calls me sweet names without my say so. And I don't plan on saying so. Let's head out, Heather. He's starting to come around."

Her words were loud enough to set the whole camp straight, but she was moving fast. She must have been afraid Jiggy would pop up from the floor and exact his revenge right then.

Heather walked around the counter with Liza and Zeke in tow.

They were almost at the door when Jiggy did just that. His eyes were sparkling and glazed, but Heather wasn't sure if that was because of the hit or because of his fascination with Liza. "Beg pardon, ma'am. May I have the privilege of taking your hand in a dance the next time Tupper tightens the hide and saws the strings? I'd be much honored. My way of apologizing for my rude behavior." He gave her a mock bow.

Liza's lips were pressed into a tight line. "I don't countenance no invitations from a man half-dressed no matter how much of a looker he is." Liza sucked in a breath. Like she hadn't meant for the last part to slip her lips. She marched past Zeke and was out the door, spine starched, rolling pin still in hand.

She was probably still in earshot when Jiggy said, "She thinks I'm a looker. That's enough for one night. Boy howdy, what a woman."

Liza darted across the mud at a near-run in front of Heather.

Zeke's warm hand took Heather's arm as she took the three big steps down to the earthy muck that was everywhere. He helped her step clean until she reached the front of the cabin she was to call home. She was glad for his help and amazed at how different she'd felt with him beside her now, than earlier this same day.

She should be more like Liza and present a rock-wall front. Even though she wasn't willing to take the chance on letting any of these men close, she wasn't good at a stony façade—especially not with Zeke, it seemed. But now, after the evening had passed, and she understood Zeke was kind and understanding and had his own girl, she felt more at ease, like she could let him in a little closer than the others.

Jasmine.

Pretty name. Heather didn't like the smell of that flower. She didn't examine that reaction too close.

Cora Mae would love hearing about Jigger Jones and Liza. Heather wondered if Archie Millikin was still making himself a pest. She should encourage Cora Mae to buy herself a rolling pin.

She laughed.

"What?" Zeke pulled her to a stop in front of the open door.

They could hear Liza banging things around, probably working off her spleen. "I was thinking of a friend from back east that might need her own rolling pin."

His smile beamed out from under his black beard. She liked the little crinkles it created at the corners of his earthy-brown eyes. "Seemed pretty effective. Too bad Cookie doesn't provide them in the box."

"Box?"

"It's a small store. Has everything the men need, but more importantly the things they want. All for a price. It's a main event when Cookie opens. It will keep us from our jobs in the woods for an extra hour, but The Bull doesn't mind as long as the timber count is adequate at the end of the day. We're ahead for this week. And the men will work harder and faster after the reward and with the hope of another great meal."

"You go out with your leg? I mean…"

He smiled at her question. "I go out to count. I can't do what I use to, yet. But Harvey, he has me tallying board foot and surveying for the future. My leg gets awful sore, but it all works."

As he told her, his dark brown eyes deepened until they seemed almost black. She wasn't sure knowing his thoughts right then would be a good idea.

He was quiet for a second and then said, "Let's get you both tucked in. Liza has the rolling pin, which should be enough, but on the off chance, remember the cowbell. I'll hear it from the loft easily enough. I'll be here in seconds if I hear it. Please drop this in place once you're settled." He pointed to the dropping board.

He sobered and stepped toward her.

Her face must have fallen and given away the deep sadness that poured over her entire being.

She was sure he would think it was because of fear for her own safety. And in a way it was. The sadness that poured over her like a rain cloud had more to do with the fact that she never really paid any attention to the color of Riley's eyes, and now here she stood in front of Zeke not missing a single detail.

She really was tired. She put up a hand to keep him from coming closer.

Stopping her heart just as effectively. No fluttering allowed. Fluttering was the beginning of love. Hadn't Mama said so? Fairy-tale love was best left in books. It was dangerous. Fatal even—nearly killed her pa to deal with that kind of love. She wouldn't have it. *I'll ignore it all.* She would make no room for love. Her chest squeezed.

She had no intentions of letting her heart be put in the same noose. She would need to toughen, not soften, if she was going to survive this troop of men. *I'm tired. That's all.* It was the end of a long day. She would sleep off her sensitivity. And she would take a mental rolling pin to any thoughts of Zeke starting right now.

He has a girl back home.

He said, "Again, I'm sorry for your loss." He reached out and tugged her black armband. "I'll see you in the morning. Sleep well." He'd drawn himself up stiff and confident and marched as straight as a soldier back through the mud—without using his cane once.

His kindness was a leveler—a sure punch that would've made Frenchie and Jiggy proud. But she was glad he was leaving. It was best if he thought her mired in grief. And she needed to get to bed before she started counting all the ways he made her feel safe in one simple evening.

Stop it. You'll only get hurt.

Chapter Thirteen

Early the next morning, all the men were lined up on the back side of the barn. Moses poured frigid water over Zeke's head and down his shoulders. Zeke shivered and braced himself for another bucket full after a glance down the line of twelve wooden drums filled with stinky, naked loggers doing the same. Zeke scrubbed and washed in record time before Moses held up the second bucket.

"Moooo?" Moses's mangled version of "more" was easy to translate after months of sharing their barrel baths in the darkness of the dawning new day.

Once free of soap, Zeke climbed out of the barrel in one swift leap, dried, and scrabbled into his woolies and tin pants. He hoped his waterproof pants still held a trace of heat. At the same time he dressed, Moses stripped and climbed in. They would all switch places before they were done, most smelling heaps better. Each man moved fast in the chilly morning. Each man was probably thinking of what they would purchase from Cookie's box. Unless they still had a mind to think about their new guests.

By the time he was pushing his last button into place, Moses was in the barrel waiting for his wetting. The sight of all Moses's scars always made Zeke's feet hesitate for the briefest of seconds. What had happened to his friend? Who had torn his flesh and tortured him so?

Zeke poured the creek water over Moses as he moaned along with every other man who was receiving the same shock. Moses was always fast. He'd be out in half the time it took the others.

Zeke turned back to fill his bucket from the trough and

looked at the thick forest behind them all, shrouded in shadows. His neck crawled with more than cold bumps.

Was there something out there? A critter maybe?

Why did it feel like he was standing in the crosshairs of a gun barrel?

Did he feel it because there really could be someone out there?

If David had killed that man and framed him, then what would keep him from coming for him? Patrick said David would come. He shook off the feeling with another shiver. *This is a day like every other.* Every other day filled with unanswered questions— primarily why did David pick him? Was it a simple case of wrong place wrong time, or was there more to it? He rubbed the hair down at the back of his neck and scanned the tree line one more time—even though the darkness hadn't receded enough for him to see anything. He was jumpy because the ladies were in camp. That's all.

Moses scrubbed and splashed. In just a few minutes, Moses and Zeke would head inside, and Moses would sit and write, "*Please forgive me.*" in his journal while he waited for his bowl of mush and molasses and cinnamon rolls to be ready—their routine.

Cinnamon rolls.

With the last bucket pouring over his friend's back, Zeke traced Moses's scars as the rinse water flushed away the suds. Moses was out and dressed before Zeke had their barrel empty and stored. Moses left the back of the bunkhouse just ahead of him. He turned the corner and disappeared just as Cookie began beating the first strands of his wake-up call on the gut-hammer.

Gong. Gong. Gong! Not that many were still asleep. Most wanted to see what was inside Cookie's box even if they couldn't buy anything.

Cookie was working up to his usual snorting and blowing and banging on the triangle before his usual whoop and holler and lines about getting up or rolling out.

Zeke came around the bunkhouse and collided with Moses's back. He'd stopped right in the path. "What is it?"

Moses waved his arms and then pointed. "Woooog. Giiiiiiilllll-sh."

Zeke looked to where Moses pointed. Heather and Liza, freshly awakened, were finding their way through the muddy path toward them.

"The girls? Oh no. They can't come this way. Uh, Miss Heather, Miss Liza. You can't come this way!" he called.

The men bathing in the freezing water didn't seem to hear. They were too busy bellowing and whooping. They sounded like someone was injured or dying even over the top of Cookie's noise. Moses still waved his hands. The girls kept coming.

Zeke ran to them. "You shouldn't be out here."

Liza moved to dart around him.

Both ladies looked like they'd flung their dresses over whatever they wore to bed. Zeke spoke more forcefully. "You're about twenty feet from getting the shock of your life."

Heather's tussled braid hung below her elbows. Her eyes were hazy with sleep. The edge of pale muslin peeked out the collar that wasn't as tight as it should be at her neck.

He tried not to think about her nightclothes.

"Are we being attacked?" Liza's dark hair spiked in all directions.

"Is someone hurt?" Heather turned her pretty face up to him.

He would have responded to her caring questions, but Liza still hadn't stopped. He reached out and grabbed a handful of the back of Liza's skirts. "No. Stop!"

Liza stiffened at his commanding bellow.

Heather flinched.

Liza bristled up, her back rigid in the same pose she'd adopted last night before she whacked Jiggy. "And why should I do what you say? Someone needs help."

Moses laughed loud and long. He even bent over and smacked his leg.

Zeke turned to him. "Seriously," he challenged. Moses never laughed. He was going to choose this moment, when Zeke couldn't relax for a second, to indulge. "They aren't hurt. I know this is your first morning here, and you aren't used to it, but the men are getting cleaned up. The bathing barrels are back there. Cookie said to be clean if they want to be included in the fun of the box. This is Cookie's way of keeping the lice and bedbugs away."

"They're bathing?" Liza's face scrunched as she listened.

"The water is very cold this time of year."

Liza folded her arms across her chest, like she didn't quite believe him—like she might just choose to see for herself. Someone's moans and complaints bounced off the forest walls.

Zeke didn't like being sized up like he was the enemy. David did that to him back in Auburn, and it still burned. He stood tall and faced down the tiny, black-haired pixie. "Jigger Jones is back there. In the buff. Cold water is being dumped on his head. He's making more noise than most, as always. I think he'd love your help scrubbing off the sweat from last night's fight. By all means, continue." He shrugged and turned back to Heather.

Her face was a lovely shade of pink—whether from the brisk morning air or from the topic. He lowered his voice for her ears alone. "They'll all be coming around that corner in a few seconds. Best if they don't see you when you're not all put together nice."

Seeing the hollow of her throat move in swallow where her dress would usually cover seemed as intimate as a married couple's secret. Zeke hated to embarrass her by speaking about things that were all together inappropriate. But if he stood a chance of keeping their reputation as safe as their innocence, thing needed to start on the right foot. He and the men would all need to work to be careful of these women's reputation. And Heather and Liza really needed to wait until they were fully presentable before they mixed with the crew.

She didn't answer. Liza darted past headed for the cabin. Steps and singing could be heard coming up behind him. French singing.

"We'll save a bowl of oats and molasses for you," Zeke called.

Heather scurried back the way she came too. The back of her

day dress wasn't fastened above the waist. The fabric fell back on one side, revealing the cream of her muslin nightclothes.

His mouth felt dry, and he was fully warmed from his frigid bath in one burst. He stood and watched until she disappeared inside. He heard the distinct clunk of the drop lock fall into place. And like that, he could breathe again.

Moses clapped him on the shoulder to start him moving again. The silent man lifted one knowing eyebrow and then winked.

"Shet your mouth, Moses. You just shet it. I can hear you thinking. And you need to stop it." Moses laughed again, and Zeke wondered at the sound. Moses was made to laugh. If he could think of anything besides a pair of silver-blue eyes, he might go about figuring how to make his friend laugh more often.

He let Moses go inside and a few of the other fellows trudged past as he stood there. He needed to let the last image of Heather go before he saw her again. His thoughts were still firing faster than bullets. The longer he stood there cooling down, the more his damp scalp and ears returned to being cold.

The chill on his neck turned to a shiver and hair stood, again. He jerked his head around. Moses was there, waiting for him on the front steps of the lodge. "Mo. I plan on taking the wagon to town this morning, after Cookie's box." He would send word back to Patrick. He'd give it one more try. "You want to come along? You'd miss a day's pay, unless Cookie needs you to take the trip. Harvey's clear on that. But it can't wait. I need to check the post." Maybe news awaited.

He was watching Moses for his usual nod or shake of the head. But Moses was fixing his gaze on the tree line over Zeke's shoulder. All the feelings of being watched from the barrel baths came alive again. "You too? I felt it when you were scrubbing. Man or animal?"

Moses shrugged. "Heeeeshh Waaaaaashhhhhgggg."

"Yes. I agree. Whatever is there is watching. We'll check after we get back from town. Check for tracks. No sense going there now when whoever it is could get the drop on us."

They went inside, and all the men shopped over the things inside Cookie's box, before both ladies entered the dining hall.

Liza walked past them all and went straight to the kitchen to help Cookie prepare to serve the simple breakfast. Heather went more slowly, smiling a kind greeting and answering a few calls of good morning. She looked inside the box, over all that Cookie had for sale before she made her way to the large coffee kettle on the woodstove.

Zeke made himself turn his back to her. Jasmine was his focus. That was the right thing to do.

Breakfast was uneventful. Moses and Zeke left for town, making short work of the items on Cookie's mercantile list—double long with the things Heather required for her recipes.

They checked for mail.

There was a letter.

Zeke was glad Moses was driving the wagon back to Camp 13. The papers crinkled under his hand when he read it through. There was too much news and too little. He burned to solve his own problems—to defend his good name to anybody who would listen.

How could this have happened? He'd done nothing wrong.

The wagon struck a root and tossed him against Moses's arm. Zeke smoothed the letter to reread it.

Patrick's handwriting was thick and heavy. Ink smudges dotted the top and bottom of the letter. His name was nowhere on it. The wax seal, broken by him, covered the words "Written by Patrick Spade." The fact that Patrick had been so careful made Zeke even more twitchy.

> *There is trouble as we suspected. David turned the town on its head looking for you and is screaming about the injustice of the visitor's murder. He even gathered a few funds from folks to hunt you down.*

I don't think he's spending it on that, however. Except, he says he had a wanted drawn up. I had the lawyer to dinner. Miss Jasmine fixed a meal for us. I used the pretext of needing Price's will explained in full, to be sure we didn't miss anything, to bring the lawyer. I knew David would find an excuse to come. I was paying attention for any detail that would help you. We talked for almost an hour before David weaseled his way in. David's meat house and livery both burned in the fire.

From what I can gather without drawing attention, David has made offers on several small businesses in town at some point or another. Some that weren't even up for sale. Many more businesses than his meager bank salary could provide for.

I'm not sure how relevant any of this is. But we need to find out everything in regard to David and his business plans. Especially after he so conveniently dropped in on my dinner with the lawyer. I'm convinced he's been watching me, or Miss Jasmine is feeding him information. Too many coincidences. She's put on quite a show of grief about you and Price. Suppose I could be wrong about it all.

We need to stay vigilant. David is willing to go the mile for this. I'm certain he is behind it and has something big at stake. We need to find out exactly what, if we are going to tip the odds back in your favor. Hang tight. I'm sure he will slip up soon.

Zeke stopped reading the letter and clenched his teeth enough to bunch the muscle alongside his jaw. *We? We need to find out all there is?* How could he do that? There was nothing for him to do. He looked around at all the brush and shrubs—trying to see the impossible—into Auburn or into David's mind. Everything looked cheery with the sun shining through the fall wind and the branches dropping their yellow leaves.

The bushes were teaming with life. Chickadees and finches searched for their winter stores. Their little lives lived simply as they provided for themselves. There had to be more answers than the letter provided. Patrick's urge to wait a little longer pinched like too small boots. He read more.

> *Since you left, David has been working to rebuild what he lost in the fire. I suspect that's where the manhunt money ended up. I'm sure he searched the mansion himself for the deed. I spied him go in when Miss Jasmine was cleaning. He didn't know I was watching. I've been pretending to go to work. I get ready in the morning and then walk out of town the usual way and circle back. He isn't expecting a fight or any kind of resistance. Won't he be surprised.*
>
> *David slipped in the low window off the main room. I'm not sure if he kept his presence hidden from Miss Jasmine or not. I have my suspicions there, nothing confirmed yet. I know you had a fancy for her, but you might prepare yourself for bad news on that front.*

Bad news concerning Jasmine? He couldn't believe it. His heart grew so heavy he nearly moaned with the weight. She can't be that two-faced. *Can she?*

> *David hitched a ride with Hank Withers, the silver mine owner. They were both dressed in their Sunday best when they drove out of town. They spent all day gone, and David seems to have settled down since they returned.*
>
> *I keep waiting for him to question me. I've conned him into thinking I'm nothing more than a dolt. He'll have to come right out and ask me for information direct, unless he searches the house again. I see him watching it often. If my suspicions are right, then he is*

truly after the deed. It's the only thing that makes sense, even with this miner Hank Withers in the picture.

He has more love in his eyes for Price Mansion than most men have on their wedding day. He is surely up to something. I cut over to Baker City. They have a sheriff there we can trust. I filled him in. But he agrees there is nothing for us until David tips his hand. If I'm correct, he'll be coming your way soon. Be sure you're ready.

Here's the plan. I left your address in a very hidden place. As soon as I know he's searched the mansion and found it, I'll send another letter, but he may beat the letter to you. Expect him to chase you. This may be your only warning. If he comes for you, it is pretty much an admission of guilt. Until then, stay warm and dry. We'll smoke 'em out eventually. I'm half inclined to thank you. I ain't had this much fun since playing hide-and-seek with my six brothers growing up. Might be something in doing this kind of work for me when all is said and done. Might have to try my hand at detecting.

Snow is in the air. If David doesn't hurry, he may not get to push his plan forward until spring thaw. And if he has wagered all I think he has on owning Price Mansion, then that delay will make him even more persistent.

Zeke read it all twice more before Moses pulled the wagon to the barn. Zeke jumped down and strode inside—letter in pocket. Arms full of baking goods. He ignored the heavenly smell of smoky meat in the air and made sure he didn't invite conversation with either of the new guests. They were more than guests, he knew, but it was easier to keep his distance if he thought of them that way.

He left the rest of the mail for the camp with Cookie in the usual spot.

He moved through the dining hall and went up the stairs to his loft, ignoring the pain in his leg, ignoring the busy work of the three people in the kitchen. He splayed the letter across the wooden table he used for payroll and log count tallies. He planned to reread the letter again and again until he could picture everything that David was doing as if he'd done it himself and then he would form a letter with specific questions for Patrick to find out. He could still help even if he wasn't there. Maybe he would think of a question that would pry loose the puzzle piece that would send all of David's house of cards spilling to the floor.

He would try. And focusing on that would keep him from imagining that Jasmine was somehow wrapped up in this. One minute he could see nothing but her sweet innocence. And the next he saw her in the road, standing over the dead man, looking at him with horror. Maybe her horror was more than suspecting him of the murder?

And what about Price. Was that a natural death? One man was dead, could it possibly be two men? He hated thinking of her this way.

During the next few days, Zeke kept distant from everyone and stewed about Jasmine's innocence. He didn't eat well, barely slept, and hardly noticed Jigger Jones's turkey strut as he showed off for Liza. He didn't come back to the present until a week passed, and Tupper was warming up on the string.

Before the music and dancing took over everything, Zeke left the dining hall and went to the barn. He tossed a blanket over a horse's back. October would greet them with snow soon. Before it did, he needed to check for signs of someone watching the camp. He told Moses they would go the day he collected his letter. He shouldn't have waited so long to check for signs of someone watching.

Zeke found a halter on its hook and put it on his ride, trying to convince himself he was here to search more than he was glad the smell of the musty barn and horses erased the sweet smell of yeasty bread and Heather that saturated even his flannel shirt.

He'd kept his distance, but couldn't help but watch and notice Heather's every move. He didn't even remember what Jasmine smelled like anymore. How long had he been away now?

He brushed the horse's flank with a few heavy strokes. He was sure to get a dressing down from Jiggy when he found out Zeke was making friends with one of his best and largest draft horses. But if he was fast going and coming, Jiggy would never know. The wiry man was all caught up in his plans for a dance with Liza. Teasing the whole camp into a jovial mood all so he could dance with the tiny woman.

Then, they all could dance with her. Maybe Miss Heather would join in?

With a practiced bound, he was on the back of the horse. He pressed his knees into the wide flank and used the mane as reins, ignoring the twinge of pain in his knee.

Wherever this animal had been raised, someone loved him. The horse seemed to enjoy coming to him and carrying him. What brought this animal so far from his roots that he found himself tethered to a load of logs, working and pulling, with Jiggy cussin' to speed him and hollering a blue streak?

He wished he could shake the foreboding that had shadowed him the moment he'd read Patrick's letter as easily as Jiggy shrugged off whatever chased him over the ocean and across the country to the foothills of the Cascade Mountains.

"Like fish out of water Jiggy was. But he doesn't seem to act it." He patted the horse's neck. "We're quite the pair." Zeke went quiet when they entered the edge of the woods. The horse seemed to sense his need to tread slow and be watchful. The itch at the back of his neck was back again. He'd worked hard on Harvey's tallies yesterday so he could break away this afternoon—fresh air before the dancing to come.

Zeke thought it would be hard to find signs, but it was relatively easy even without dismounting.

Several boot prints marred the soil at the base of a fir tree that would take two men's arms to span in a hug. A perfect line of sight to where he and Moses stood the day of the barrel baths.

He should've checked sooner. It wasn't just a feeling. *This is real. Someone is watching. But who?* Had David been really fast and found the address and come after him, beating the warning letter from Patrick?

Were they watching him or Liza and Heather? Or one of the other loggers? There was no way to find out. He pressed the horse to walk the footpath all the way around to the next tree the watcher used, glad the rains had been light of late—not enough to wash away the prints.

Whoever was watching wasn't too concerned about leaving a trail. Was that good or bad?

Zeke sat atop the warm, gentle draft horse and let the rippling of the nearby creek settle him. From there, outside Camp 13, he tried to see things objectively.

His chest tightened. The horse nickered and flicked him with his tail. "Sorry, boy." He released his thighs that squeezed the horse. He thought about leading this horse right out of camp, right down the road to Oregon City. He could catch passage up the Colombia and be home in a couple weeks. Faster, if he packed food and tack and rode hard. Why was he staying here?

He could spy on David and Jasmine if he was in Auburn, just like this stranger spied on them here. He climbed down and wiped away the prints so he could tell if the stalker returned.

Hitting the trail and returning the way he came all sounded good until the niggling possibility of hanging from a tree by his throat entered his mind.

He used a downed tree to mount the draft horse again. Across the way, the back door of the lodge opened, and Heather struggled out, manhandling a bucket of water. She was obviously heading toward the last spindling plants in the garden. Growing season was nearly over. The first frost was only days away, and yet she tended the sad plants. She would tend whatever she was responsible for.

A warmth, the very opposite of thinking about being hanged from a tree, spread throughout his chest. All he wanted to do was hold onto that warmth. To feel safe and valued. Had he ever had that? Had he ever had anyone tend him?

Thinking of Heather waking up next to him in the bed that was once his and was now hers bent his head low. He wouldn't let himself look at her as she worked the greens. He had no right. Not with Jasmine still in his plans. That wasn't fair or wise to any of them. He couldn't trespass Jasmine or himself by carrying on behind her back—even in his mind. *Even if Jasmine was guilty?*

He sighed.

Hanging or not, he needed answers, or he needed to leave soon. Even if he had to face a hanging tree. Heather had been through enough without taking on the unknown mess *he* was dragging around—even if the thought of holding her close on a cold morning sounded as near to heaven as he could get.

So much of his life was waiting for him in the future. What was he supposed to do now? He couldn't fix anything tonight. He would do his part to keep Liza and Heather safe, if someone was watching, and he would keep an eye on the loggers at the same time. For now, he would go back to the lodge, get cleaned up, and do as everyone else—he would dance.

If they smiled and laughed and talked, he would too. But in no uncertain terms would he find himself exclusively beside Miss Heather's side—for himself, but if she needed him...

Heather finished in the garden and was closing the door behind her, returning to the kitchen, when he broke from the forest into view. The horse moved forward before Zeke tapped his side, knowing his desire to return to the barn and lodge before he did himself.

He put the draft horse away, rubbing at the place on his knee that was over tight. If they were going to dance, and he was going to dance, then he didn't want to embarrass Miss Heather by limping and wobbling to Tupper's tunes.

Chapter Fourteen

*H*eather pressed a fork into one of forty baked potatoes nestled beside the massive venison roast, nearly the whole hind quarter of the buck Bjorn butchered specifically for tonight sizzled in its juices.

Things had slipped into a semblance of a routine during the past week while Liza had kept Jiggy at a distance. But the moment of reckoning was upon them.

Tonight was the dance.

Jiggy would claim Liza's hand.

Heather looked at the mass amount of food steaming before her and hoped the men thought it tasted better than she thought it smelled. It was the first venison she'd cooked on this end of the Trail. *The deer meat must be different somehow.* Because the smell made her stomach swim.

"Smells good."

"Glad you think so, Cookie. What are you looking for?"

He was searching through the pegs on the walls that held many a man's drying shirts, coats, and tin pants.

"Two of the fellas told me they're missing things. Boots and long underwear. Not stuff that usually goes missing." Cookie moved through the things and then left, presumably for the bunkhouse. He wouldn't dare accuse anyone of stealing, if he didn't check for misplaced items first. If there was a thief in camp, then the air would be more than charged for a storm—the dance would be the least of their concerns. She was sure.

She turned back to her meal.

Cookie's random declarations that it smelled good appeased

her a little. The men would eat it, even if it wasn't savory. They ate everything that wasn't nailed down. She'd prepared so much food, enough food, since she arrived, to keep her body sore and tired.

Cooking for the crew left her no time to mope. Thoughts of Riley drew a lonely ache but still no tears. Tears would take energy she couldn't spare—even with Liza working alongside her every step. And why would tears come for Riley when they still didn't budge for Mama?

She drizzled a thin stream of molasses over the heap of carrots on her way past. There was too much to do. No time to tend her sadness. It helped that no one asked questions. No one pried into her past. Whether that was because they were men or because each held his own secrets, she didn't know—she suspected both.

The men's boots clomped on the hardwood floor as they pushed the tables up against the walls for room. They seemed to be as excited as Cora Mae on Christmas morning. Too bad Cora Mae couldn't be here for the dance—she would stand shoulder to shoulder with Liza, defending her from Jiggy's advances. Heather almost laughed. Earlier, when she was preparing the venison, Cookie told her the dance was almost as exciting as the Fourth of July, when all the loggers went carousing in town at the same time.

She pressed her lip between her teeth and stirred the heavy brown gravy, ignoring the fatigue that settled in her bones and down to the arches of her feet. She would dance if they asked her. They needed that.

Some more than others.

The empty looks on some of the men's faces reminded her of Pa in the days before he left. Both Frenchie and Moses carried a yoke of heaviness thicker than her gravy. Anyone could see it on them.

She didn't dare ask them about it. That would break the unwritten rule. And that would invite them to ask her questions in return. She couldn't ask. But she could wonder. Was it love? Had they loved like Pa and Ma? Had it left them gutted like an empty eggshell?

Even now as she worked about the kitchen, she could see Moses scribbling in his journal as he did every morning and evening before his meals. The scars on his cheek and down his neck puckered under his frown. If only the writing would bring him a measure of peace. If only he would find the way to the peace and share it with her.

Must be love. Nothing destroyed so thoroughly. Nothing hurt so much. She would always hold Riley in the highest, sweetest regard for his willingness to rescue her, but she would also be ever grateful that she didn't now carry the crushing anvil of love lost. She cared for him, and it hurt plenty to have him gone, but she knew deep down it wasn't the same.

She stood entranced, captivated by the movement of Moses's hands as he pulled a knife from his pocket and sharpened his lead. The tiny flecks of wood flicked in the direction of the barrel stove. She tried to understand Moses's pain from across the room. Could this full house of rowdy men draw him from his pain—his memories—for even a moment?

Or would it all be a lame attempt at a grand distraction that left him weary enough to sleep for a week straight, as it did her?

She checked under the striped ticking that covered her rising rolls hidden like chicks warming under a brooding hen. They would go in the oven that she'd just taken two dozen out of. She inhaled the deep, yeasty scent to replace the smell of roast in her nose.

The rolls would be the final touch to the meal. Even if she was wrong about Moses and his scars, tonight, she would be the distraction. She would leave old memories, hers and theirs, on the benches and in the corners as she joined the playing and dancing. She would do her part to bring medicine and, hopefully, some of it would rub off on her *own* heart and make it so she could feel again.

The boom of many laughs as they ribbed at each other filled the hall. She needed to hear it again—a million times over—to draw out the sting of death and loss. She'd heard Moses's laugh once. What would Zeke's sound like?

He seemed eager to be around her and Liza at the beginning, but ever since that first wake-up call with the barrel baths, he'd kept his distance. Had he changed? Or had she read him wrong?

She should be happy he was staying away. Every time he was near, she felt like she was frying in a pan. *He is no more or less to me than any of these other men.* She lifted the rolls and sniffed in another deep breath, pressing a hand to her flopping belly before she reached to scoop up the pan to put in the oven.

A pair of strong arms came around her from behind and, without even brushing her sleeves, efficiently took the hot rolls and led the way back to the tables. *Zeke. So close, yet so silent and distant.*

Not even a hello or a greeting. Just efficient and strong arms. Had she done something? Had she known him long enough to even wonder such a thing? And why did she care?

Why did it bother her that he set the rolls down and left with nothing more than a nod? She didn't need the extra confusion. She didn't need the questions. None of the other loggers' comings and goings mattered to her.

She dusted a puff of white flour off her sleeve. He was the first connection she and Liza made in this new life. He and Cookie made her feel safe. *That's all.* It was only natural that she wanted to feel close to him. *Liar.* Cookie never made her feel ruffled. Cookie was always talking to her. Or rather barking an order or asking for a recipe.

Maybe Zeke was treating her the same as everyone else. She wanted to huff again, but decided a breath of the rain-washed, clean air would be better for her temperamental tummy and roiling emotions than another breath of the cooking meat.

She let the men dish up. The second batch of rolls would be consumed the instant they were done. When all had been served and the room was filled with men's chatter and scraping forks, she stepped out the back door that opened onto a large garden plot that was the biggest she'd ever seen but was still way too small to meet the needs of this crew. She took a deep breath and wiped her brow. Every time she saw it, she decided what she would add and where it would go if she was here come spring.

It would frost soon and harden everything in sight. With thoughts of winter came thoughts of her future, when would she have enough money to reach Rebecca? Definitely no later than next spring, if she had any say in the matter.

She stayed out there until the heat of the ovens turned to chill on her skin. When she came back inside, the room was coming alive to Tupper's fiddle. Plates were empty, and Liza was clearing them all away. Tupper stopped to twist and turn the knobs, making a game out of touching a note here and there. Underneath his serious front he was a showman. How many of the men around the room were like him, creating a mask to show the people around them to cover their softer side? Liza did that. Did she?

She squeezed nails into her palms when her eyes betrayed her and sought out Zeke's broad shoulders first. Was the distance he was creating between them a cover? Was she sending him a message to stay away? She probably was. She should be happy about that. It was easier than carrying around a rolling pin. She smiled at that idea.

He must have felt her gaze. He looked up from his almost clean plate and met her eyes. She didn't look away. She didn't let the smile fade or sweep a hand up to check for loose curls. Her hair would loosen before the night was over. It would fall into a heap of soft rings around her face and neck after the first dance even though she'd used twice the pins to anchor it.

Zeke's gaze stayed on her until one of the other men stumbled into the back of his chair on his way past.

When he looked away, she let herself reach up and touch her special ribbon. The one she had twisted through her pins and curls. She missed her sister-friends enough that the piece of cloth with its fading pattern on blue added a homesick kick to her swirling stomach.

The ribbon marked the promise sewn in the back of Victoria, Cora Mae's fancy porcelain doll. The doll that witnessed her life-pact, her forever promise. The slim material made her feel like someone was witnessing these days of her life, someone who loved her and cared what happened or how hard things were.

Liza was a dear, and Heather appreciated having her around, especially in the small cabin at night when the walls shook with the sound of snoring men. But Liza was still getting to know her, and she was still getting to know Liza. Cora Mae, Rose, and Rebecca wouldn't need more than a look to know she was done in.

Then Zeke was beside her, dropping his tin plate in Liza's clearly marked crate before he was there, standing at her elbow. All the distance he'd created throughout the past days evaporated like the steam on the nearly gone roast. She hadn't seen him approach, she was so lost in thoughts of her dear friends. Maybe he would take another trip to town. Maybe she could write another letter. She could send news of where she was and how she was managing. Zeke had collected the mail last time, maybe he could take one to town and mail it for her.

"The meal was satisfying. The crew is keeping you and Liza a secret. Did you know that?" Zeke said.

"A secret? From whom?"

"From everyone. From the other camps. News travels fast around these mountains and hills. Especially amongst the loggers. As soon as the others figure out you cook like this." He waved his hand to the room full of men enjoying their last bites and full bellies. "Then there will be a waiting line for new hires to work here. And none of these loggers will get to stay, if they don't put in their best, twelve hours a day. Things could get intense."

She felt him studying her.

"Are you done here?" he asked. "Do you want to take a seat? You look like you put in your twelve already. Not that you don't look lovely."

It felt good to have someone notice, but did she want him to see how uncertain he made her feel? Maybe he was used to being around women and reading their feelings…more so than the others. She didn't answer but followed as he led her to a chair. She would sit and collect her energy. The activity of the room slowly increased as more men finished chewing and put their tin plates in the crate—and Tupper's tunes filled the hall.

"More intensity? This place doesn't need that," Heather said.

He added, "No they don't. Like a rough handled keg of powder never knows when it will go boom."

"Camp 13 doesn't need any more…" She nodded to where Liza was working. Jiggy was creating a stir and drawing everyone's eye as he circled Liza as she wiped the oilcloths clean that covered each table to protect the wood from food stains.

"It was nice of whoever it was to bring the oilcloths to Liza. She smiled for most of the morning when she found them."

"The men are mighty addicted to that little smile—rare as hen's teeth that it is—Jiggy most of all. I suspect there will be more surprises in the future. It's nice to have something to think on other than whether the springboard that is holding you forty feet off the ground is set proper or whether the tree will land where your saw told it to, or if, God forbid, it lands on top of you."

"That sounds worrisome. Do you like counting trees for Harvey? Would you rather work up there with the papers or up on the springboards sawing?" She pointed to his loft and tried not to think of him sleeping up there. She'd only come into the kitchen once when she could still hear his heavy breathing. He spent part of each day out in the forest counting—but he was never gone from Liza and Heather's side long enough to worry Cookie.

He shrugged. "It's all work."

A big laugh boomed from Cookie. "This is gonna be one heck of a night. They are all going to sleep until I ring the gut-hammer in the morning."

She nodded. Most of the time, Liza woke her before Cookie rang the triangle. How her friend managed to wake before it, after working as hard as they did, was a mystery to Heather.

Heather felt like she could lay down and sleep for a week straight right then, if everyone left her to it. She couldn't think about her bed now, or her head would swim and take her stomach with it. She would start yawning as everyone else started dancing.

Zeke was still answering her question. "I like testing my leg, and I like seeing the land. That's what I did before coming here. I was a surveyor. I don't mind the tallies. I miss how fast the days went when swinging an axe and pulling a saw."

She bobbed a quick curtsy so he would know she heard. What else was there to say. When he didn't say more, she watched Liza and Jiggy. "I think, if Mr. Jiggy has his way, then you'll have an opportunity to test your leg tonight along with Liza."

"How long do you think it will take for him to wear her down?" Zeke asked.

"We're about to find out."

Tupper's hands were flying over the strings. The men were turned on their seats to watch the show. A few trickles of pipe or cigar smoke filtered up to the main support beam—a massive log above their heads.

Bjorn clapped his hands to the beat and spit a stream of tobacco to sizzle on the barrel stove in rhythm with Tupper's stomping foot.

Jiggy's graceful voice carried above the music for all to hear. "I'm fully clothed, Miss Liza, I hope you do appreciate I put on my best Sunday shirt just for you. Lord Ashburton over there wanted to tie a cravat around my neck all fancy like, but I'm done with those. Shall I make you an offer for the next dance?"

"You can make it if you want to, wearing whatever kind of necktie suits your fancy." She spit.

"I suppose you'd only be happy if my tie was made of rope with the other end hanging from a tree?"

Heather should have been watching Jiggy and Liza spar, like everyone else, but once again her mind had drifted, and she'd been staring at Zeke's handsome face and dark beard. She saw the complete whites of his eyes and the compulsive rub of his neck when they bantered about hanging. *Why is he afraid of a hangman's noose?* What could this kind man have possibly done? Did it have something to do with why he was way out in this godforsaken backwoods logging camp?

Zeke caught her staring and said, "Liza might as well have

used a white glove and slapped his cheek like they do in England, where he's from. A good old-fashioned duel might be a little less dramatic."

"I thought he was from France."

"He is. Both France and England. He probably has a title too, if I remember right."

They both watched Liza slide her tiny boots together until no space was between her feet.

She crossed her arms over her chest. "You think so poorly of me? I wouldn't wish nary a soul to swing from a hangman's noose, and yet you'd be willing to dance with someone who'd wish that upon ya? No accounting for taste."

"Hear that Ashburton? She's questioning my taste. Don't you wish Mother could hear her say it?"

They knew each other's families?

The two old friends shared a laugh.

Heather didn't know if it was the tension between Liza and Jiggy, or the new questions about Zeke's past, or the lingering smell and heat from cooking the venison, but her stomach turned again. She wanted the two to quit bantering like roosters and start the dancing, so she could fall into her bed and sleep away the aches in her feet and lower back.

Jiggy turned from Ashburton back to Liza, made a little bow, and turned up the charm. "You should know, where Ashburton and I come from, not only do I have a reputation for only appreciating the finest things, but I've been known to set a trend or two with but a glance of interest. You, my dear, would be considered nothing short of the most incomparable of the season with all of my efforts."

"Well that, kind sir, sounds exhausting." She jutted her chin.

Jiggy threw his head back and roared. Smiles cracked through scraggly beards, some missing a tooth here or there, all around the room at the sound. Next they knew, Jiggy was extending his arm. "Would you do me the honor?"

"I will on one condition." Liza tapped her boot, arms still crossed.

He quirked an eyebrow.

"I meant what I said about not needing no man to nestle up beside me. I also don't need every-last-one of you blokes gazing on while Jiggy makes a fool of me. I will dance one dance with each one of you, *if* you all keep the dance floor full. And I'll dance with Moses first, since he's the most sensible one and never gives nobody any lip and fuss."

Zeke grinned at the look of confusion on Moses's face as Liza darted around Jiggy and came to his side. Moses had secreted himself in the corner behind the barrel stove, as far away from the commotion as possible. He'd been writing in his journal when Liza said his name.

Zeke bent down and whispered in Heather's ear. It sent a shiver down her neck. "He looks scared."

"I think you're right." Heather put a hand to her lips to keep her giggle in check. Liza might not appreciate the humor of it.

Liza didn't waste any time coming to Moses and extending her arm as Jiggy had to her.

Chapter Fifteen

❦

*M*oses and Liza bounced into motion, matching the rhythm of the music. Zeke looked down at Heather. She was so petite next to him; she didn't even come up to his shoulder. But he was happy to see the spark of joy bounce into her cool-blues with a grin to match. And her tiny foot began tapping out the rhythm.

She said, "Moses is scared. Scared and shocked. I wonder if he knows how to dance?" Moses's dark skin made Liza's seem all the paler, and his large shoulders made Liza's look all the tinier.

Tupper switched up the tune. He twisted and turned the notes until the whole room felt his energy.

Zeke wanted to dance with Heather, so he would have to do his part to meet Liza's demands.

He wanted to shelter Heather in his arms, but he shouldn't—couldn't. Not without his thoughts betraying Jasmine and pricking his conscience like a wood sliver.

He couldn't dance with her until he, at least, danced with Liza, and a handful of the fellas danced with Heather. He needed to treat her the same as everyone else in the room—the same way he treated Liza. His leg would be tested for sure—because he would be dancing a lot—to dance with Heather. He would hold his head up high as he danced. His integrity was all he had left. It was his shield and his pride, even if it was being destroyed back in Auburn by David and his lies.

Frenchie made a show and pounced into the fray in the middle of the dance floor with a fancy step and a little shuffle as he worked his way to Heather. Zeke had to fold his fingers to keep from blocking Heather from ending up in his arms—the other man's energy was so contagious.

Frenchie bowed over Heather's hand, and she acquiesced. Leaving Zeke to speculate as he watched. She seemed so gentle and caring. Why was she out here in this rugged place? She was even careful enough to not put her hand on the part of Frenchie's shoulder that most assuredly was covered with red scabs under his shirt in the shape of the spikes on the bottom of Jiggy's boots from her first night in camp.

Liza shouted above the music, "All of ya! You wanna dance with me or Miss Heather, you better be doing your part. Not just sitting there with your eyes popping out of yer heads."

Suitably chastised, Zeke stood with the rest of the men and tried to find moves to the song without being in the way of the two dancing pairs. Bjorn with all his height and girth found the only fellow that was small enough to compete with wiry Jiggy for size. Bjorn bowed and offered his hand. Bjorn looked to Liza, but before Liza could add her two cents, the little man tapped Bjorn on the shoulder and bowed over Bjorn's hand—the little man would be lead.

The room erupted with ribbing jests as Bjorn presented a curtsy and batted his eyelashes.

Liza was grinning at the pair when they went flying past her. Both men seemed to know the intricate steps to a formal dance. They peacocked their moves until a glisten of sweat marked their foreheads.

Half the men joined in. Some romped and stomped and others executed precise polished moves. All revealed a little more of themselves to the whole.

Moses passed Liza to Jiggy only a few notes before Frenchie placed Heather's hand in Zeke's.

Home.

The moment her hand touched his, his heart beat like the thundering hooves of the oxen and draft horses heading back to the barn after a long day of pulling.

There was no *deciding* to dance with her or not. Frenchie took the decision out of his hands, and now he was holding her. He pulled her close enough to maneuver the song and protect her from getting slammed by a few overzealous loggers.

Heather smelled like honeysuckle and fresh rain. Her hand trembled slightly in his. Was she nervous too? He was ready to start them around the room when Tupper, with a mischievous grin, turned his fiddle to the waltz. The room slowed in unison. A few more guffaws were heard as the men dancing with other men made a show of embracing each other in the closeness of the dance.

"May I?" he asked.

She nodded, and he moved to hold her in the proper position, glad his mother had pretended to have parties from time to time and showed him the way of it. He'd only ever danced the waltz with her, and he wasn't all that sure that his mother knew the right moves. When a clod-footed pair nearly crashed into him from the side, he figured it didn't matter. He pulled her close. Telling himself that it was for her safety.

"Do you think Jiggy paid Mr. Tupper off?" she asked.

"Anything is possible. Jigger Jones is a force when he's determined."

"Liza will test his merit, I imagine. But they do look lovely together. I wonder how she learned the steps."

"She didn't. He has her scooped on his chest. Look at her feet. They barely touch. He is calling the shots on this one. And she looks none too happy—like a feisty kitten."

Heather's soft laugh touched more than his ears. "I wonder what it would look like if she was enjoying herself. She might not know what that feels like. Things have been rough for her."

"For you too? You still look a little tired. I hope you won't let Cookie work you into a sick."

"I'm fine. It will be easier as I figure out the routine. Cookie agrees. There's been a lot to get used to. And I haven't slept as well as I thought I would. Have you heard the noise they all make? It shakes the walls."

"Why do you think I bartered to sleep up there?" He nodded toward the loft and kept them moving around the floor. "You should hear the snores when you're in the bunkhouse. The first week, I kept waking thinking a thunderstorm was crashing through."

"Yes! Exactly. Liza sleeps through it like it was nothing and wakes before Cookie beats the gut-hammer every morning. I haven't adjusted quite so well."

"Cookie says the snoring is why he made his bed in that small pantry behind the kitchen. But he could snore five men under the table."

"Does he keep you awake in here?" He caught her checking a yawn even as the room twirled by. He smiled at her. "All this talk of sleep."

She smiled back.

"No. I had weeks to get used to the sound. You'll be fine in a few more days."

"Yes." And like that, she was removed from his arms by a hairy-faced woodsman only to be passed off from one logger to the next.

Liza and Heather danced almost a full hour before Cookie called a break for the girls. He brought them to the counter and surprised them with lemonade.

Zeke moved to sit in Moses's chair after he took his turn with Liza. He could watch the whole room and have a better view of the ladies and Cookie. No fire burned in the belly of the giant stove on a night like tonight. The large room was overwarm with all the fun.

Cookie was proud of his surprise. "It's not full-on lemonade. There were only two lemons. But it should cut the thirst better than water. I even sweetened it a little with the honey that you boys collected for Miss Liza."

All the dancers slowed, all but Jiggy and Bjorn.

When Tupper found it was just them, he tripped the music to double time, his pace on the strings a challenge to the dancers. The two men danced and tossed and spun each other in a crazy, powerful, unconventional, yet somehow a perfectly timed, rampage of a dance. Heather and Liza sipped their drinks and stayed out of the way of the moving pair. Everyone else joined with stomps and clapped and hooted them on. Catcalls and whistles intertwined with the tune swirling around them.

In the midst of all the fun, Zeke noticed Heather's eyes roll back and her glass fall. He sprang toward her as she was going down—from heat or fatigue Zeke didn't know. With a sliding dive from his place in the chair to the counter, he kept her head from hitting the floor, barely just, ignoring the flash of pain that shot through his knee.

Tupper scraped the last note. Silence followed. And then pandemonium burst. He didn't know who spoke except Moses's mumbled cry of Heather's name. "Heeeerrrra."

"Get a blanket to cover her."

"And a pillow."

"Do you have more lemonade, Cookie?"

"Heather. I'm here, Heather." Liza didn't try to take Heather out of Zeke's arms, where he bundled her, but Liza did scoop up her free hand and patted the back, hoping to bring her around.

Every logger in the room was circled around, crowding them.

After a few more long moments, Heather did come around and she was instantly sick on the wooden floor beside them.

Some of the men groaned and others gagged, but most simply stepped back.

Cookie took charge, "All right now. End of the fun. Head to your bunks. The Bull will be expecting the normal count tomorrow no matter how late you stay up. That's right. Clear out and let us tend to Miss Heather. I'm sure I just worked her too hard, and she got motion sick flinging around the room with all you ugly scrubs."

"You do work her hard. Harder than Jiggy does the oxen," one logger shouted.

The fellow that hollered it probably expected Cookie to be offended and give as good as he got like usual.

The room emptied faster when Cookie sounded unsure. "You might be right. Expect beans and grits for the next few days. The girls both deserve a few days rest after cooking and fetching and caring for your sorry hides these past days. Might be I forgot to give them a day off. Off with you now."

Everyone was moving to clear the room. "Does that mean there won't be cinnamon rolls in the morning?" One loan comment broke the exit.

"Git. Go on now. Leave us to it."

Heather heard the men talking above her but couldn't focus on what they were saying. She felt a slight better after being sick, but the room still whirled. Even Zeke's face mere inches above hers didn't distract her from the queasiness in her gut that was mounting for another attack.

Liza patted the back of her hand until it was pure red with the slaps. "Are you ill? I don't want you to die. Connie Evans died when I was in school with her. And she just got all-the-sudden-sick like this." Liza's voice quavered.

Heather chuckled. "I'm not sure. I don't plan on dying." She slipped her poor hand from Liza's grasp and started to sit up.

"Here, let me help you." Zeke tucked himself behind her, so she could have a place to lean as she gained her bearings. His injured leg stretched straight.

Cookie came back from bolting the last logger out of the front door. If her head wasn't pounding, she would have laughed again as the chubby man scurried to the kitchen for an empty bucket and another filled with rags and toweling. His feet moved faster than she'd seen them go—even when the batch of snickerdoodles was burning.

Cookie knelt with a huff and started to clean up her sick. "Here. Keep this close. In case there's a repeat." He handed the bucket to Heather.

Zeke grabbed it and balanced it on her outstretched legs—at hand, if she needed it.

"I'm afraid those boys might be right. I may have overworked you. Love having two extra pairs of hands. But I should have known better. My Clare was a delicate thing. I made sure she wasn't burnt to the sockets especially when—" Cookie stopped mid-stroke on the floor and stared at Heather like she had the pox.

His eyes bulged.

She started to move, and Zeke was there to give an arm up. "What? I think I'm fine. I could even get up now."

"Wait. Not yet. There is something I need to ask you—a mite personal question. Changes a lot of things, if I'm right." Cookie looked at Liza and Zeke and scanned the room before his worried face met Heather's. He came in closer and spoke his question in the merest of whispers. "Is there any way you could possibly be in the family way? My Clare always got the faints when she was carrying my brood."

"The family way? Uh. What? Oh."

Zeke tensed behind her.

She could almost feel each of her thoughts as they processed. Each new one thumped in until the final one fell heavy, like a tree in the forest. "Maybe, I mean yes." She put a hand to her face as if to keep them all from seeing her.

"Whatever the case may be. You're here. You're not alone," Zeke said with her back rested on his chest. She could feel his chest thrum.

"A baby? Is that what you said?" Liza seemed just as rocked as Heather. "Are you going to have a baby? That's a sight better than dying."

"And how." Cookie laughed. "Better than dying, but it can take a while for the idea to settle in and take root. Quite a shock if this is the first you—"

Heather's head was spinning, and the room went black for a second time.

"Oh, dear," Liza added.

Before Heather could do anything, Zeke scooped her into his arms, careful not to drop her...and the baby.

A baby?

Her vision cleared as he lifted her. She could be growing a person inside her. *Her own family.*

And the world stopped spinning just as Zeke sat, with her on his lap, on one of the benches that lined the walls.

Cookie placed the bucket on the table next to them, so it would be close if she grew sick again. "Let me go grab some bread. Helped my wife. Maybe it will help you?" Cookie was off.

Heather put her hand to her head. "A baby. I'm not sure. How am I? What am I supposed to do?" Riley was gone. Oh, Lord.

Cookie was back with the crust of bread on a small plate and a cool wet cloth for her neck.

After she took a small mouthful of the bread and Liza placed the towel on her neck, Zeke's voice prayed into her confusion. Peace instantly made her take a deep breath.

"Comfort my friend in this great moment. Help her understand Your plans for her future and keep her safe and help us know how to come alongside and give her what she needs as she grows and tends her child...her family."

Heather didn't try to leave his lap. "Thank you. But I don't know. How am I to know these things?"

Zeke was glad she was looking at Cookie for the answer and not him. The shock of the possibility still hadn't fully registered in his mind. And he wasn't the one involved.

"Tell you what. You take tomorrow off and sleep in well and tight. Then, in the afternoon, I'll send Zeke and Liza with you to town. I'll have you fetch goods for the kitchen, the mail, and whatever else I can think of, so none of the boys will worry. But Zeke, while you're in town, seek out Doctor Corbin. He will have answers to her questions, and he will know for sure. What do you think?" He was asking Heather.

"I suppose that's best. I have to find out. After all this my mind won't stop turning over the possibility until I know one way or the other. And sleep sounds divine. I've been bone-tired all day."

"You should've spoken up. You should have said something."

Heather smiled at Liza.

"A baby. I can't get my heart to stop beating as fast as Tupper's music. I'm still so glad you ain't dying. You ain't, are ya?" Liza felt Heather's forehead. "But we don't know for sure?"

Liza's comment was absurd. Heather gave a weak laugh.

Zeke squeezed her to his chest.

Heather answered, "No. I don't actually know. On either account. All I know is Zeke's prayer makes me want to pray a few hundred prayers of my own and sleep for a week." She broke off a small hunk of the bread and ate it.

Zeke stood, and Heather squeaked her surprise as she flung her arms to hold him around the neck. "Let's get you settled for the night."

She dropped the bread.

"I've got you."

But did he? Would his knee take the weight of a second person? Could he take the weight of another responsibility when his life seemed to be weak and limping?

"Liza, help me gather what she'll need for the night. You'll have to keep a watch on her until morning. If it isn't a wee one that took her down, then it might get worse. We might need to bring the doctor in." Cookie finished cleaning the mess and was barking orders at Liza as Zeke carried Heather to the door.

Zeke was stepping with sure confident steps. Other than a lot of joint popping, his leg was holding up.

"Thank you, and I'm sorry." Heather tucked her chin, so he couldn't see her face.

"Nothing to be sorry for. Nothing to thank me for. There is a lot for you to think on."

"Hard to consider or believe. Could Cookie be right?" She looked at him then. Her cool-blue eyes, mere inches from his own, seeking his honest opinion.

He wanted to say so much but couldn't; his face blushed warm under his beard.

She'd embarrassed him. But who had time to think about that when it felt like the whole world shifted. *Married then widowed, then a child. Her child.* A whole person she hadn't even met yet was hers to care for. She would go from one person to two.

Zeke's voice rumbled under her as he stepped over the worst of the mud. "A lot to take in. I can see why you fainted. But if it's true, then just think, you have a new family member coming—counting on us to take care of you. In my world, family was my most precious possession."

Liza came out of the lodge with the bucket and other things. She zipped past them, opening the cabin door and leading the way inside their little home. When Zeke carried her inside, Liza handed Heather another hunk of bread and then unloaded the things in her arms onto a small table. Zeke held her for one extra moment, and then released her legs, so they dangled to the floor. He kept a tight hold until he was sure she had her balance, and then he stepped back. Heather stared at his face—where the blush had been—still thinking of the changes that could be.

He probably thought she was lost in thought, but she wasn't. A long minute passed. "Family."

He nodded. "I'll see you tomorrow. I'll fill the water barrel before I turn in tonight in case you have need of fresh water. Don't rush. Be well, Miss Heather." And with that he turned and left her standing and chewing the dry bread as lost and frightened on the outside as she was on the inside.

Her stomach turned again.

She watched while he found a pair of empty buckets right outside the door and headed to the creek to fill them.

Zeke was lost to his thoughts as the nearly frozen mud beneath his feet crunched the path down to the stream. He drew the water in slow measured scoops, giving his mind a chance to catch hold of one unsettled thought at a time.

He would stay by her side. She didn't seem to have anyone but Liza, and Liza could only do so much. As far as he could tell, they were two women alone. *And I'm alone.* When they went into town tomorrow, he would check for a letter, but if there was nothing from Patrick, he would wait patiently until he sent news, and he would consider the lack of new information as direction from the Lord. Maybe he was here to help Heather in her time of need. Maybe supporting her was the thing he could help with while he couldn't do anything for himself. He liked that idea.

A baby.

For the first time in weeks, in this moment, he felt a settling peace. Even when he thought of Jasmine—of possibly losing Jasmine—he stayed at rest. He carried the first pair of full water buckets back and dumped them in the barrel outside the girls' front door and went back for one more round.

The dark of night settled in around him, and the snores from the men in the bunkhouse rumbled through the walls. A screech owl objected to the noise. Zeke looked to find the owl in the darkness and caught sight of glowing embers of a pipe or cigar. As fast as he saw it, it was flicked to the ground and snuffed out.

"Who's there?" Who watched him? And why? It could be one of the men unable to sleep. It could be nothing. Should he track whoever it was?

No. He would tell Cookie and Moses and the men, and they would all be more vigilant, but the girls couldn't know.

They had enough to worry about without adding something new to the changes in their lives. It could be as simple as a logger from another camp of men checking if the rumors of new lady cooks were legitimate. He would make sure to be extra watchful tomorrow on his way to town. And he would be sure to alert the

men to do the same.

Chapter Sixteen

Every bone in Heather's body rattled free of its moorings as the wheels of the wagon bumped over the ruts. The wagon ride to town was winding and slow. Beautiful ferns and tall grasses faded from green to brown at the feet of the cedars and the oaks on both sides of the skid road. Milk Creek was full and rolled past them, snaking between the tree trunks. Trees with girths as big around as flour barrels in every direction. The sounds and the beauty couldn't distract her from the possibility that Riley's child could even now be growing inside her.

"Cookie asked if we could swing by the mercantile and buy Frenchie a new mackinaw while we're in town. His went missing a few days back." Zeke's leg pressed warm against hers.

Heather murmured her agreement.

"Has he been out working without a coat? No one should be left to freeze like that." Liza was always making sure the men were warm and dry.

"Most of the fellas have two coats, so one can dry while they wear the other. His second is missing. None of the other fellas have it, but he's not freezing."

"How can he know his is missing? You look like a line of matching twins when you have them on all at the same time."

"The men can tell his apart from the others. His had a notch out of the collar. He took a fall off his springboard, sixty feet up, and only lived because his collar caught on a snag breaking his fall. It didn't hold. It tore away, but it slowed him down and made his feet hit the ground first. No one in camp would take his lucky charm."

Heather appreciated what they were trying to do. Both Liza and Zeke were distracting her from what was coming.

Me a mother? A baby without a husband? Her wagon ride wasn't the only thing being shaken. How would she provide for this little one? How would she work and tend the baby? If she couldn't work through the winter and into spring, how would she save enough to make the trip to find Rebecca?

Rebecca and the rest of her heart-sisters, what would they think? Was she the first among them to become a mother? They would want to know as soon as she did. She would write them. She still hadn't told them what Camp 13 was like. She ignored thoughts of Zeke. There was nothing to tell. If Cora Mae, Rose, and Rebecca knew what she was up against, then she wasn't alone, that was the pact—to witness each other's lives—to care.

Liza, on the outside section of the wagon seat, kept placing a bracing arm across Heather's lap to ensure she not fall off. And she scooted so close to Heather's side that she was forced to press against Zeke.

She didn't mind. Last night, at the dance, she'd been so conscious of every move Zeke made—even though she was extra sure not to draw his attention. Now, she cared for none of that. The warmth of his side felt solid when her whole world was mixed up. "Jesus." She nearly moaned her prayer. She wanted to lay her head back on Zeke's shoulder and sleep for hours—if the wagon would just hold still.

A baby.

Could that really be why she fainted? She pressed a hand to her flat stomach.

The brim of Zeke's hat bobbed into her view. He must've seen her hand slide to her belly. He didn't say anything, but compassion gentled his eyes.

They rode on in silence. Heather watched the leaves fall from the trees, trying not to jump ahead of whatever the doctor's news would be.

Along the way, a farmhouse came into view. A pair of horses spooked at the wagon noise and ran in tandem in the tall grass—

tails high. They galloped to the end of their pasture before one kicked out at the other. If she could be so free. If she could kick back at all that was happening to her—that had happened to her.

The clanking of a smithy sounded nearby. A dog barked. They were almost to town. Then the wagon came to a stop. Zeke stepped down and tied the reins to the post that ran the length of the boardwalk.

Heather read the sign on the building right in front of her. DOCTOR MEDICAL. Her chest squeezed, and her breath hitched. No going back. *That's true, even if I don't let the doctor check me.*

Zeke came back to her side of the wagon. "Can you two manage? Do you need me to stay with you? I could at least introduce you to the doctor. I spent a little time with him when this first happened." He rubbed an open hand down the side of his leg and rested his large palm on his injured knee. "He's a good doctor—and clean. Doesn't believe in bloodletting. He'll go on and on about it." He seemed nervous.

Heather studied the worn-out, brown toes of her boots. Did she want him in there with her? The doctor was sure to ask as many questions. Her face heated. "Thank you. I can manage. Liza will support me well enough. I imagine this appointment would be more uncomfortable for us both, if you stayed. But thank you." She couldn't delay any longer. Any moment she should stand up. Any moment, she should climb down from the wagon, and any moment she should step into whatever her future had for her.

I can't move, Father.

Mama's words came just in time. *"The Lord's mercies are new every morning—thank God for it. It's up to you whether or not you take them up. Pure wasteful not to."* Her mother always rattled on about the Lord's mercies on the hard days. Was that why Heather remembered her words now—because this was hard?

Heather swallowed and reached out from an inside place—deep in her belly—toward those promised mercies. *Help.*

Before Heather could muster a move, Liza nudged an elbow into her ribs "I've got your back. If this doctor don't know his stuff." She clutched Heather's wrist. "I'd rather he tells you that you're to be a ma, than that you're terrible sick. But he could say either. I've been watching you...how green you grew on the ride. You sure you ain't death-sick?"

Heather stood—standing in place to let her stomach settle and to let powerless doom roll over and turn into determination.

Liza let go of her arm as Heather spoke, "The wagon ride made me feel woozy, but only from the rocking. I assure you I'm fine." She wasn't a damsel in distress. She never had that luxury. This was different than Ma and Riley. She'd buried them and left them behind, but this she had to face. She could start by knowing the truth—no matter how big.

Zeke lent Heather a hand to help her down.

"I'll be fine, truly." She said it for herself and for Zeke and Liza to hear. She moved toward the boardwalk muttering for no one but herself. "Might not be true a year from now, having a youngin' in tow—having to provide for us both." She turned to face Zeke and spoke up, "Right now, I need answers to a hundred questions, and they are in there."

"I understand needing answers to hard questions."

She remembered the way Zeke fingered his neck when the jokes about hanging ran the room. He probably did have big questions. That made her feel strangely not alone.

Liza jumped from the wagon, landed with a two-footed thump on the packed dirt street, and trotted up beside her while Zeke filled them in. "Doc should be in. When he isn't doctorin' folks, he makes furniture to stay busy and make extra coin. If he doesn't answer the knock go ahead around the back—that way." Zeke pointed to a path wide enough to fit a wagon between the wooden buildings. "I'll leave you ladies to it. I'll collect Camp 13's mail and the wanted posters that Cookie loves so much. Then I'll get the coat. I'll wait in the wagon, here, when I'm done. No need to hurry on my account. Cookie told us to take the whole day."

Zeke left their side, with a courteous lift of his hat, and walked down the middle of the street. Not a solitary other person could be seen on the walkway from one end of town to the other. The street was as empty as Heather's heart felt. Were all the people minding their farms?

Smoke rolling out of the chimneys here and there and the sounds of laughing children came from a long way off. *Laughing children.* She brushed over her stomach again.

Liza put her arm on Heather's and tugged her forward. "The mail must be delivered to the mercantile, that must be why he's going there. You ready? Should we get inside? Get this over with?"

Heather didn't answer but walked up the steps to the door, not letting go of Liza's arm. Liza knocked for them both, and then her tiny friend opened the heavy door and hollered in her I'm-in-charge voice. "Hello? Doctor?"

A thick-chested man with a horseshoe mustache came to them from a back room. "Howdy, ladies. Doc here, but I suppose you figured that. Come on in and tell me what I can do for you while I wash the wood dust from my hands."

"Is she dying, or is she having a baby?" Heather blushed at Liza's crazy-blurt.

"A baby or death—are those our only two options?" Doc used the soap as he answered.

Heather patted Liza's hand on her arm. The trembling in Liza matched her own knocking knees.

Heather asked, "I'm not rightly sure, doctor? I come with a lot of questions, and I hope you can answer them. Those were the only two guesses we came up with. Maybe you'll give us more to choose from?" She tried to be lighthearted to match the doctor's jovial nature, but the swimming feeling returned to her stomach, and she felt like she was wilting.

Once his hands were clean and dry, he patted the long bed-sized bench, "Here, come sit down. Either option is scary enough to give the strongest person weak knees." The doctor switched from an apron that had woodworking tools hidden in several deep pockets to one that hung stiff and clean from a peg on the wall. "I can give your situation a try. But to answer your questions, I'll hafta ask plenty of my own. You can have a seat over there, miss. And you can move that chair beside your friend."

Liza scraped the chair as she dragged it beside Heather. Liza's face was as white as the curtain that hung across the doorway to separate the space they were in from the rest of the room. Heather wanted to put her at ease, but how could she when her life would change behind this curtain…in mere moments.

But I have to know.

David ran a hand through his hair and messed it up. Where was Zeke Bradley, and where was *his* deed? Would Zeke ever come back? It was time to find out what happened to Price Mansion, if Zeke never returned—maybe he could maneuver his way around the deed.

He didn't knock before he entered the lawyer's office, but he did school his features into the professional calm that always got him the sale. The lawyer was probably sitting stuffing his face and licking his fingers. *Did the man do anything but eat?*

Apparently, he did. The lawyer was struggling to put on his jacket.

"Good evening, sir."

"What can I do for you, Mr. Vickner? I'm about done for the day. A steak over at the diner has my name on it."

And there it is, food again. "Please, call me David. I won't keep you from your meal for long. I thought I would ask you a tough question I've been wondering about since that stranger was murdered by Zeke Bradley." He waited for the lawyer to finish sliding one of his chubby arms into his coat. "Now that he's a wanted man, what happens to the Price Mansion? Will it go up for auction? It really would be a shame to let it fall into disrepair or even stay empty for too long. Those old places need care." And it was like a king's throne, his throne, and *he* would sit on his throne— beg, borrow, or steal.

"You'll have to wait until the law decides if Mr. Bradley is guilty or innocent. It's a matter for the town or the sheriff to decide—probably won't happen until there is some sort of news on Zeke." The lawyer finally wiggled his chubby arm into the ill-fitted sleeve. He was floundering like a fish on a riverbank to reach the other sleeve.

"But if he doesn't come back? If they never find him?"

"No worries on that score. I've a source that gave me some news, and as long as he is alive, has the deed, and hasn't been charged by the sheriff or the town, the house is his to use as he sees fit." He coughed up a dust, and after finally wrestling his jacket across his shoulders, he had to use a hankie to mop his sweat.

This was the second time this man had stymied him with news—and he was again behind. David hated to be at a disadvantage. He prided himself on staying one step ahead of his opponent—of everyone. And this greasy mess of a man had maneuvered the Price Mansion out from under him twice.

He was repulsed by the lawyer's manner and behavior, but he still needed his favor. "You heard from him? That's fine news. Did you send for the sheriff of Baker City to go after him? He is wanted. We should see him hang."

The lawyer stopped and looked at him.

David settled his features to tell the story the lawyer most likely wanted to read.

"Wanted for questioning at this point. No talk of hanging."

"Yet."

The lawyer pulled a hat that easily molded to his bald head off the shelf and began to move past David toward the door.

David went on, "He was there beside the dead man. I saw him with my own eyes." And the lawyer was dismissing him for a steak.

"That may be the case, but where I come from printing your own wanted poster and putting your own money up for reward smacks of something more than altruism."

"Careful." David wanted to say so much more.

"Oh, I am. Careful as a rattlesnake—a hungry one who is ready for his steak." He pointed toward the door. "After you."

Did this lawyer with three chins have any idea what could befall him in his sleep if he threatened him? He could poison him like he had Mr. Price. He could bash him like the stranger. But he would prefer to see his eyes bulge like the original David Vickner, the banker he'd killed—that man now knew not to accuse him. *Patience. Stick to the plan. Move slow.* "Rattlesnake or not, a man died. I happen to think that someone should pay the price for that crime. And this town needs justice."

The lawyer didn't answer. He closed the door and made obvious work of locking it behind him. "This town has muddled along without you and your concern for many years. I think she can stand on her own feet. Would you like to share my dinner table? They're making roasted potatoes to go with the steak. One of Porter's cows—best around."

"I'll pass, but thank you."

The lawyer waddled off.

David put a hand through his hair, smoothing down the ire that raised the flesh on the back of his neck. Once he was settled, he made a show of his practiced nonchalance as he retraced his steps back to the bank. *His bank.* If he could get Price Mansion, then he was one step closer to owning this town—he could buy off another lawyer.

The bank would be closing in minutes.

The lawyer would be carving into his beef any minute and forgetting about him. He would never notice that David circled back around the buildings. He would never notice David using another skill he taught himself—when he was only eleven.

Back at Price Mansion, he checked for Patrick, and when there was no sign of him, he popped the lock free and was inside in seconds. He lit a match and found a single candle and holder. He set flame to wick and held his hand to keep the dancing light muted as he perused Patrick's room, his desk, and all the pockets of his clothes. Where would he keep a letter—assuming his news about Zeke came in a letter—assuming the letter was given to Patrick before the lawyer. The lawyer said his *source* told him…

Only five minutes later, he stepped out the door with a smile on his face. He waited to be sure no one watched. Snowflakes landed on his head and shoulders. The only evidence that remained from his little visit was the directions to a certain Camp 13 seared into his memory forever.

Mr. Zeke Bradley, I'm coming for you, and I want my mansion.

The game was on. He rehearsed all his options and planned his next move.

By the time he reached the porch of his boardinghouse, the whole town was covered in white powder. His smile died. He growled. He finally had the lead, a chance to do something, and the weather cast its lot against him.

No matter.

He would take it in stride. He'd have to shift things around at the bank to be sure he would keep things running smooth until spring, but once the weather warmed, he would hunt down that deed and leave nary a witness.

Too bad he couldn't celebrate with Jasmine out in the open—for all to see. Soon, but for now they had to protect their cover. For the con to work, she had to play a hardworking widow who he'd seen around town, here and there, like any of the other townsfolk.

They had seen each other all right. He grinned at his joke. Things were turning in his favor. *Finally.*

Chapter Seventeen

⁂

Zeke beat Heather and Liza back to the wagon, as he expected, but he didn't figure on how much worrying he would do all through his errands. Or that he would sit and have a staring match with the doctor's front door. He wanted to go to them—to Heather—and see if she needed help and support. But she needed privacy more.

And how much support would he be really? He was nothing to either of these two ladies. He knew very little about them and their history, and they didn't know a thing about him. Who knew anything about him? The little Patrick knew from swapping stories with Old Man Price could hardly count.

All these secrets.

They kept him isolated and alone. If the girls knew them, they would've asked for someone else to escort them to town.

He could move on. He could pack up and find a new place and write Patrick of the change. How would it be possible for him to help care for Heather, if she found herself both a widow and a mother, if leaving was his choice.

A mother.

She could be a mother. The baby would grow and be born and…the wonder of it tightened his chest and made him miss his mother.

Heather would have her own little family. Son or daughter—didn't matter—she wouldn't be alone. He tried not to be jealous. What she would be facing would be the hardest. A baby's livelihood was at stake.

What a powerful thing. He didn't want her to be burdened or

buried by the responsibilities and changes a child would bring, but boy howdy, a family sounded nice.

He stood next to the horses and rubbed their noses. *A family.*

The doctor's office door opened, and Heather's tiny brown leather boot was the first thing he saw. The second was her dazed smile.

And he knew with one glance. *A baby.*

He darted past the horse—the animal bounced his head up in alarm. Zeke vaulted up the stairs in one swift move and was by her side lending her his arm—his strength. He could see the white of fear circling each of her normally soft-blue eyes. He wanted to crush the fear in a fierce hug—but he didn't. He couldn't. And he couldn't say anything that would help. All he could do was lead her down the stairs and get the three of them home.

He could tell Heather didn't really see him after that first look. She was caught up in thought as he helped her make her way to the wagon, Liza beside her. He flicked the reins and turned the wagon in the street until they were retracing their tracks. Did Heather wish she could circle back so easy? Go back to before her husband died, maybe to before her husband? Or did she love her husband even now? Would she crumble under the pressures?

She seemed like the feisty type—not in an outward way like Liza was with Jiggy, but she fought her battles. Each day in the kitchen she did or said something to shape the way Cookie ran his dining hall. She never backed down, but she wasn't mean or rude either.

She had grit, but she didn't flail about announcing it to everyone who passed.

She could always share the work of a child, by marrying one of the other loggers. Zeke shied away from that idea. "By the look on your face it's good news? Not dying? The doctor had answers? Was he sure?"

Liza spoke for Heather. "Sure as water flows downhill. I double-checked after Heather double-checked. Ain't no doubt. It's a baby. She's not gonna croak."

"No doubt in the doctor's mind anyway." Heather wrung her hands in her lap.

"When is it to be?" He let his leg bump hers beside him. If only he could offer her protection and safety. But he couldn't even guarantee his own.

"April."

"You sure?"

"Yes, I know." She ducked her head, presumably to hide her embarrassment. But she'd been married. There could be no shame. Should he tell her that she would make a great mother? Did he know her well enough to believe that?

He flicked the reins to speed them home.

The doctor's confirmation made everything so real and permanent—even the air around them seemed heavier to breathe in. They rolled out of town as silently as they'd rolled in.

When they came close to Milk Creek the wagon hit a rut and shuddered. Zeke heard Heather's tiny moan. Her normally rosy cheeks were so white. He turned the horses into the grassy pasture on the side of the road and pulled them to a stop. "Heather, you need a rest and a chance to catch your bearings. That's the whole reason Cookie concocted this plan for us all three to head to town."

"For that and to see the doctor." Liza helped Zeke's words along and then held her skirts with one hand and jumped down. Liza claimed the handles of the picnic basket Cookie sent along from the back of the wagon. She hefted it up over the side and made her way toward the brook. "Let's feed her. She only ate a half piece of buttered bread this morning."

It didn't seem to faze Heather that Liza was taking charge and talking to him like she wasn't even there.

The dry grass was sparse, most of it beaten down by weather or animal at some point in the season. What was left standing brushed the underside of Liza's elbows as she hoisted the basket to the base of a tree—what leaves were left on it were turned from green to gold.

Zeke faced Heather on the bench of the wagon. "We can stay here for a while. As long as you need, really.

Heather stood in the wagon bench and let him take her waist to lift her down. "I can't seem to take it in. Then my stomach rolls and convinces me of the truth."

He lifted her down as slow and gentle as if she was the newborn. "They are making their presence known."

"They. Don't do that. You made my heart leap. Let's stick with one please. Thank you very much."

Zeke chuckled. She was still pale but shocking her added a pink flush to her skin. He would encourage her and help her aim for the best, and that started today.

He kept her in his arms. She stared at his chest for so long he wanted to look and see if there was a spot of food on his shirt.

She would live.

She would raise a child.

Will I be alive to see him or her grow? He rubbed his throat and swallowed deep.

They weren't out here by the water deciding his fate—they were stopped to help her figure out hers. When he looked down, she was watching him.

"I've seen you rub your neck before. We can go back to the doctor if you need to be checked." She reached up and splayed her tiny hand across his forehead. The contact sent a rush of stampeding horses to each of his limbs. He was sure his reactions showed in his eyes.

She pulled her hand back too quickly not to be telling.

He was caught.

He broke away from her, so as not to embarrass her. "I'm fine. Must be a nervous habit or something. I'm trying to imagine what you must be thinking, and I'm failing to do anything calming. I think I could be good at making you more nervous." He picked the mailbag for Camp 13 out of the wagon bed. The mail and the wanted posters were in there. He usually looked at both before he left town, but this day had bigger things to think about.

If they settled her for a time, in the cool breeze and sunshine, he could look at them.

They walked in silence over to Liza. The tree with the colorful leaves they chose to sit under ended up being an apple tree loaded with fruit waiting for the first hard frost to sweeten them.

"Have a seat. Be comfortable and simply think on things." Zeke picked a couple apples for each of the horses and placed them at the animals' feet. He needed a chance to catch his fears and hog-tie them before he could offer Heather any sort of encouragement.

He wished he could just tell her what he ran from. He was innocent. Why did he even hesitate?

He looked back at the bag of mail wondering if his picture would be in there after what Patrick told him in his last letter. He stopped himself from reaching for his throat and rubbing it again. If he wasn't careful, he would give away his secret.

The best way to keep people from knowing your business is to keep your own counsel. Hadn't Price said that to him?

It couldn't be that much longer before Patrick found out something useful or gave him a plan of action. For now, he could keep checking the wanteds, like Cookie always did, to see if his face—or perhaps David's face—showed up.

He rejoined the ladies, and Liza handed him a piece of cut cheese and a hunk of bread, broken and spread with butter and honey, from her place in the grass.

Heather already had her own.

"This should help with your queasiness, at least I saw Ma always eating this. Maybe she just liked it," Liza said with a shrug.

"More than my belly is queasy. My whole world tipped and wobbled, like one chair leg is shorter than the rest and it won't set right. Riley's pa is still around, back in Meramec, but he's mean—really mean. I would never subject anyone to him. I can't tell him about this." She clutched her waist. "That would've made Riley worse than mad. But I'll need to tell Cora Mae, Rose, and Rebecca. I've told you both a little about my friends back home, right?" she asked, but didn't wait for them to answer.

"I still haven't had a chance to tell them about Camp 13. The last letter or letters—I sent two in the same day—they were short and probably pretty shocking. This will be too." Heather snatched a peek at Zeke. Then she put her hand on her flat stomach again.

Liza took a nibble of her bread. "Can you believe a whole person is growing in there?" She caught a drip of honey with her finger and licked it off. "If keeping a wee one safe and being the only one responsible for getting him three square meals a day wasn't a part of raising a little one, then I'd be right glad to have a child. I loved each one of my little brothers and sisters. Each one so beautiful, different, and each one a big pain in my backside. But they're so full of life and living—they can make playing with dirt and rocks an adventure. But keeping them alive and fed business can be tricky."

"Would you wed Jigger Jones to have one? I've overheard him talk to Frenchie. He has a soft heart and loves the Lord. He's a good man." Heather peeked at her.

Liza bolted up to a stand, flinging her bread.

Heather laughed. "Got ya."

Zeke raised his eyebrows. Heather showed more color with that tease than she had since before she fainted.

Liza's arms flapped. "Marrying Jiggy would be like marrying a baby minus the nappy changes." She knocked the honey jar over and righted it in one movement. "And don't you ever say anything like that around Camp 13. Or I'll need more than a rolling pin to beat off the leech. You give Jiggy any such idea, and I'll tan your hide worse than my mama used to tan mine."

Heather laughed. The tinkling sound was as pleasant as the brook that rolled past them. He could drown in the happy sound. *She laughed.*

Levity during the heavy. Would Heather stand her ground and do right by her child? *Not all parents did.* Some gave up— even when they knew they'd be missed. *Even when they are still needed.* Some—without a fight at all. The picture of his father's face the last time he saw it—the last time he breathed on earth.

Heather seemed next to normal. "Did you go through the mail yet? Is there one in there for me?"

"I haven't." Zeke shuffled through the burlap sack and pulled out several letters for the different men in camp. The wanteds spilled onto the grass. Heat poured through him, causing sweat to bead on his brow. Why did he feel so guilty? But if there was a picture of him, it was based on a lie. He knew that. He thought Liza and Heather would understand, if he explained. But that didn't take the shame of it away. He didn't make a fast move, but he did stop sorting the letters and gathered the wanteds into one pile.

Liza picked up the poster on top. "I've seen him before. Long time ago. He hung out with Charley for a night. His eyes were more twitchy than a hound covered in fleas."

Heather took the paper from Liza's hand, so she could read it. "Says he stole from a widow. Her money and her horses. Why do you have all these?" She pointed to the rest of the pile he was picking up.

"Cookie likes to keep tabs on the crew." More sweat beads covered his forehead. *Would they notice?*

Heather gave the paper back to Liza, who said, "No surprise he was a thief. Too bad I didn't know he was wanted back then. He was worth a lot of money. But then I would've escaped before I met you, Heather." Liza tossed the wanted poster back to Zeke and picked up another. She glanced at it and then threw it back on the stack too.

Zeke clutched all the posters. He turned them over out of sight and went through letters. He found some. "Look. One for you, Heather. And one for me too."

"Yes? Oh good." Her eyes lit up like he'd given her the moon. "All the more reason to be glad we came to town."

When Heather opened her letter, Liza pulled the stack of wanteds—about twenty in all—back into her lap and was inspecting each of the ink-drawn faces while Heather read her letter. Zeke was torn between seeing if Liza found his face on a wanted and watching Heather smile as she traced the lines of writing with her finger.

His letter was from Patrick. *News.* Finally. But did he dare rip into it like Heather did hers? What if David or whoever set him up got away with it—banishing him from Auburn? Would folks believe him a murderer?

Even if the news he craved wasn't inside, he had to clear his name. He would clear his name. His name was all he had left. And *he* wouldn't give it up without a fight.

He popped the wax seal. He unfolded the thick yellow paper. There was a second piece of paper inside. He could see ink bleeding through the back of the paper. It was a wanted poster not too unlike the ones in Liza's lap.

Maybe David's face is on there.

He opened it fast. Maybe this was the end of the mess. Maybe he could go home. By the time he had the papers half opened, he thought his heart would stop with the heavy jolt. His own face stared back at him. His hand shook until he fumbled the papers. If he thought he was sweating before, he was mistaken. His whole body flashed hot.

Heather read through half a paragraph. The urge to cry almost broke the surface of her dry soul. She waited…almost hoping.

It passed.

It was so nice to hear from home—her sisters. The mercantile owner back in Milford must've sent this along to the Camp 13—presuming she and Liza got the job. But her letters, the one about Riley's accident and her moving to Camp 13, couldn't have made the trip across the Trail yet. They were responding to one she'd written when she first got off the Trail.

Her friends asked about the farm, the tiny cabin, and if she was eating her tomatoes yet. Cora Mae scratched a sloppy question down the side. Her handwriting was the finest of the four of them, when she was patient enough to make it neat, but this had ink blotches everywhere.

Rose thinks its tactless and immodest of me to ask, but I want to know. Is there a baby on the way?

The question mark scratched across the body of the letter. Rose must have taken the pen back.

Her friends would be so excited to hear about a baby—the baby. But what would they think of finding out about him or her and finding out she was a widow at the same time? She would make them terribly happy, terribly sad, and scared for her with one letter.

They would be almost as scared as she was.

She was still thinking on it all when Zeke's hands trembled enough to make his letters crinkle. It was easier to watch his hands than notice hers were too.

He dropped his letter like it was a hot pan fresh from the oven. Before he could pluck it back up, she saw the edges of a drawing—a wanted poster. And this time, she too had met the wanted man.

It was Zeke.

She kept her eyes on the letter from her sisters, but the words went out of focus as she tried to take in the shock of what she'd just seen. It was almost as hard for her to absorb as the doctor's news.

What had he done? She hadn't seen the bottom of the paper. It was folded away from her. And even now, Zeke was stuffing the offensive poster back into his breast pocket.

He touched his neck again. Was he wanted for something that would get him hanged, or was it truly a nervous habit?

A baby was a lot, but it didn't cause her to look over her shoulder like Zeke was doing now.

Zeke made short work of loading their lunch back into the picnic basket. So much for staying until she felt settled—not that she could feel settled about the baby in one sitting. Not that she could feel settled with Zeke. Was she safe with this gentle stranger—who had shown her every kindness? Was her future son or daughter safe?

Something was wrong—yet there was no way she was going to ask him what was in the letter. *But I must know.* She would find out. She had to think of the baby's future too, and Zeke had stayed close since day one. Did they know Zeke at all?

She made sure her voice didn't tremble. She was done being out here with the unknowns—just her and Liza. And there was no way Liza would even think about scratching out Zeke's eyes, like she'd warned her she would back when they first came, even if things turned to trouble right here and now. She wouldn't believe Zeke was a problem. He'd become a friend.

What am I saying? Even she didn't believe Zeke was a problem. Goose prickles danced across her arms. She would have to wait for her chance, but she would read that poster.

"Thank you for the meal, Liza," Heather said. "We should get back now. I'm sure Cookie will worry until he sees us come rolling in."

Chapter Eighteen

*H*eather cracked the back door enough to look outside and see if Liza had all the men's attention on her garden expansion project. Two weeks had passed since her doctor's visit. All the men finally quit watching her like she carried the Black Plague in her belly or like she was their mother's favorite china dish teetering on the edge of a rocky cliff—both looks grew wearisome.

All she could do was behave as normal as possible. She baked, peeled, washed, mixed, and scrubbed the last two weeks away. With a nap every afternoon that Cookie insisted upon. The few times she'd grown sick, she managed to utilize the scrap bucket with no one the wiser—except Liza and Cookie, who both understood.

Liza was a great confidant when it came to the baby. Liza's mother had so many pregnancies that she was more the expert than Heather. When they climbed into their shared bed at night, Liza talked about all the little things her mother used to complain about from swollen ankles to an itchy belly.

Liza didn't know what all needed to be done to assist in a birth, but she could remember how her mother prepared and how she behaved. All of which was a comfort.

Now, as she watched out the window, men swarmed around Liza as she barked orders. Each man eager to please her tiny friend. Some men plied shovels others pulled up the split-log fencing and prepared to enlarge the garden grounds. By the end of the next couple hours, they would have the earth turned over, mulch and manure spread, and they would have added a couple dozen new fruit trees to the orchard to be settled and waiting for spring.

Liza was quite the visionary when it came to planting potatoes and growing corn. She thought bigger than Cookie and Heather put together.

Cookie's snores from the back of the kitchen were steady and muffled by the wall separating them.

This was her chance.

She hadn't had a good night's sleep since she saw the wanted poster in Zeke's hands. Now was the time to settle matters—maybe the only time she could sneak up to Zeke's loft-space and see what was in that last letter. There always seemed to be someone around—Liza, Cookie, Zeke.

He'd been so caring and attentive during the past two weeks. *Kind*. She'd tried to learn more. He evaded talk of himself or his past. He loved the outdoors and working the land, that he appreciated fine craftsmanship and had a solid work ethic, was easy to see. But what of the details?

She left the dining hall and started up the stairs.

They creaked under her weight.

She froze and looked around. When she saw no one, she hiked her skirts and darted to the top, staying as close to the back wall as possible. If someone did come in, she wanted to be able to hide from their view.

The loft was big. She walked past his neatly made bed, ignoring his shaving kit and traveling gear tucked into the squares of two stacked wooden crates and went straight to his desk. Would he keep his personal letters with the office books? She flipped through the stack of letters and the account book on the desk, sure to leave things just as she found them.

Nothing—all Camp 13 related.

An organized man. Where would you keep your letters, Zeke?

She scanned the room a second time.

Talk to me.

And then she spied it. An old cracker tin on the floor beside his Sunday boots. In the perfect place to be easy for him to reread at night before he fell asleep. She crossed to it—wishing for good news, expecting another hit.

She knelt and pulled the top off, cringing when it gave with a loud *Thrump*.

She flipped several letters in the tin but stopped when she recognized the color of the wanted poster folded with the letter on top. She pulled it out and set the tin on Zeke's bed while she stood there and opened it. And there was Zeke's face, minus the beard, looking back at her—kind eyes included, and below his name was the words: "Wanted for murder with a $1,000 reward."

All the air went out of her. She sat with a plop on his bed. Each breath required a conscious draw. *A murderer?* Out of all the men to find her and help her, she had to pick a murderer. She couldn't believe it.

There must be a reason or explanation. Was there any explanation that would justify letting a murderer close to her and her baby—and Liza?

She wasn't interested in loving deep and hard like her parents had. It wasn't worth the pain for them. It wouldn't be for her either—the cost if you lost them buried you, but if the pain in her chest was any indication, she might be too late.

But he's a murderer.

What was she going to do? Should she remain his friend? Should she confront him? Should she cut him direct? She couldn't cut him, that would draw more attention to her. *No.* But she could turn him in for his reward, like Cookie did the others. A thousand dollars would set her and the baby up for a nice long while. *But this was Zeke.* It felt like a barrel of flour sat right on her chest.

She shouldn't read his letter—she had to. If her scruples wouldn't let her read his mail, she shouldn't be up here snooping in the first place. She opened it before she could get in an argument with herself.

Nothing new really. Here is David's handiwork. It won't be long now until he chases—unless he lets this weather best him. The snow is really coming down. No drastic moves beyond this wanted poster. It's plastered all over town. Good likeness. He's thorough and he doesn't flush easy. But we'll get him yet. The sheriff in Baker checked things over. Even talked to me about you. I told him my suspicions, but there is nothing for him to go on. You should stay hidden. It's not safe yet.

If David comes for you, maybe then. But if you come now, he wins. You will swing for murder.

Heather stopped reading.

Murder. Swing. She rubbed her throat. This was why he was always watchful. Zeke killed someone and he was hiding from the sheriff. And obviously someone was helping him get away with it. This was all the proof she needed. Zeke wasn't to be trusted.

She should claim the reward and never look back.

She rubbed her throat again. But he would hang—almost by her hand. Did she want that? She better finish reading the letter and get back to her work before Cookie woke and came looking for her.

The lawyer knows about Camp 13. I made sure he knew. And I'm sure David found the address I hid for him. David will be mad as two wives married to the same fool, if he has to wait much longer to see his plans through. He won't snap unless we force him to it. So that's what we'll do.

Danger is coming your way with a loaded gun. We've come too far to throw in the towel. Stick to the plan. And watch your back.

Heather's hands were shaking. She had to fold the letter twice to get it to its original shape. She stuffed it on top of the other letters and closed the tin. She put it back exactly as she found it and took the stairs two at a time, hand under her belly to support her small, growing mound.

She put herself to work in the kitchen turning a bucket of apples that were crunchy sweet into a dozen apple pies. She could think better when her hands were busy peeling and quartering and cutting dough.

Was she better off reading that letter? *A murderer. And who sent the letter—who was coming with a gun?* She ended up with more questions and more concerns than she had before.

"You want help slicing? That's a lot of apples. I'm done with my part in Liza's garden show."

"*Yeep.*" Heather darted back and turned the tiny paring knife in her hand on him. "Zeke! You scared me." She moved the knife away.

"Didn't mean to sneak up on you."

"I was lost in thought while peeling and didn't hear you approach."

"Whatever were you thinking about that made you that jumpy? Might be worth forgetting." He picked the wrong kind of knife out of one of her canisters on the counter. The big handle looked small in his large hands.

He took as much of the apple flesh as the peel when he cut into the first, but she couldn't chase him off without making him suspicious.

"You've been lost in your thoughts a lot lately. Is it the baby?"

Now was another chance. She could try and get more answers and get to know him. If he was a dangerous man, then she could be a thousand dollars richer. If he wasn't, then she might gain a friend.

Her list of friends wasn't very long. "Some. I think the baby is in or behind every thought or decision I make. But I was thinking about some of the folks back where I came from. Some not so nice. Riley's pa, for one. How can people turn out so cruel... murderers even? Did it start with how they were raised? How they were mothered?" She left the apples to him and started the batter mix for the crusts.

"I suppose some folks turn cruel to match their parents' evil." He popped a cube of apple in his mouth.

She held the silence until he continued.

"And some to spurn their parents' neglect—you know, hurting people hurt people. But murdering takes a whole different kind of thinking. No parenting involved…"

That was the best she could do. Would he confide in her right there? Would he spill his side of whatever was happening? Would he tell her who David was? She pressed on. "So, all those faces on Cookie's wanteds made a *choice* to kill?"

"Possibly. Some of those men kill as easy as harvesting a chicken for dinner, with nary a thought, but I've learned not to trust everything on those posters. Sometimes, folks—even sheriffs—get it wrong. Sometimes, the facts are skewed. Sometimes, those easy-killing types figure out how to use those posters to serve their plans."

"You think some of those men are innocent?"

"Yes. And proving it and restoring their good name would be like putting this skin back on this apple." He held up a long thread of peel that twisted in circles. "I think Cookie would agree. I've looked at those wanted posters as close as he. There are a few faces in there that have come through camp, earned a few meals, and moved on. Cookie never turned them in, he passed up the reward, because there was something not-murderer about them."

Was his picture in Cookie's stack? She might have to check on that. And could she believe him? Guilty men always professed their innocence, didn't they? She pulled the stack of a dozen tin plates that Liza had scrubbed and put away just this morning. The baked egg, cheese, and bacon breakfast went over well with the loggers. The tins were still a tad moist. She went about drying them before she flipped one over to trace for the shape and size of the crusts.

"Was Riley's father a murderer?"

"No," she rushed. "I didn't mean to give you that impression. I was thinking about the long-term fruit of this parenting role I'm about to begin."

"I don't see why you'll have any trouble. You seem to roll with the dough when things go sideways around here." He smiled at his quip. "You didn't even get riled up when Tupper tipped the whole stew pot off the counter—you reached for the sandwich fixings and cheese and put a pot of eggs to boil on the stove. The men went to bed with full bellies and woke to an even bigger breakfast. No fussing about it. You would respond to a kid like that, I think."

"I suppose." If she could get up the nerve to ask him outright if he killed someone, then she would know whether to collect the money and run or be a friend. If she turned him in, the sheriff would ask the questions and she would receive the money.

But she gazed at him sideways through her lashes. It wasn't that simple. She had to be right. And she was coming to care for him.

Not love, she refused that.

She would never do that, but care, yes. Just like she did for all the loggers who were trying in their way to help her. She stuck out her chin. She was defensive of her disbelieving thoughts.

The wanted poster was clear. It was the letter that muddled her. She couldn't believe the man who'd carried her after she'd fainted could be a killer. He may not be free of guilt, but who of the men around here were?

"Love bears all things, believes all things, hopes all things and endures all things." Mother's voice came to her *now*? And scripture no less? About love? She nearly snorted out loud.

Believes all things?

Could she? She wished...

The money.

She couldn't be too impetuous. Like Zeke said, she needed to go with the flow no matter what she faced, for the baby's sake.

"This is a lot of apples." He plucked an empty metal bucket off the top shelf and flipped it over for a seat. He stretched the leg with the healing knee out straight and went back to peeling. The apples were chunky and lumpy compared to what she would come up with, but she wouldn't turn down help peeling apples for twelve pies, especially when she planned to peel potatoes for breakfast later.

"I spend most of my time peeling and chopping." She didn't feel threatened by him. Was she a bad judge of character? She thought about all the loggers and her impression of each. She didn't think so. There were some she wouldn't want to be left outside alone in the dark with—the way their eyes watched her— but she could name them. Which group should Zeke be in?

"You still have that frown on your face. Expecting mothers are supposed to be planning to sew outfits, coming up with boy and girl names, and making nappies. More excitement than worry."

How could she not smile at that? She turned to him, keeping her fingers busy rolling dough, and crimping one crust after another. "Thanks to some of the loggers, I have enough nappy cotton to account for five infants."

"They must've figured on how many nappies *they* would need." His booming chuckle filled the space. "And baby names?"

"I don't know. I have a few. If it's a girl I'd name her after my mama. And for a boy I was thinking, Daniel or David? Bible names would've made my mother happy."

There she did it. The last arrow in her arsenal. How would he handle hearing David's name? She watched his face out of the corner of her eye, so he wouldn't feel her staring.

"David is a good Bible name, but I've had a bad association with it."

"Hmm. How so?"

"The only David I know is a liar and a cheat. He would swindle his own mother."

He sounded innocent. Sad even. That was as close as she was going to get to the hidden truth. But how could she find out more from an unbiased source? And why did she want to know so badly? Was the reward motivating her? Or did she want Zeke to be innocent? "So, no to David. Easy enough. What names would you pick if you had a child?"

His hands stilled in his peeling.

This time she did stop working and met his eyes. "What?"

"I've never thought about naming a child. It would have to be special. Family is forever. Kinda makes me jealous. I haven't had any blood family in a long while. My folks loved me good and hard, but they've been gone. Some things you miss the feel of."

Heather wasn't comfortable digging any more. She could feel his sorrow from across the room. She gathered the large bowl, sugar, flour, spices, and butter to mix the apples. "If it would help, you can stick around and take a middle-of-the-night shift. Cookie keeps telling me all his tricks he used to settle his colicky babies. After what he describes…if I could run from this, I would."

Zeke continued to peel his way through the apples. After a long pause, he asked, "Would you really?"

"Really what?" She mixed.

"Run from your child?"

"I'm so unprepared, but oh heavens no. I'm all he or she has. I could never abandon my child. I was being flip." She should tell him about Pa's leaving. But she could feel the anger tighten in her middle. She'd only known about the baby growing in her for two weeks and she could never imagine walking away. She rolled the dough with a little added force. "And…"

"And?"

"…besides a few dear friends, I suppose this baby is my only family too."

The smell of cinnamon filled the space between them, and Cookie started banging around in his room. His nap was over, and it was time to begin dinner prep. Liza would be in from the garden soon.

Zeke kept peeling and said, "When my folks took sick, Ma went first. Pa was sick, but not as bad as Ma. She was already worn down by work and never having enough. But Pa, he could've fought it. He could've survived, he didn't want to stay. He left me." The last three words he said on a whisper.

Her hands stilled.

She moved to wash the pastry off her fingers, and then she went closer to his side. Here he was, finally sharing something real from his past, and all she could think of was more grilling questions than ever. Could she trust this man, or was he the best swindler around?

Either way, she couldn't have made herself walk away from him if she wanted—she knew how that felt. She stepped close enough their shoulders nearly touched. "I'm sure he would've lived, if he could. Influenza, right? That's what you told me before?" She asked her question as if she hadn't memorized every detail about him.

"My folks were God-fearing people. They taught me to love, pray, and work hard. But that day, he quit. He asked me to be strong and let him go. He didn't want to live without Ma. They had the kind of love everyone envies and wishes for." A chunk of apple peel dropped outside his bowl. He picked it up and put it back in.

She put her hand on his shoulder as he was sitting there.

He looked at her hand and drew a deep, settling breath.

Cookie shouted from the back room. "You okay with meatloaf, Miss Heather? I feel like a fast dinner tonight. Ten meatloaves and a barrel of rice."

"I started apple pies!" she called back.

"Good. That will round out the meal." The plump man never came from his space in the back room.

Heather brought Zeke back to their conversation. "My folks had that kind of love too. Pa would've taken Ma's sick on himself, if he could. Since he couldn't, he let it rip him apart from the inside. It was like watching two people die slow—until he up and ran from it and left me to tend Ma until she passed. Not sure that kind of love is worth the pain. At least, I don't think it's worth it."

She took his bowl of apple slices and mixed them with her sugar and spice for her pies.

Zeke stood from his bucket and came to her side. He placed one hand on her hand to stop her work and used the other to turn her and catch her chin. He bent over her face just a little—demanding her attention. Once he had it, he said, "That kind of love is the only thing worth the pain."

He touched his fingers to her nose, then grabbed one of the

sugar-coated apples, plopped it in his mouth and left her, leaving out the back door probably to check on the garden plot additions.

He took her breath with him.

He was so sincere. *So serious.*

She felt something in her soften. The paper said murderer, but he'd worked himself into her heart like one of the worms that found these sweet apples. He made her think twice about loving like her parents. He made it sound like a treasure worth hunting for.

If she didn't have so much—a baby to take care of, pies to make, and a Rebecca to go find—she might let herself consider it.

Meramec, Missouri
November 1847

Rose received a letter from Heather. The beautiful script with her name across the front was the only thing that had made Rose smile since the last time Cora Mae and she were together. So many of her days were the same, simpering around Cecil, obeying his orders, pandering to his pride.

Rose called up to her brother, "Cecil, Mr. Reynolds's order came in. Would you like me to take it to him or wait for him to come in and claim it?" She knew what he'd answer before she asked.

"It's better if he and I stay on opposite sides of the street," Cecil called down from the loft.

Rose was across the mercantile and out the door before he went on to explain what she'd listened to him say daily for weeks—multiple times daily.

He'd been squawking on about the all-too-high-and-mighty Abe Reynolds ever since their exchange about Cecil's condescending attempt to pay for a new pair of shoes for Abe Reynolds's daughter, Cora Mae, after Cora Mae gave hers to Rebecca.

Rebecca had been blown out of hers when her father blew up their cabin while making whiskey.

Cecil could offend a flea given the time.

The worst of it was, Rose didn't need him to tell her anything. She was there. She saw Cecil's idiocy firsthand.

Rose crossed the street and got far enough down the boardwalk to be considered out of earshot from the mercantile before she slowed her step.

Then she ignored the incessant curiosity to know what was in the letter from her sister-friend as she sucked in a breath of fresh air and looked around the lovely town.

Meramec was a great town.

She could enjoy the people and the way of life—if she had a life of her own. She sighed, because it always came back to Cecil, even on such a fine day.

Cora Mae popped out of a shop and spied her. She was running across the street waving Rose down with all the freedom and energy of a hummingbird.

Rose lifted her hand with the letter.

They both turned in unison to the bench with spent and drying flowers around it. "I was coming to find you. I'm so glad we have a letter. I need something new to think about when I try to tune Cecil out."

"What do you think they're up too? I still can't believe Rebecca has been married over a year. And we haven't met him."

Rose opened the newest letter, which turned out to be two bound together, and read the first before they could fall into their most repeated conversation. She breathed through the pressure in her chest. She wished she could be on an adventure. The words squelched her frustration.

> *Riley is dead. Farming accident. Please tell his father.*

Other than her name there was nothing else written. Cora Mae said, "What? That can't be right." She tugged the paper out of Rose's hand.

Rose read the second note. It was only a little longer.

> *Headed to a logging camp to bake and cook so I can get enough money to find Rebecca. Pray I get the job. I'm not going alone. There is this girl our age named Liza. I will write more later.*

Cora Mae must've been reading over her shoulder. "That's better than this one. Liza? A job? Every time I get frustrated with Archie and Father, I threaten to run away inside my head. But that sounds miserable and hard—to find a new job—to be all on your own. Do we even know how far this Milford is from Eagle Creek?"

Rose flipped the papers over to see the address.

"Do you think what they are doing is harder than waiting here for word from them?" Cora Mae asked.

Rose swallowed.

The letters were barely news. They made her ask more questions than they gave answers, and they made her worry. She did that enough for herself already. She would *so* much rather be the one finding her way out there in Milford and Eagle Creek than repeating the same mind-numbing drudge each day as Cecil expected her to do.

She told Cora Mae, "I'd rather be with them. I'd rather have my own life—even if I was like Riley in the end—it would be better."

Cora Mae reached over and clutched her hand, rumpling their letters. "Me too. But I'd be scared if I was her. I'd want you—or one of you—with me."

They both sat and thought—and worried.

Chapter Nineteen

*D*avid tucked his head against the cold. Jasmine rode the horse behind his, as miserable as he was. "We aren't stopping again. Not until dark. I told you this wasn't a pleasure trip—that we'd be riding hard."

"I knew what I was getting into, but I'm *done* for the day. My fingers are frozen to the reins, and I think this horse is gonna die right out from under me. If I freeze to death, I'm telling your mother how you disrespected me." She sniffed her red nose.

Jasmine had never threatened him or spoken back in all the years they'd made their way out of the pit of humanity. *She must really be worn to a frazzle.*

He liked having her with him.

The feel of her at night, beside him, kept the flames of fear licking at his heels away. He was barely holding things together back in Auburn. It had been a long, careful winter. Folks were within a few days of discovering his smoke and mirrors. If he stayed behind and waited for Zeke to turn up—he was sunk. He needed the deed. If he had it, he could pull a loan from the bank and soothe all the feathers that wanted their money. If he got the loan, he would get another year, or so, to skim money and maneuver men until his business pulled a profit.

Things had to go his way when he made it to Camp 13. *I'll make it go my way.* He didn't want to lose Jasmine if he didn't have to. He'd worked too hard for his image, and she was a part of it.

They left Auburn separately with different stories—his business, hers distant family. They met up and traveled together as soon as they thought it would be safe—no one from Auburn would see them.

She complained, "Next time steal a smoother ride. This one has bruised me through. I won't be walking straight for a week, and don't you think you'll be taking any favors." Her voice trembled.

If he didn't stop, he was going to have a crying, irritated woman on his hands. He knew all the signs. He'd spent his early years surrounded by women of all shapes and sizes—learning about all the vagaries a woman could provide in a house of ill repute—his mother's trade.

All their schemes and manipulations were his primary education.

I'm glad for it too. He was impervious to curves and tears alike. And he knew how to trick a lady. His mother was instrumental in pointing out each and every way. He nearly smiled, "Dear heart, you need a rest?" Fool woman was slowing him down anyway.

"Yes, I do, David." She winced as the horse took a rough step amongst the lava rock and sage. "Here?"

He grunted.

A turnout on the trail led to a copse. A neat tight place that would work for the night. "This will have to do." He paused, so she could enjoy her moment of relief. "Mind you, we have to shove off before light in the morning. Neither of us should be gone for long, and we have people to find and a deed to steal."

She didn't answer him as she slid out of the saddle, groaning and moaning the whole while.

"And, when we get there, I'm gonna need a few days to get a feel for the lay of the land and plan. I only have one chance at this. Our future hangs in the balance. I won't be able to *marry* you next spring, if I can't pull this off." He watched her from the corner of his eye as he began to unsaddle their horse.

Take the bait?

"Marry me? You mean it? Next spring?" She rushed him and wrapped her arms around his back and clasped her hands over his middle. She held on like a drowning child.

And like that, I set the hook. She would do his bidding for weeks and might possibly warm his bed, soreness and all, for a few well-chosen words that could be retracted or delayed, if need be.

He didn't mind the idea of marrying Jasmine.

Better her than any other. She knew him and didn't shy away. And she knew him enough to fear him. *Best of both worlds.* He turned in her arms with his back against the warmth of the horse's flank and dipped his head for a greedy kiss. He poured all his frustrations and all his desire into that kiss, pretending he was settled in the Price Mansion with a table full of mining tycoons asking him for advice. Each man admiring Jasmine, their beautiful hostess.

It all came down to Zeke.

David's kisses grew rougher, and Jasmine protested but didn't step back.

Zeke would be no more if he stood in David's way. He *would* have that deed in a week or two, one way or another, and all would be set right—as he planned it.

Heather couldn't think of anything better than church at Camp 13. Preacher only made it around once a month, weather permitting. The snow had come and gone, the daffodils had bloomed and faded, and the lilacs laced the air with their cheery scent, by the time Preacher Marks made it back to camp—she was near starved for a good church service.

The Sunday lunchtime meal was twice as large, with twice the normal choices. All the loggers were still slick and wet from their Sunday cleanup. Liza was fussing, and Heather was wiping down the tables to help her, so they could both sit and listen.

Bjorn came lumbering forward. "Before you get started, Preacher Marks. We would like to give a few things to Miss Heather—for the little one. We'll be right back. The things are in the bunkhouse." Bjorn and Frenchie made their way to the door, and two more men followed.

Heather stopped wiping and looked across the room. Men of all shapes and sizes looked back at her—all trim and fit from hard days in the forest. Each stared at her with a different sort of compassion in their eyes—some soft with tenderness, others wide or pinched with a hint of fear and concern directed at her expanding middle.

"What are you boys up to?" Liza, done with the plate scraping, cut even squares of the crumble cake and loaded small bowls. "You all worked double hard to be spit-polished for the preacher. Some of you even bought soap when Cookie opened the store yesterday. Some of you even used it—smells like a field of spring flowers in here. And after being frozen in with you all winter, I could almost say a prayer of thanks. You deserve extra dessert." Liza cracked a brief smile at her sallies.

Heather went back to wiping tables even as Liza balanced seven plates along her arms and wrists—a trick she'd learned during the past months—as she went around the room and served the men who hadn't left. She was talking all the while. "Now you're giving things to Heather? Preacher's gonna think you're trying to good-work your way into his good graces." She set the tin bowl in front of one man after another and then went back to Heather's side.

"My good graces ain't needed, Miss—wouldn't be worth a wad of used tobacco," the preacher said with his hat rolling between his hands. "But I'd like a slice of what you're serving, if the fellas are willing to share." The lean, bowlegged preacher stepped over a log bench and sat down while Liza served him a slice. "Thank you kindly. Mighty gracious of ya."

"Not gracious at all, I'm simply serving it up. She's the cook. And Cookie wants you to come back more often, so he had us make a good meal and sweet treat to put these boys in a good mood for whatever you slap them with."

"And she told us she wouldn't let us fall asleep on you, Preacher," Tupper said without taking his eyes off the dessert.

Liza bumped Jiggy's ankles off the bench with a thud.

"Hey, g—"

"Don't do it. Don't you let those curses fly. I may not believe in what this here preacher preaches, but if God listens to him when he prays, then you best stay on his good side or else."

Heather was surprised Liza even touched Jiggy. The winter really was thawing.

Jiggy hopped up and followed behind her. "Or else what?" He snagged a full coffeepot from the hot stove with a wad of toweling and followed her, filling loggers' mugs beside her.

"Or else I'll find a better use for Heather's soap—like scrubbing out the mouth of a foul-mouthed logger." Liza turned to the whole room. "I could catch any one of you." They all knew she couldn't, but they let her have her threat.

Jiggy leaned over her and whispered, but everyone could hear him. "Almost tempts me to start cussing, but I'm a God-fearing man."

Liza huffed and went back for more tins of dessert until all the men were served.

Heather watched Liza work the room with her feisty banter, glad Liza stuck with her all those months ago. If she wasn't serving the spice cake and Jiggy wasn't serving the coffee, Heather didn't know how she would be keeping up. She needed their help. *Now more than ever.* She passed a hand over her round middle, but she did it fast. The baby seemed to dance, like Jiggy, inside of her. She was glad for the movement, but nothing made the room full of men more restless than if she drew too much attention to her oversized middle—and man was it oversized these days.

This strange group of men and Liza felt more and more like a family as the days passed.

She would always feel small and fragile amongst their lean, muscled bodies and big appetites. But there could be no place safer for her or her baby—like a room full of older brothers always watching.

Liza bantered and played amongst them. A few openly flirted with Liza. She hoped Jiggy would one day win their massive game of tug-of-war and steal Liza's heart. But, for her, brothers are all any of them would ever be—Zeke included.

Too many unknowns.

She couldn't afford to risk more—she wouldn't open her heart to any of them.

The door opened. Four men came in. The first two carried a heavy rocking chair with thick, curved runners and an ornately carved headrest. They set it down with a thud. One tipped it to show the action.

"We all took turns on shaping these. Some cut and fit, others sanded and smoothed. Moses did the art. He has as fine a hand as a lady's at painting landscapes," Frenchie said.

Bjorn added, "Moses drew a couple pictures in his book for us to choose from. We liked the one with the trees."

"Looks like being out in the field a morning, before the logging begins," a logger in the back called.

"Kind of hopeful," Cookie said.

Liza squeezed between the men, never touching one, to see what they had given Heather. Barely clearing their shoulders, she inspected the carving.

All Heather could do was continue to take in her surroundings. Before her mother's death, this moment would have her flooding with enough tears to drown the men, but even though her heart squeezed, her eyes remained dry.

How long would this drought last? How long, Lord?

What would have to happen before she could feel again? She remembered what Riley said about when his arm grew numb. Would her feelings ever shake free? Had Mother taken Heather's tears to the grave with her? She made eye contact with Moses who sat silent in his corner beside the potbelly stove. He'd stopped scribbling in his journal long enough to watch her see the chair.

She saved her words and sat in it, smoothing her hands down

the arms and setting the rocking motion into play. She would hold her child here—her own flesh and blood like Zeke described when they had their talk over apple pie fillings. "I've never seen anything finer," she announced.

The chests of the men around her seemed to swell.

Would she raise a son? A son that would grow into a man as kind as the ones that stood before her? Or would she raise the leaving kind—like father?

She pushed the image of Pa's anguished face away before her irritation and sadness showed on her face.

Zeke came forward carrying one end of a cradle. Jiggy held the other end. Zeke said, "And this here is for you too. We made it double-large, so it would last long enough for the little tyke to be big enough to sleep on his own pallet when he outgrows this. Cookie told us how big it needed to be. Should be nice and safe."

"The wood is beautiful. Look at the swirling pattern in the grain." She traced her fingers over the finer points. Other loggers brought smaller gifts and useful things and put them inside the cradle. She thanked each one.

Cookie chipped in, "Harder than woodpecker lips too—wild cherrywood. No way a little scrub could get out or chew through it. At least, not without your knowin'."

"The cradle is perfect. And needed. Thank you. This calls for a special round of fritters tomorrow."

The groans of pleasure had the men returning to their seats to down the cake Liza had set in place—most in only two or three spoonfuls.

"You boys ready for me to begin?" The preacher splayed his black leather Bible, that seemed more broke in than a good cast-iron pan, in his long-fingered palm.

Heather watched Liza speed up her movements as she took the coffee from Jiggy and splashed more coffee into empty cups. Her dark hair gave a gentle bounce with each of her staccato steps as she offered each man a second hit.

The preacher's voice was low and smooth but loud enough to be heard in all the corners of the room. "Moses and I had ourselves a nice long chat about forgiveness and the benefits of believing that Jesus really is the Son of God."

Liza spilled the hot brew she was pouring, and Jiggy sputtered and pulled his scalded hand back. Liza bopped him with her spoon. "Shh."

"Hey! What was that for? I was listening. You burnt me."

"Your eyes were closed."

"I was wincing in pain. That's hot."

The men around the room sniggered and chuckled. They would snigger and chuckle anytime Liza whacked Jiggy with the spoon—or rolling pin.

Liza raised an eyebrow at him.

"Fine then. I was praying for my ma back home. That's why my eyes were closed. She'd like what Preacher Marks is saying too. Not sure you do." He pinned her with his gaze. No joking in his tone.

"Don't rightly matter if I like what he says or not. Jesus cain't help nor hurt a body, if they don't ask for His help. And I don't plan on askin'. I'm taking care of myself just fine." She gave the preacher a mulish glare.

Jiggy rubbed the spot on his head that she'd smacked with the spoon. "That's too bad." Jiggy's tone held no adoration.

Liza stopped staring down the preacher and turned her glare on Jiggy. The whole room watched the pair. Heather rocked in her beautiful new chair. Would the preacher ever get to share his message? He hadn't made more than a few sentences so far.

"Too bad?" Liza sputtered. "Too bad that I don't ask for God's help, or that I'm taking care of myself?" Everything about Liza was poised to defend. "Careful." She pointed the spoon at him. "I'll smack you double if you try any of that dandy talk on me."

Jiggy scraped his chair back and gave a little space between him and the diminutive, dark-haired hot pepper. He stayed seated, but Heather could see sadness droop the corners of his eyes.

Why sadness?

What was he getting on about? Heather leaned back and relaxed her head into the headrest and enjoyed being off her feet and not being the center of attention.

Jiggy spoke soft, "It's too bad you don't trust anyone but yourself. And even worse that my Lord Jesus is on the list of those you don't trust." Jiggy lowered his voice and studied the back of his hand. "I've been down that road, and it has more pain in it than you can imagine—no matter how self-sufficient you think you are." Jiggy swallowed heavy and drew his shoulders up. He took a deep breath with eyes only on Liza's face.

"I never want to go back to making all the calls for my own life—being the only one making a way for myself. I've never been so soul-weary than when I lived like that. Trusting Jesus is the best, and one of the only, smart moves of my life. I wouldn't want to partner with *anyone*, business or otherwise, if they didn't humbly feel the same."

Liza bristled even more than usual. "How can you say that? Believe that? This preacher here is peddling horse dookie. He's nothing more than a fast-tongued salesman selling something you can't even see. I've met his kind." She stabbed the coffee kettle in the direction of the preacher and gripped the wooden spoon on her hip until her fingers creased white. "He's sitting there telling us all he had a chat with Moses. Moses? And he is sayin' it with a straight face. That should be your first warning."

"But I did, young miss—I do beg pardon." The preacher's words drew all eyes before they skipped to Moses. They didn't know this preacher very well.

Heather knew the men would only take the word of one they trusted—one they'd worked alongside.

"Moses?" the preacher asked.

"Yeeeeessh." Moses let the whole room know he agreed.

Chapter Twenty

Zeke was amazed that Moses would venture a word in such a full room. He rarely spoke even when they were felling trees. The words he'd shared around the campfire the first day they met were about the most talkative Zeke had ever found him to be.

"I talked to Moses, and he told me his story. About each of his scars and the one thing he's most sorry for." The preacher walked to Moses and placed a long-fingered hand on his shoulder.

Zeke was glad his friend didn't have to carry the weight of whatever it was alone. Zeke had fallen asleep many nights wondering if he should ask. And when he was convinced he should ask, he spent the rest of the night trying to figure what to say and how to bring it up.

Would it help Moses to talk about those three words—*Please forgive me?* What else were friends for, if not to talk and help shoulder the burden.

But if he asked Moses about his past, then Moses could reciprocate, and he was sure that wouldn't lead to anything good. That conversation wouldn't be healthy for him or Mo.

Moses pulled the leather journal he wrote in every night by the fire into his lap. He opened the pages, flipping through until he found the one he longed for, and spread them flat with his big, scarred-up hands.

Moses looked at Liza.

Liza wasn't able to hide behind her bossiness. She stood, spoon in one hand, coffee kettle in the other, eyes darting like a cornered chipmunk watching for a chance to escape.

Moses took out his nub pencil and wet the tip on his tongue

before he scratched on the page. The pastor turned so he could read it and nodded at the man before he lifted Moses's journal out of his lap and carried it across the room to stand before Liza. "Moses's story is Moses's to tell. But some of the pain he bore in his body was done to protect his family—his baby."

The preacher turned to include Heather.

Heather stopped rocking.

"He did something that no man should have to do to keep his child alive—but he did it, and he would do it again. If you know what you're about to do is wrong and especially wrong before God and you do it anyway, it can leave a heavy weight on your shoulders. I hope you never have to feel that weight, Miss Liza. But if you find yourself in those straits, as Moses did, and don't have a clear understanding of how big God's forgiveness is—then all the worse. His grace is sufficient."

He ran a hand over Moses's journal. The preacher's words came slow and smooth—nothing fancy, nothing flashy. Zeke figured he could talk a bank robber out of his loot with that tone. "Miss Liza, you don't have to trust me. I ain't worth a cup of spit. But Jesus? I help folks trust Jesus. And I'd guess every man in this room has done something to be in the same place Moses has been. And knowing Jesus forgives is the only hope we have. Some are sinking in the mud of their mistakes and choices. Else, some wouldn't be way out here at Camp 13, in the middle of nowhere."

Zeke started to nod. He had to stop it. If someone saw him agree, they might ask.

The room filled with a bunch of murmured agreements.

Liza stepped closer to the preacher, lifting her stubborn chin. "If Moses was defending his child, then he should be praised for his courage not buried beneath guilt." Liza's words zipped.

"Do you know what he did to save his child?" The preacher's words were even quieter. But Zeke felt each one.

"No." Liza's stance shifted. She let her arms fall to her sides and tucked the spoon away. Jiggy came in behind her and carefully lifted the kettle away.

"I won't tell what is only Moses's to say, but does this look like the heart of a man free from guilt?" He opened the book and flipped through many pages.

Zeke knew full well what was crammed neatly on every space on every page. Jiggy stood beside Liza and put his hand gently on her arm.

Zeke envied Jiggy, not with Liza but with Heather. Jiggy was making a stand with Liza—protecting her so she wouldn't feel alone or threatened. Even by the preacher's words.

"'Please forgive me' is written over and over," Jiggy said it loud enough for all the men to hear. They all probably wondered what Moses worked on every evening and after every meal.

Jiggy reached forward and flipped the pages as the preacher held the book, searching for the last entry. The one Moses just wrote. *I am forgiven.*

Liza looked up at Jiggy. "I don't know if I could ever trust something I can't see." Liza turned her back on the preacher and moved toward the kitchen. Jiggy went after her, then halted. The tiny woman stayed in the room, turned, and knelt at the foot of the rocking chair in front of Heather.

Zeke moved closer behind Heather.

Liza said, "I can't see Him, Heather. But you talk to Him like He is good and kind. If He is good and kind, then why did He leave you to fend for yourself? Why did He make things so hard for me? For you? There ain't nothing kind about going hungry or being so cold you can't feel your feet, and you have to eat grubs, or you'll die. And that was when I was a kid. Who is so cruel to a child?"

Zeke wondered what Heather would say. His heart felt abandon and exposed—left to fend for himself a few times of late. It seemed like the only time he got answers was if he shook the tree hard enough to make apples drop on his own—like Liza was used to doing. Was God in his mess somewhere?

Heather squeezed Liza's hand. "But you got away from awful Charley, and you found me...and I found you. Doesn't that count for kindness?"

"You make it seem so simple. Every night, I hear you, and I try to think like you. You never get mad at God for messing up your life—with a passed-away ma and husband and a growing babe. I would be plumb ticked—and I'd tell Him so. Might of told Him, for you, a time or two."

A few men laughed. Jiggy smiled when Heather chuckled.

"I've been mad, Liza, and plenty scared. But God isn't afraid of that. And I would be doomed if He ever abandoned me. Don't you see? God is the only thing that we *can* count on. Everything else shifts and moves." Heather turned her head and met Zeke's gaze.

Shifts and moves?

Zeke felt scalded and burned, like the back of Jiggy's hand. She'd aimed that last comment at him. *She had.* She was disappointed in him—maybe hurt or sad. *At me?*

Was she upset that he kept his distance? He thrilled at that. Was she irritated that he sometimes moved to protect her? Like now, standing behind her chair.

He wasn't sure why, but she was most certainly speaking to him between her sentences. He could still feel the pressure of her gaze. He'd let her down even before he knew she was counting on him.

And why shouldn't she be disappointed? He was practically lying to her each time he didn't tell her about the things happening back in Auburn.

But if he told her, then he would surely lose her respect and friendship—and maybe his freedom. He cut his gaze to the location behind the counter where Cookie kept his wanted posters.

The posters mocked him from their shelf.

His brow beaded with sweat, and his neck grew itchy. He could almost feel the hemp in the rope scraping against his soft skin.

Heather may be frustrated, but that couldn't matter. He would never breathe a word of his woes to her precious ears and make her burdens double overnight. *Besides. I'm just being fearful. What could she know? I never told her anything.* Maybe that was part of it. Maybe she could tell.

Heather was clutching Liza's hands.

Moses stood from his chair beside the preacher. He gathered his journal back from the circuit rider before he squatted beside Liza. His hulking form almost making Liza look like a child.

The whites of Moses's eyes gleamed with a joy Zeke had never seen on his friend's face. Moses passed the journal to Liza and, when she took it, he clasped both her hands around the book and demanded her focus.

Then Moses tapped his chest and pointed and made the sign of a cross. He nodded for Liza to see and then he pointed one long finger and touched near her collarbone.

"You trust the preacher, Mo? You think he knows what he's talking about?" she asked.

"Yaaaa." He nodded.

"I'll think on it."

He pushed his journal toward her and let go, meaning for her to keep it. Then he stood and reached deep into his breast pocket and pulled out a small wooden ring—the kind used as a baby teether.

He handed it to Heather. Heather held it reverently. Zeke could see that it was well crafted but used.

"Mmmmyyy." Moses made the sign of rocking a baby.

"This was your baby's?"

Moses nodded.

"I'm honored. Thank you." Almost tears, but dry.

Moses walked out the door and when his back disappeared the preacher said, "That's church, boys."

Cookie cleared his throat. He rubbed the kinks from his back as he hollered instructions. "All you men, Harvey will have my hide if you flake tomorrow after having done this today. So, Sunday lunch is over, dinner will be served at five, not six. Best not be late. And early to bed with you. Have them heading out an hour before daylight in the morning, Zeke."

"Yes, sir," Zeke answered. "You heard him."

Men shifted and moved in every direction. Some gathering their supplies to darn socks, others adding goose grease to their boots or tin pants. Others sharpened their axes.

"Do you want help moving these things to your cabin?" Jiggy asked.

Heather answered, "The cradle should be put in the cabin. But I'd like this left here, maybe pushed a little closer to the wood heat, until this baby makes itself known."

Jiggy and some others carried the things to their cabin.

Heather stood.

Zeke moved the rocker, "Not long now, right?"

"Shouldn't be—but I've never done this before, and Cookie can only remember some things. I'll just have to be patient." The room emptied during the next several minutes.

Heather sat down again, put her head back in the rocker, and soothed her belly. *How much longer?* "Seems like I've been waiting my whole life for one thing or another—for Pa to come home, for Ma to get better—and now for this little one."

"Waiting is almost as hard as not knowing what to expect." Zeke said it with his back to her, wishing he could share everything and see if she had any ideas about what he could try.

When he turned and could see her face, she was looking around the room as if checking for listeners. She leaned forward and put a hand on his forearm, "You can tell me, Zeke. Whatever it is."

He tugged his arm back as if he'd touched the woodstove. And then wished he could put it back. Heather was offering him support, and he rebuffed her out of instinct. He hated that he made the kind light fade from her eyes.

"I see. Forget I asked." She stood and went to the kitchen, Zeke on her heels.

What could he say? It was everything or nothing. There was no halfway with what was following on his trail. He couldn't risk putting her in harm's way. Besides, what could she possibly think of or do that he hadn't considered? "Heather?"

She faced him. And he could see. She knew he held back.

"If I could," he said.

"I understand," she replied.

But did she?

She walked away, leaving him no other choice but to focus on where the camp would cut and clear tomorrow. And count how many downed trees would be required to make the boss man happy.

Chapter Twenty-One

The next day, when they were out in the forest, Moses darted past Zeke carrying an axe over his shoulder and a bucket of wedges balanced in his other hand. Moses lit across the top of the logs, leaping one to the next with the balance and grace of a cougar.

Zeke had counted early and was ready to test his leg for the strength required for logging. He would still tally logs for the boss, but he could work the saws again—if he was strong enough.

Zeke was right behind Mo. He picked up his pace. His knee near mended. Before his accident, Lord Ashburton, the foreman, assigned Zeke and Moses to the same trees. Zeke jumped from the end of one fallen tree to the next, keeping an eye out for the stable surface he would step on next. He was only a few paces behind Moses's broad back.

Neither were winded.

As they moved to their next project, men's voices hollered different instructions all around them. Chopping and sawing sounds cut the air in a sort of wild rhythm. After the first tree was down, the air smelled like moved earth and fresh cut wood.

The first week Zeke was a logger, he was sore everywhere, even his fingertips and earlobes. But now, even after several months down with his knee, he could keep up with everyone except Jigger Jones and a logger named Bear. *Most* couldn't keep up with either of them. Jigger Jones was half crazy, and Bear was compact and stout, built like his namesake and just as hairy. He could scale a tree with his bare hands and bare feet.

Moses jumped off the end of the log and trotted to the massive fir that would be their next conquest. Zeke was about to copy him when another logger yelled, "Tiiiiiimbeeerrrrrr!"

Zeke looked back to see the commotion. The falling tree was thick enough it would take a string of eighteen mules to pull it out of the ravine. He turned his back to begin the felling of his tree, ready to begin climbing. He took two steps.

Moses screamed. "Ooooookkkk oooouuuu!"

Before Zeke could react, Moses was running down the log toward him. The whites of his eyes as round as owls. Moses slammed into him harder than a donkey kick.

The breath rushed from Zeke's lungs. As he was falling off the butt of the log into nothingness, a treetop came down, end first, crushing the log Zeke would have been standing on.

The weight of the impact caused their log to come up with equal force—almost standing it up before it crashed back down.

Moses was caught and launched toward the blue sky.

"Mo!" Zeke shouted when Moses was batted like a rag doll into the air. His massive body flung wild.

Zeke's breath burst from his chest when his back hit the dirt, leaving him airless for several long seconds. The back of his head bounced off the hard earth.

But how could he care, when he didn't know how Moses fared? As soon as he could, he wrenched himself over, gasping for a full breath. He staggered to his feet and turned to the place the other loggers were all running toward.

Tupper, the closest thing the camp had to a doctor, was the first to Moses's side.

Zeke gasped and hobbled his way over. *No! Don't be…He saved me, Lord. Help him! He saved me. I should be under that tree.*

But even before he reached Moses's side, he knew. The other loggers turned their backs on what they saw and pulled their hats off their heads. Some swore. Some cried out. Others pressed thumbs over their eyes.

Then Zeke saw for himself. Moses's body wrecked. No match for the flight or the landing. He'd landed on a broken-off limb.

Skewered through. Neck lying at a wrong angle. Gone before he'd landed.

Zeke fell to his knees several feet from Moses's side. There was nothing he could do.

If he'd kept his eyes on the tree, Moses would still be alive. *My mistake cost Moses his life.* The air was stripped from his lungs in a different way.

Zeke stayed on his knees and looked away from the broken body of his friend and gazed instead at the patch of blue in the sky above him. He wasn't even supposed to be here. This was temporary. Moses had followed him here, to his death. *For what?*

Men from all around came down off their springboards notched into the side of trees twenty feet or more up, others came over carrying their axes and saws.

Two of the men brought shovels. They picked a place only two paces away from Moses's bleeding and broken body and began digging his grave.

The low thrum of an old, hummed hymn came rumbling through the chest of one man and began to echo in each neighbor's gravelly throat. The sound more sorrowful than a woman keening for a dead child bounced off the forest walls.

There would be no church service.

There would be no coffin.

Brown earth clung to the end of the shovels being passed from man to man as they each took a turn digging. This was the way each man said his piece and good-bye.

When Zeke's breath finally returned to his lungs, he held it. His body shook with the wail that wanted to escape his belly. *Mo.*

Moses had only been free of his journal for less than a day. All for what? So Zeke could hide in the forest and lick his wounded pride as he waited for a breakthrough in Auburn.

He was a ninny.

He had to go back.

He had to make Moses's sacrifice worth something. Moses had died to save him. What was he going to do with that?

Zeke couldn't bring himself to study the contorted shape of

Moses's body. No one removed Moses from the tree. His grave digging would come first. Zeke wanted to scream and punch. But who? Instead, he skipped over and plucked the shovel from Tupper's hands and dug like he'd never dug before.

He scooped and he shoved into the brown earth. Again and again. His palms hot as they rubbed the handle—sure to have blister memorials tomorrow. Still he dug. His back ached and his nose ran from the tears that burned the back of his eyes and throat.

Moses is gone.

For what?

Zeke had to come clean.

The snow had melted. He wouldn't wait much longer to go back to Auburn. Only until after Heather had her baby. But then, he would go, and he would make Moses's death worth something, even if he had to squeeze the life out of David with his own hands in trade. Not that he really would. He growled in pain and frustration.

No more secrets. No more hiding.

When Moses was laid to rest, right in the heart of the forest, Zeke would head back to tell the girls, and before his sore head hit the pillow, he would tell Heather and Cookie his story. He was done hiding. He was done with secrets. His secrets killed Mo.

Yes, he would tell Cookie and Heather. Two people he considered friends.

Two people who could turn me in.

If he had told Moses about Auburn and its dangers, Moses might have helped him with David. Moses obviously had a run-in, or twenty, with hard situations. His scars told that story. *Would things have been different?* Zeke thought of the noose but would not rub his neck this time. This wasn't about his hide anymore. This was about Mo.

When the hole was deep enough to keep Moses in and predators out, ten men each held a piece of Moses and lifted in unison.

His body resisted and then came free from his impalement.

One man removed Moses's boots.

Tradition.

Zeke wasn't even surprised when he saw scars lined the bottoms of his friend's pink-soled feet. Was there any part of Moses without a scar? Someone tortured Mo, but it was Zeke's fault he was dead.

I am forgiven.

The word written in Moses's hand found Zeke.

Directions murmured by Tupper guided the group's steps until Moses was carefully laid into the bottom of his forest grave. All did their part to cover him, and Moses's boots were hooked on the tree that marked his burial better than any headstone. The loggers had been undertakers before—they would be again.

Moses's boots would be the only marker—until the forest consumed them, long after the earth consumed Mo.

Some of the weather-beaten men went silently back to their springboards and saws, but Zeke couldn't. He stayed by the raw earth that covered Moses for the whole of the workday. When the count was finally done. Zeke left ahead of everyone. It was only right that he be the bearer of the news to camp.

Would Heather even be able to look at him? Would she hate him as much as he hated himself when she heard that Moses's death was the fruit of cowardice—his cowardice? If he hadn't run from his trouble, Moses wouldn't even be here. He wouldn't have died here.

His steps back to camp, toward Heather and Liza and Cookie, turned to giant strides as he tried to outrun the gapping chasm that was life without Mo. If he slowed, if he stopped before he reached his confessors, the ground that was turning into a dark pit behind him was sure to find its way to the space beneath his feet. He would fall as sure as not. He too would be consumed by the dark earth that Moses's body was even now being sucked into.

"Heather!" His chest was tight and heaving as he gulped for air. His knee burned but he ignored it, refusing to limp. The massive lodge came into view, but it was still a ways up ahead. Smoke curled from both the potbelly stove and the chimney of Heather's ovens. Though he knew she couldn't hear him, he called again. "Heather!"

Cookie and Liza would need to know, but Heather was the one he needed to tell. He was well and truly alone until he told her everything. If she ran for the hills, then he would deal with that.

"Run for the hills?" The irony in his choice of words ripped a tormented laugh from him. He looked around. *Run for the hills.* Trees thick and green and trees naked and bare clustered around him in every direction, blocking his view of Mount Hood. He'd trailed between the Douglas fir trunks. He'd climbed to the sky on the strength of their branches. He'd already run for the hills. There was no place to go from here that would lead to truth except telling the truth.

If Heather could see fit to look him in the eyes after what happened this morning and what he had to tell her, then he would keep talking to her until she understood about David, his parents, his dreams of having a family—all of it.

Thoughts of Jasmine buffeted him. He couldn't remember ever having a need to pour anything out before Jasmine. He couldn't remember anything personal about Jasmine. Did he know her at all?

Heather was here. Heather was now. Heather knew Mo. Could she understand?

He was beside the bunkhouse, still sorting himself and searching for what his first words would be, when he heard a snap from behind the bunkhouse.

He stopped short. "Hello? Who is there?" Did one of the men beat him back? They couldn't have. None of them ran with the devil on his tail like he did. Did one of the men cut work? "Harvey won't like finding out you're trying to pull one over on him."

It was still and silent. Whoever was there was hiding.

Did he care to find out who it was? Not as much as he needed to dump the contents of his soul for Heather to sort. He would find out later who wasn't on shift and dock his pay. *If* he still had a job after he told Cookie who he was. He stood in front of the closed lodge door. Once he opened it there was no going back.

It was time for the truth.

Chapter Twenty-Two

"No! Not Mo!" Liza burst before Zeke had finished his sentence.

Heather felt all the breath leave her chest at Zeke's words. She moved from the kitchen to her rocker and sunk low before she fell over. *Another loss.*

"The risk is always high on this job." Cookie lifted a meaty hand and wiped it down the whole of his face.

"Mo? I can't believe it. The preacher was here yesterday and he—I can't believe it." Liza began pacing.

Heather watched her friend wind herself up into a frenzy while everything in her plummeted until her heart felt like it was going to stop beating and fall to the floor. They held themselves in opposite ways, Liza and her, one pacing and trying to understand and the other sitting without rocking.

The rest of the loggers filed in—heads low, hats off—silent.

Liza didn't seem to care that the others came in. "He was a good man. I can't see how. I can't see why." Liza walked faster—to and fro—without fussing with any cleaning. Her skirts flared each time she turned to a new direction.

Heather watched it as if by each turn her friend made, she could be sure that time was passing and that she was alive to witness it. Her breath slowly came back to her chest.

Zeke was at her feet. "Heather. I can't—"

"I know." Heather didn't have to say it again. She closed her eyes and laid her head back on the carved headpiece of the rocking chair. Moses drew the art intricately there. The carving was a piece of him. She needed to be close to it. Moses was wordless, but not silent. Could he feel how much she cared? How much she would miss him? He'd influenced the whole camp. Moses never gave up—through the most horrible pain and loss a person could face.

Zeke clutched at her hand. He lowered his voice and leaned in for her ears alone. "I need to speak with you. There is more I have to say."

Heather wondered if he was finally going to tell her he killed people and ran from the law or something equally sinister.

Liza alternated between wringing her hands and flailing them out beside her like bird wings. "Cookie, these men can't waltz in here and tell me Moses is gone. They can't. I can't believe it iffen I don't see it with my own eyes. So how can they just say it? I've gotta see."

Cookie moved to Liza who was still pacing all about the room. When she came within his reach, Cookie scooped her to him and hugged her tight. Her head only came to his shoulders and Cookie, more round than tall, hugged solid and pure.

Heather wished the old man was holding her. She felt his solid embrace in her body from her place in the rocker across the room. He seemed to hug all her places of loss—from standing at the foot of her mother's bed, her body cold and still, to when she was alone shoveling earth over Riley's open eyes, chasing the birds away.

Zeke hadn't let her fingers go since he asked to talk with her. She dug her fingers into his palm, pressing back against the anguish in her chest. It made her belly tight and created a dull pang in her back.

She looked at his face. *No words.* How was she supposed to listen to him, to whatever he had to say with Moses gone?

She felt her nails press into his skin. She loosened her hold. "Sorry."

"Don't be sorry. I'm the one who is sorry—I need you to know." He pulled her hand back into his.

Across the room, Liza lifted her head off Cookie's chest. "I can't see my way through, Cookie. I have to go to him. I have to see where he is."

"We'll take you, Miss Liza," Jiggy called to her from the group of loggers still clustered by the door. The men shifted and grunted their agreement. They moved closer to Liza and shielded her in their own way. Jiggy at the front of the pack.

"Jiggy. Moses is gone. He was kilt." Liza said it like she was the one informing them.

"Yes, miss." Jiggy wrung his hat in his hands and then opened his arms wide from his place next to her—an invitation she could take or leave on her terms.

Liza stunned the whole room by darting to Jiggy and falling into his arms. He held her while she whimpered. "I need to see, Jiggy. Moses was gonna show me. He believed that preacher man. I need to go to him. I need you to help me see things like Mo— like his journal. I slept with it under my pillow." She sobbed.

"We'll take you. And I'll show you. You can trust me. I know who Moses found—I can help you find Him too."

Heather knew who Jiggy was referring to—who Moses had found forgiveness with—Jesus. The biggest love of all. Could she trust His love, or would it cost too much? Would He take even more from her?

Jiggy tucked Liza's tiny form under his arm. She was a perfect fit to his side. "We'll all take you. Once you see, it will be a mite easier—but only a mite."

Cookie scraped a large pot of food across the stovetop until it was away from the main heat. "I'm coming too. Supper will be after we get back." Cookie pulled his apron over his head and replaced it with his winter coat.

"I'll stay here, with Heather. Unless you want to go?" Zeke turned to ask her. "It's a long walk."

Heather let go of Zeke's hand. She was grateful Zeke included her. But she was close enough to Moses just being in the chair that he'd helped carve. She set the chair to rocking, ignoring the pain that pulled at her lower back. "It's better if I stay. I'd slow you all down."

"We could hitch a draft," Bjorn offered.

"I'm not sure I could or should be up on a horse." She patted her belly and the group all moved to the door without her. Jiggy and Liza first. Then they all moved down the skid road toward Moses's earthen grave.

When the last man left and pulled the door behind him, the quiet of the room settled in around her and Zeke.

Zeke continued to kneel in front of her chair while she rocked. "I'm so sorry. I have to say these things. They can't stay hidden for even one moment longer."

She was so tired of all the things in her life that she couldn't control. None of how things had played out had been her desired plan. Even the timing of this moment—his terrible news. And it would be terrible. That was all she'd ever had. All life had given her so far—even the baby was a surprise. No hope for better now.

She couldn't feel anything. Not for the man in front of her. Not for Mo. Not for sweet Mama. Life kept handing her misery, and she was forced to take it in, absorb it, be changed by it. And yet still have no say.

Zeke's news would be the same. He would pile the weight of his burden on her, and she would be buried beneath it like Riley and Moses were.

It would kill her.

She stopped rocking. She'd sat by, serving and caring, so many times. *Enough.* She looked Zeke straight in the eye. "Did you kill someone?" She felt the heat of anger poison her tongue.

"Mo? No! But he saved me. I should have—"

"Not him. I saw the wanted poster." She didn't have to tell him she'd snuck to his loft and rifled his things like a common thief. But if she did tell him, there would be one less thing to carry. And her body was weighted down with so much, the pressure was so great, and it all rested tight in the roundness of her belly.

If she didn't fight back and fuel the anger rising in her chest she would—"I saw it the day we came home from the doctor. After that, I went through your things when I got the chance. I've waited for you to say. I've asked questions. Did you kill the man they said you murdered?"

"No. That's what I'm trying to tell you about. I have secrets and a reason to hide, but it's not my sin that chases me away from home."

The ache in her back moved around the front, making her skin as hard as an unbaked potato. Sitting was uncomfortable. She stood. She would hear all he had to say. She'd guessed and speculated about him all winter.

Spring would bring truth.

And his confession could rip away the only sense of safety she'd had since before Mother took sick. Safety she could see now, in this moment, when it was about to slip away from her.

Zeke would no longer be a solid place for her to lean—someone in her corner championing her—like he did the first day she and Liza arrived. She would hear him out, but she couldn't face what he would say without busy fingers.

"I'll listen, but come with me. I'm gonna make cookies. Moses loves…loved…my molasses cookies." She hated that her words sounded clipped and angry. But there was no help for it. This was survival.

"Thank you. I need to be free. Maybe you can see a way for me to be free."

She left him before he could leave her, by moving with practiced ease around the counter to the shelves that held all the things that she understood and could control: salt, nutmeg, soda.

She could take a measure of each or leave each.

She could mix them.

She could blend them.

She could make them behave the way she wanted—creating things others enjoyed or found filling. But today, she needed to control these things. She needed to blend them and bend them into the thing she desired. Because if she didn't bend them, she was sure the words coming from Zeke would double her over until she splintered like a branch bent wrong.

Her hands found the familiar wooden scoop she used to measure the sugar and flour. She lingered with it in her grasp, rubbing the smoothness. Her taut belly pressed into the counter in front of her as heavy as if she were carrying a gunnysack full of grain under her calico.

The weight pulled at her back.

She couldn't do anything about that either. She'd let this huge kitchen be her comfort. She tiptoed up and pulled the most tangible reminder of her mother's love down off the shelf. Opening the recipe box, the first thing she saw was mama's ribbon with the tiny flowers stitched down the center.

The ribbon spoke of a love between a man and a woman. Her mother and father. It spoke of a shackle that bound you and tied you up until you had nothing left like a bowl of eggs dropped on the wooden floor.

Maybe marriage wasn't the only place love left you dry and worn down to ruin. Maybe friendship was the same. She found the paper slip with Mama's delicate script on it. She poured and separated and stirred the ingredients as if she was on a short candle. Any moment, all the light was going to disappear, and she would be alone in the dark…again.

She stabbed at the dough with the heavy wooden spoon.

Zeke hovered all around her. "Are you sure you don't want to go back and sit. We could finish this later. Do you need to rest?"

Zeke had the potential to devastate her, and she'd stayed away as best she could, but still he took care of her like she was valuable—precious even.

She fussed and mixed. Flour spilled onto the rough-hewn counter. She forced herself to stay focused and not to turn and look into his dark eyes. "Who is Patrick?" She must have shocked him because he took a small step back from her and she heard him jam his hands into his pockets.

She wanted him to hurry up and talk—to hurry up and tell her whatever it was that he was hiding. To hurry up and admit that he couldn't stay—that he would leave her, just like Pa and Riley.

She stirred and scooped and kept at the work, because if she didn't keep her hands busy, she would cover her ears and block out every detail.

Moses was gone.

He wouldn't see the child in her belly. He wouldn't be there to see her child hold his child's wooden toy.

Love.

Again, she faced the evils of that word. She didn't love Moses like a woman loved a man or like Pa loved Ma, but still, his loss ripped, fileting her like the fish Bjorn caught and cleaned for her right after she first came.

"I didn't kill anyone. I was new to town, kept to myself, made few friends, had no real family, so it made it easy for the man who did do the killing to pin it on me. His reputation in town is quite fixed. He accused me on word alone. But with no proof, I can't defend myself against the charge."

She measured out the same ingredients into three large bowls, tripling her mother's recipe in each. The men would eat more in their sadness. The cookies wouldn't even make it until morning. "If you know who did it, why don't you accuse him back?"

"I have no proof. It would be his word to mine. He's been in town sometime longer than me, but he works at the bank and everyone knows him—trusts him, even if they shouldn't. He is crafty. And I..." Zeke started from the beginning. He told her all the things she needed to know. He talked about his friends—Patrick and Mr. Price. And he talked about Jasmine. She listened to him as she stirred the coals in the stove to life and mixed all the dry ingredients.

She pulled the eggs she would need out of the sand barrel and was fixing to crack the first, when he said, "I can show you the deed. I can show you the papers from Patrick. He's talking to the town lawyer and the sheriff in Baker while I'm away. He is trying to find out why or find proof."

His voice pleaded. Even his hands were open to her. Asking. He needed her to understand. To believe. To trust. But she had nothing left to give. All she had to offer him was an empty shell, like the one she held in her hand.

Why did it matter what she answered him? If she let him see how empty she was, that she had nothing to offer, nothing for him to love, he would retract his friendship and whatever else he had in mind. *For sure*, he wouldn't fall for her like Pa did Ma. His leaving would be easier on them both. "If you tell me that is how it happened, then I believe you." Her voice sounded flat even in her ears.

She turned back to her bowls, holding the second egg ready to crack. "I have found nothing about you cruel. Only a cruel man could willingly bludgeon a man. I choose to believe you."

Before she could even finish her words, Zeke spun her to face him, bending until his eyes were a mere inch from hers. She would've stepped back but the counter was in her way.

Without breaking eye contact he placed both his hands on her shoulders and slid their warmth down her sleeves to her elbows. She let her arms settle to her sides, lowering the egg.

"You believe me? You trust me? Even after all of it? Even after Moses?" His tan face and dark-as-tree-bark eyes showed signs of unshed tears. He would cry simply because she believed him?

She lifted her hand not holding the egg and rested it against his cheek. He pressed into it. And before she knew what was coming, he pulled her to him.

She let him, needing the comfort he was offering.

Her belly pressed between them as he leaned across the small space and pressed his lips against hers in the gentlest, sweetest kiss she'd ever experienced.

He murmured, "Thank you," right into her lips. He looked for something—acceptance maybe—in her eyes and must've found it because he settled her more firmly against his chest and bent his head to kiss again. This time for the kiss's sake and not for the thank you.

Heather folded into him.

She let herself feel every ounce of support he offered her weighted body. She closed her eyes and let his lips claim hers for several long moments before she moved to put her arms up and around his broad shoulders, still holding on to the egg. Just as she relaxed into a contented sigh against his solid warmth, something slipped from inside her and spilled on the floor.

She stepped back from him, dropping the egg in the process. She would have knocked one of the bowls of dough off the counter in her haste, if Zeke's reflexes hadn't prevented it.

"I'm sorry. I shouldn't have taken such liberties. I—"

"It's the baby." Heather held her stomach as a strong spasm sucked her breath away. "I think the baby is coming. I don't kn—" She groaned as pain came fast.

"We need the doctor. I'll get the doctor."

She clutched his arm before he could turn away from her. "You can't go. I need you here." The pain continued its deep clutching. "*Ahh!*"

Before the pain ended, Zeke scooped her into his arms and left the kitchen at almost a run. "I'll take you to the cabin. Then I can go find Liza."

She curled her lips into her teeth and squeezed her eyes against the bobbing landscape. The weight in her belly increased and demanded, tightening with each of his jostling steps until all she could do was groan. She bowed her head into his neck. His dark beard tickled her cheek as she clutched his woodsy-smelling sleeve.

When the pain let up, she lifted her head. He'd opened her cabin door with the hand at her back. He kicked it wide to make room for them both. Before he even placed her on the straw tick mattress and moved back a step, another pain gripped her belly. She groaned out, "You can't leave me."

"I need to get you something. What?" He looked like a hunted rabbit ready to bolt.

"Liza had me gather supplies, towels, and sheets." She pointed to a neatly folded stack on the barrel that had been cut down to make up a small table. A melted candle stood in its holder next to her stack. She clutched a hand to her cramping belly. "But I will need the hot water set on top of the stove in the lodge and fresh cold water from the creek first. I'm not sure what all I'll need it for, Liza's been talking about it, but I need her—"

Zeke darted out the door before she could finish her sentence, leaving the door swinging wide. She heard the clank of the water buckets.

Oh, please come back.

When the pain lifted enough she could move and breathe, she reached down and unhooked her well-worn shoes and looped a finger in her woolen stockings to drag them off as well. Being bent over brought the next pain on. She had to prepare herself for what was coming before Zeke came back—if he came back. When the cramp let up, she stood carefully and slow.

"Oh, Mama, I wish you were here. Or Liza." Liza told her that her mother worked on a birthing for more than one day, sometimes more than two—that she had plenty of time to gather her things and change into a sleeping gown and bring the doctor—but it didn't look like Heather was going to have that luxury. The pressure was so heavy she was more concerned the baby would fall out.

There was no way she was going to give birth in her night rail—mortally embarrassing her and Zeke both. She would burn down the shanty with the heat pouring off her face from embarrassment, if she was asked to be that undressed in front of him. But the baby was coming.

She lifted her skirts and untied the familiar knot at the back of her petticoats. She'd quit wearing her stays weeks ago. Her petticoats dropped to the floor in a white cloud. Should she shed her bloomers too?

It only makes sense. The baby wasn't exactly going to push her clothing aside on the way out. The door to the lodge across the way banged shut.

Zeke would burst back through the door any moment. And another pain was coming.

She stepped out of her bloomers. With another quick move, she had all her underclothing tucked away out of sight.

She felt a modicum of relief when the extra garments released their pressure from her body. She was standing at the foot of the bed grabbing the wooden railing as the new pain encompassing her whole body tore through her.

Zeke barreled through the doorway. Zeke was there.

You came back.

He put the buckets aside without dripping a single drop and came close enough she could clutch his hand. Sweat broke out on her upper lip before the pain released enough for her to breathe.

"What's next. Should you lay down?"

"I tried." She shook her head. "I can't lay down. The pain is more. I don't want to do this. I need this to stop."

Zeke tugged her until she stepped backward from the bed. He tucked Heather into his chest and supported her. She stayed there—quiet and breathing for what seemed like too short a time. When her belly tightened again, she leaned over, into the cramping, without letting go of him. Her small white toes peeked out from beneath the hem of her dress. His boots looked like armed guards standing sentry over her exposed white skin. And that was just what he was—her guard and her protector.

There was no way he would leave her to fend for herself at such a moment. He wouldn't leave now. Later maybe. But now was all she could think on. She was going to have a baby.

He shifted.

She clutched his arm. "Don't go. I need you here." She ducked her head away. She'd just comforted herself with the fact that he would stay.

"I'm here. You're safe. I can't help you with this"—he pressed himself around her like a hug—"but I'm staying right here."

His words reassured her some.

"Here comes another." She stayed face forward. She let him hold her. She pressed her lips tight against the demand of her belly. She leaned into him and let her head rest on his shoulder as they stood at the end of the bed. *He's here. I'm not alone.* She breathed in through her nose.

He didn't move. Time after time, she used him to anchor the swells of pain that crashed over her.

When a moment of pause came, Zeke reached for a piece of toweling from the stack he'd placed on the end of the bed. He wiped her brow and tucked the soft blond curls damp with sweat behind her dainty ears.

She was so tiny—delicate to look at even with exertion leaving her cheeks flushed pink. She pressed her eyes closed against all. He studied her heart-shaped face from his vantage.

Did she realize how beautiful she was, at this moment, as she served her body's needs? Did she know her baby would be born on the same day Moses left? That seemed like more than a happenstance. There was hope in it somehow.

"Don't leave," she crooned.

Another pain struck full and deep. He felt her belly harden and strain with his forearms, her grip squeezing his hands as hard as the pains wracked her.

"No doctor, no Liza, no idea what to do when the baby comes." She panted. "Except tying off the cord."

"That's more than I know."

She pressed her eyes shut and spaced her legs a little. She checked a controlled scream by turning her face to the side into his arm. The rough fabric of his sleeve brushed coarse against her face. She turned in front of him. Still clutching his arms. Her back to his chest.

She was so small against him. He felt like he could wrap his arms double around her without even trying.

What comfort could he offer? What did someone say to a person giving birth?

He stayed behind her. Several more pains came and went. She was a limp rag against his chest when something about her movements changed.

Heather bent forward and looked to the floor. Zeke looked with her and then wasn't sure if he should. The inevitable was about to happen. He'd had no part in making this child, yet he would see its first moments right alongside Heather.

Heather lifted her skirts and fumbled around beneath them.

He made himself into a human chair—balancing her lest she fall.

"I feel him. He's right there. It won't be long now."

And like that, she was hunkered over herself with both hands buried beneath her skirts, legs wide. She bore down almost to a squat, her weight relentlessly against him.

Then, in a moment, she was pulling a wet, crying baby covered with chalky-white goo out from hiding for his inspection. His birth cord still tethered to beneath her skirts.

Zeke grabbed a wad of the sheeting and brought it to the underside of the baby. He helped her hold the slippery child as his small cries rent the air, growing louder and more insistent as the baby's legs kicked and jerked.

"It's a boy. He's here."

"You did it." Zeke clutched both mother and child tighter to him, ignoring the mess that puddled at their feet.

"A boy, Zeke, I have a son. I'm a mother." Joy crowned her lovely face and his threatened to match at the wonder he saw there. What it would be like to have a family. What it would be like to have a son.

He glanced at the ceiling to keep her from glimpsing his bone-aching lack in that moment that was her prize. "You will be the greatest mother of them all. And he is quite the son. Look at him."

The squirmy pink flesh wiggled and cried between them—chin quivering.

"Zeke, I'd like you to meet Riley Moses."

"Riley Moses. A sound name. And a gift to the men in this camp. A much-needed gift."

Just then words could be heard coming from the alleyway that ran between the lodge and her cabin. The crew was back.

Zeke left Heather's side only to call Liza to her aid, "Liza! The baby!"

The cold that filled in where the warmth of her body had been felt as permanent as a tattoo etched in his flesh.

She wasn't his.

Riley Moses wasn't his.

He was as alone as he'd ever been only more so.

Chapter Twenty-Three

avid kept himself and Jasmine hidden when a whole crew of loggers walked the road to the largest lodge he'd ever seen. There was a bunch of hollering and running about. It wasn't safe for him to steal a look. He was just relieved this was the right place.

It had taken him and Jasmine longer than expected to track Zeke to this backwoods operation. David had made double sure that he didn't tip his hand by alerting the locals that he sought one man.

Once they traveled out of the snow into warmer country, Jasmine seemed to take to this godforsaken place, like a mule to a pack, but he'd had enough of sleeping outdoors. When he got back to Auburn, with the deed to the mansion in his hands, he would soak in the full-sized copper tub for a week to get all the grime out. He was built for more than this plebeian life. Jasmine was too—she just didn't know it yet.

When it seemed more settled, David slipped forward and peered around the end of the building just in time to see Zeke carrying a woman across the path, going from a smaller cabin to the log home.

The same building they'd been hiding behind earlier, when Zeke came up the road and called out.

"Hear that? I told you I heard a baby earlier. After the scream you said was a mountain lion." Jasmine shivered and tucked herself under his arm as she'd made a habit of doing since he said he would marry her. "Maybe we could have one of our own someday."

A lightning bolt of terror stiffened David from heel to elbow. *A child.* Him? Had he ever even considered the possibility? He couldn't and wouldn't answer her secret plea. There were too many things that needed his attention first. Too many things that needed to fall into line—or be forced into line—before he could turn domestic.

"A baby would be perfect don't you think?" She tried again.

He went back to spying on Zeke. *Wait.* An infant was the perfect leverage for what he had in mind. If the careful way Zeke handled the bundle of feminine charms in his arms was any indication, then David's luck was finally turning. "In more ways than one."

Jasmine clung to him, joy radiating from every part of her.

Now. *It comes down to timing.* He held the advantage of surprise. If he could play it to its full potential, then he could be heading back to Auburn to claim his prize before the end of the week.

"Take Heather right to her rocker, Zeke. No need for her to strain herself. She's been through a lot." Liza walked ahead of Zeke and the sea of loggers parted in front of them.

Every last man was scrubbed and polished—hair slicked, hands cleaned. Bjorn passed a hand down his face, scrubbing tears that fell unabashedly down his ruddy cheeks and into his beard. "Miss Heather, I'm so delighted that all is well with you and your bairn." His heavy accent clogged with emotion. "It's not always the case. I cast many a prayer for you the last weeks."

Zeke carefully let Heather take her feet. He kept his arm protectively around her shoulder to be sure she had her balance, wishing the flip-flopping of his heart would settle down. Liza shoved him out the door like all the other gawking loggers and closed it in his face with orders for him to come back in two hours. And it was like all the intensity and terror of the birthing had waited to come visiting until after it was all done. His knees nearly buckled at first.

Two hours was long enough for Cookie to have what smelled like a king's feast on the stove as well as finishing up the molasses cookies Heather had started.

Heather offered a smiled of comfort to Bjorn for the loss he'd faced at a birthing. "Your prayers must have greased the wheels because this little man came out like his feet were on fire."

"I've never heard of such a thing." Liza claimed Riley from Heather until she was seated and comfortable.

A few of the men came close enough to see little Riley, who was stretching and worming around in Liza's arms.

As soon as Heather settled, Liza handed her baby back. Heather smiled, and as far as Zeke was concerned, the heavens parted. He'd never seen a look so pure and sweet. Sheer joy radiated from Heather's tender smile.

Again, he ignored the stab of jealousy that hitched inside him. He could wish this little family was his all he wanted, but that didn't change facts. He was nearly a criminal—or he was one, depending on who you asked. He wouldn't spoil this perfection with his troubles. What kind of man would that make him?

Zeke took up a place at the back of Heather's rocker and watched as the logging camp met Riley Moses—Cookie first in the line.

"Riley Moses," Cookie said. "That has a nice ring to it. Riley Moses, get your backside over here! Yup. It will do. It passes the boy-in-trouble test." Cookie moved back to tend his ovens while the others took their turn.

Several men lingered. When most had seen Riley Moses, a small ruckus started between two men.

"Is that my canteen? I've been missing mine for nigh on two weeks now, and it's been chapping me." He went to check the canteen and when it was obviously not his he set it down and turned to face the rocking chair. The whole room was quiet and looking at him. "Sorry. I didn't mean to speak of something so— on Riley's special day. On Moses's day. I just thought that was it."

"I'm missing my second pair of boots, too."

Cookie blustered, "Not this again. Harvey will have to hear about it." He didn't make eye contact with any of the men.

"Don't know when it went missing, but my second bedroll is gone. I thought the preacher might've taken it along with him when he left."

"Preacher wouldn't've taken your stuff. Not without asking." Liza's words sounded foreign to Zeke's ears.

Protecting the preacher whom she nearly attacked a few days ago?

"I could tell someone rifled through my stuff the other day, but the only thing that came up missing was the lavender soap that you made us, Miss Heather. I figured whoever took it must really need it. So, which one of you warthogs took my soap?"

And like that it was as if a striker match was flicked and lit inside him.

Zeke remembered hearing someone in the bunkhouse when he was racing to tell Heather, Liza, and Cookie about Moses and to confess his secrets to Heather. Then he remembered the tracks he'd seen in the tree line before the snow came. Tracks he'd dismissed and forgotten out of hand months ago. He spoke to the whole room. "I don't think it was anyone in camp."

Everyone stopped.

They all waited on Zeke but looked at Baby Riley, who seemed determined to capture every heart in the room with his little manly grunts. Heather had unbundled him since they were plenty warm by the stove so that every man could see him.

"You think someone is stealing from camp." Heather's soft voice plucked at his core like a musician took one string at a time on his guitar. How could something so impersonal move him?

"I do. I don't know who or why, but I think they've been watching us for a while now. Moses and I figured as much the first week you and Miss Liza arrived. I forgot to tell you all about the footprints in the woods. We were being watched months ago. Who's to say that someone willing to spy on a camp full of men wasn't also willing to pinch a thing or two."

"Makes sense. A coat. Bedding. Boots. The feller has probably staked himself a hiding place through the winter and run his gear through." Cookie balanced the lid of a wooden barrel, piled high with cookies, on his chubby hands as he worked his way around the room delivering the warm goodness. Beginning with the ladies first.

The cookies and Riley's whimpers that turned into a full cry took the thieving clean out of everyone's minds except Zeke's. Who was watching and why? Was it David? Had David been able to track him?

Zeke could see out the window from where he stood guard behind Heather. He scanned the trees for movement, hoping to catch the thief out. But what were the chances of that?

He would double his vigilance. He wouldn't let her out of his sight, if at all possible. Heather lifted little Riley around until his tiny feet were kicking free of his blankets. She swooped in and kissed the baby on his tiny cheek and neck.

Did she even think about their kiss?

He wouldn't ever forget it. But delivering a baby had a way of putting things out of your mind. Or at least giving you a little perspective.

Cookie came around delivering a second round of cookies. "Stew will be ready in an hour, but I'm afraid that will be too long for our new mother. Take a few more of these and find your bunks and tend your things until supper. Let's give her the hall for a while. I'd like a complete list of anything missing by this evening. We'll soon know the truth of it."

Each man came in turn and said something to Heather or the baby.

"Thank you all. I can't believe he's here."

Zeke didn't let Cookie's words dictate to him. He planned to be there to help Heather back to her cabin, if that's what she wanted. He would stand at her door until the girls dropped the drop lock in place. He couldn't afford to leave them unprotected if they were still being watched.

Cookie came to Heather's side. "And you two ladies, what do

you say about the three of us moseying our way into town tomorrow? I'm sure you're tired, Heather. But I'd feel a mite better if the doctor could take a look at you both. Riley Moses made his appearance in quite a rush." Cookie stood to his full height and gave Zeke a raised eyebrow once-over. "We can't be too careful. We could take our time. All day if we need to."

The cook was giving him, not quite a challenge, but a boundary.

"I could manage that. I mean, we could manage that." Heather's face glowed with the light of her smile. The months he'd known her she'd seemed happy enough. But next to this new warmth and delight, he knew different. She'd been hiding as much of herself as he had. What would it take to keep that smile on her face? He wished he could claim a spot beside her to find out.

"Zeke, I'll need you to play foreman tomorrow." Like that, Cookie doused him with the cold bucket of reality. He was nothing to Heather and her son. He could be nothing until his future was settled.

"Will you check in at the post and see if there is any mail?" *If Patrick would send word.* He checked a frustrated sigh.

"Always do. Collecting letters and wanteds is more fun than a Sunday social. Is there anything you need to make the night watch more comfortable, ladies?"

"I'm making her some peppermint tea and putting a plate of food together for her. Gotta keep her blood healthy, so her milk will be rich."

Liza's words had the last of the straggling loggers scrambling to clear the room like nothing Cookie had said. Even Zeke was uncomfortable thinking about little Riley's milk. But how uncomfortable could he be after holding a woman in his arms as she was delivered of child? *Oh, Lord.*

Wonder and gratitude rolled through him as he remembered. "Every good gift and every perfect gift comes from above, and comes down from the Father of lights," he said over them.

"I love that. Say it again?" Heather asked.

"My mother said it all the time to me and Pa." The snatch of Scripture was liniment for his aching soul. He hadn't meant to share it aloud.

Heather didn't turn to him. Her gaze was trained on the sleeping Riley. His little fingers were wrapped around hers.

Zeke repeated the words and then he stood in silence for a long while, watching as mother learned about her son.

Riley soon made his hunger known to the whole camp. Liza bundled the babe and barked instructions to Zeke. "Bring Heather with me. This one won't be put off a moment longer. And once he is fed, she needs to sleep."

Heather made to rise, and Zeke stepped in and supported her upper arm. He was going to lift her.

"I think I can manage." She looked up at him. Weariness drooped her eyes. "At least I'd like to try. I'd prefer it if you didn't leave me to walk alone."

A mule kick to the chest would have left less of a mark than her words. He knew she was just talking about getting her back to her cabin, but how could he ever leave her after what they shared? But he was poison until the murder charge was lifted.

God. Did God know what to do with one-word prayers?

As they crossed the muddy and sodden area between the lodge and the cabin, the hairs on the back of Zeke's neck raised. They were being watched. He could feel it—same as before. He wanted to scan the trees for the thief, but he didn't want to alarm Heather. He stole surreptitious glances and contented himself by checking the strength of the drop lock.

By the time they were all settled into the tiny shack the feeling of being watched was over.

Zeke marched off to find out what all had been taken. If someone had a firearm missing, then they needed to know that.

Chapter Twenty-Four

Baby Riley had Heather and Liza up before dawn the next day. Heather was so thankful to have Liza's assistance. She helped them both prepare for a day in the wagon, by the time it was light outside.

Riley suckled.

And minus this feeding, not a moment too soon.

Cookie rang the bell with his winding-up motion and his great bellow. Riley didn't even flinch in her arms.

"Likely he's used to that racket after all these months. Let's shake a leg. The sooner we get on the road, the sooner we can have you both back here tucked in for a long nap."

"The nap sounds like heaven. Even though I slept more than I thought I would last night. Especially after hearing all Cookie's tales of his children—thanks to you."

Riley made eating noises while Liza flapped a heavy quilt and folded it down until it was the size of the wagon bench seat. "This will pad you where you need it most. Jiggy said he'd bring the wagon round after Cookie rang the gut-hammer." A rumbling came through the walls. "And that would be him."

The jangling of harnesses and the jostling of wagon grew louder until it came to a stop outside the door.

Jostling. Ugh. Heather wasn't sure whether to hope for Cookie to drive slow and gentle or speed along so the trip could be over. She looked down at her son snuggling against her chest. He was more asleep than awake, contentedly suckling all the while.

Did it even matter how long today's journey would take? She had this little man with her forever and always. He stole her heart for the hundredth time since he made his appearance the day before.

She thought about how things had unfolded and how much Zeke witnessed. Self-conscious heat washed over her, but not shame. How could she be ashamed of something so perfect.

She passed her hand over Riley's downy hair. Riley. *I love you, son.* Then she was standing. Handing her child to Liza's waiting arms.

She fastened up the front of her dress while her friend tucked her son into a woven basket. The perfect shape for an infant. Her infant.

The love that poured out of her was more than she could comprehend. She knew it was the same kind of love her pa felt for her ma—the kind of love she intended to avoid at all costs, because it crippled you and left you to walk a living death if it was severed.

Had Pa felt this way about me?

She couldn't think about it without being overcome by the loss of both of her parents.

She'd committed herself to never loving someone so deep. It wasn't safe. What was she going to do now? She let Riley's crying complaints at being stowed in the basket, the concerns of the day, and the aches in her body distract her from finding out.

All but a few men were long out of sight, probably already balanced on springboards, pulling their saws in long, full strokes.

Zeke was glad no one noticed him standing at the door to the dining hall with it cracked open a sliver, so he could watch the wagon leave the camp. Was he spooked because of the reports that poured in from missing items around camp, or was he more protective after watching Heather give birth? He didn't know, but he couldn't help it. It felt like his life breath was leaving his chest in equal measure to the distance Heather and the wagon rolled away.

Zeke listened until he couldn't hear them anymore.

He wrapped up his paperwork and was running out of reasons to stay back at camp. He would have to head out and count trees before long. Why hadn't he worked harder to be on that wagon with them? He shuffled his paperwork and moved to head back up to the loft.

Jiggy burst through the door he'd just closed, talking as he jogged closer and waving two pistols in the air.

Zeke turned back from his place on the stairs. "Whoa! Whoa. Slow down and be careful with those things. You could hit me up here. What is going on?"

Zeke bounded down the steps, two at a time, and was by Jiggy's side when he finally made sense.

"The other men said they heard someone in my barns this morning when I was helping the ladies into their wagon. Every logger in camp knows to stay clear of my beasts, if they value their lives and their scar-free faces."

"You're right about that. All know it's your domain."

"The oxen love me. They trust me, and I know how to treat them to get the best work out of them."

"But why are you here waving those?" Zeke tapped the side of a black powder pistol that was an identical to the one in Jiggy's other hand.

"I only now figured out that a horse and saddle are missing. The new guy from last week was getting a slow start today—cooling his feet in the creek. He is still first-week sore. He said he saw a man on a horse come out the back of the barn and follow the path along the creek before crossing onto the skid road."

"Someone left, riding behind the wagon?"

"He stole a horse and was sneaking out of here like a stray dog with a stolen bone. He is a coward, and cowards are not to be trusted." Jiggy was back to swinging the blunderbusses around wildly.

"Easy with those. Where did you get them anyway?"

"They're part of the reason I find myself here in backcountry, instead of England. I killed a man in a duel. Justified—and I would do it again if I had too—but he died, and there's rules. But

Mama was ashamed and sent me away until things settled down. I wouldn't go to Paris and be a fashionable coward. I came here and brought these with me." He jammed one pearl-handled gun into Zeke's chest.

"Let's go. I can catch him with the oxen if we hurry."

That was all the invitation Zeke needed. Any chance to be within sight of Heather and the baby, and possibly whoever was following them was enough for him. "I'm right behind you."

The oxen team of six pairs—the one the loggers were expecting—was standing restless right outside the door. Jiggy leaped to the lead reins and was shouting and cracking his whips, stirring the animals into a fury before Zeke was all the way on the wagon bench. Zeke hunkered down and braced his weight with all his strength against the growing speed and bouncing—legs spread, hands gripping the wooden rail in front of him.

Jiggy abandoned his place beside him in the wagon and leaped onto the backs of the two rear oxen—Jiggy's home away from home—balancing the movements of both animals, calling and coaxing and hollering. His Caulk boots tamped with the right combination of serious intention and care of a bullwhacker with years of experience. His gun was tucked in the waist of his trousers.

Zeke released his grip long enough to push his gun down between his belt and his pants. The beasts moaned and bawled their complaints, but their feet were picking up the pace. Zeke had ridden faster on horseback, but he'd never felt the power or heard the sound of twelve beasts in eager, almost frenzied matched steps. The wagon was like a limp doll bobbing and bouncing down the rutted skid road in their wake.

Heather. I'm coming.

Heather looked to the back of the wagon and smiled. They had more provision for today's usually short trip to town than she had the whole way across the Oregon Trail.

It took Cookie twice as long as expected to settle her, Liza, and the baby in the wagon. But they'd been gently rolling over the mucky ruts for a half hour. Cookie was singing and whistling away as if they had all day.

She supposed they did.

Many of the loggers had offered their blankets and goose-down pillows. Enough food to feed the whole camp was settled in several different baskets—some from Cookie, most from the others. There was even a wooden chair anchored in the back of the wagon for if the wagon bench grew too hard for her to sit on.

They were nearing the turnout by the creek that Zeke had used all those weeks ago—where she'd first spied his wanted poster, when a man called out, "Hello, the road! Can you help us? My wife is in need."

A lean man in a long coat came out from underneath the apple trees. A fair-skinned blond came with him looking a little wrinkled and worn. They kept coming until he was nearly standing in the middle of the road, blocking their path. At the last moment, he stepped off the road and came up on Cookie's side.

Heather hitched Riley higher in her lap, and Liza made her usual grunt of disapproval. The one she'd practiced on Jiggy since they first came.

The man turned as if waiting for his wife to catch up as he started talking. "Thank you for stopping. My wife took a spill off her horse back there and—"

Before Heather could do anything, the man pulled something from inside his coat and swung it high, bashing Cookie on the crown of his forehead. Cookie tumbled over the side of the wagon and landed with a heavy thud.

The man didn't step away. He was close enough Heather could hear his breathing.

The horses shuffled a few paces to the side. Bending the traces, they came to a stand even with the reins spilling over the edge with Cookie. Liza stepped beside Heather, working to catch her balance at the wagon's awkward movement.

The man waved a gun.

"Whoa." Liza held her hands out.

The woman came forward and reached for Riley. And like that, she was tugging the baby from Heather's arms.

"What are you doing? He's mine!" Heather's voice was screechy and breathless. She would've stood to protest louder, but Liza was stepping over her to gain a closer vantage.

The woman kept tugging on Riley's blanket.

"You will stop right there, if you know what is good for you—and the baby. Both of you." The man's voice was dead serious. He stepped even closer.

They all held still for a moment. With her back to Heather, Liza braced her strong arms on either side of Heather's chest—caging her in behind her—but Heather let the woman take Riley, lest he be injured.

Riley screamed at his rude jostling.

The sound of a click nearly shattered Heather's soul.

She turned to see around Liza's waist. The barrel of a handgun was pointed at the woman—at Riley.

"David!" His wife's face leeched white. "Don't point that at him. He's just a baby."

"Baby or no, we *will* get what we came for." David was staring at Heather while his arm aimed at her son.

Liza stiffened.

He wasn't aiming the gun at her or Liza. That would be bad enough. He was aiming it at her son. He must have known it would create instant compliance.

It did. She would do whatever he asked.

"My wife will keep your son for now. Naught will happen to him, *if* you get me what I want."

"You can have anything. There is extra food in the back." Heather felt the tremble in her voice throughout her whole body.

"It's not food I'm needing."

Heather wavered. This man was taking Riley. She couldn't lose him. She loved him. Her whole body started to shake.

Liza's fingernails bit into Heather's shoulder as she kept her body between her and the madman. Liza said, "Speak your mind, mister, or give us back what's ours and go on your way."

Heather was glad for the pain of Liza's grip. It kept the trembling steady.

The fair-haired woman curled her arms around Riley and slowly turned her shoulders and back to her husband, hunching over the baby. Either she was afraid her husband meant every word he threatened, or she was faking it to make Heather more afraid.

She believed the first. This man would kill Riley to get what he wanted.

The bottom fell out of her heart.

"Who are you? And what do you want? Don't hurt him!" Liza's demands interrupted her silent plea.

Heather's skin went ice cold. Riley's newborn wail ripped her heart.

"You do as I ask and things will be settled right and tight before the little one needs his next meal." Gun steady, he was in charge.

The blond began a bouncing rhythm with her knees to pacify the infant as she continued to twist and step farther away from the gun—first ten feet, then fifteen.

Heather could only watch.

"Jasmine, make him be quiet."

"I'm trying."

Jasmine. Heather knew that name. "Jasmine? Are you Zeke's girl?"

"She's *my* girl, and you're going to get the deed to *my* house from Zeke in exchange for *your* son's life. And you're going to do it now. You!" He pointed at Liza with his gun-free hand that still clutched the stick he'd used on Cookie.

If Liza was a taller, longer-armed woman, she could have reached out and touched the stick. He was that close to the wagon.

"Turn the wagon around."

Heather was shaking so badly, she couldn't even stand in the wagon, let alone steer. She could see the side of Liza's face. Her friend was more silent than Heather had ever seen her, but something in her stance would have made the devil hesitate.

She wrapped her arms around Liza's waist to settle herself as Liza reach to collect the first and then the second rein.

Cookie moaned from the ground at the same time they heard many pounding hooves coming from the road behind them—from Camp 13.

"Heather!" Zeke's bellow, still too far off, echoed louder than the sound of a stampede.

Help was coming, but would it be soon enough?

Before Zeke came into view, Heather, Liza, and the gunman turned to see a lone horseman crossing the creek and moving under the apple tree beside them—closer than anyone should be that wasn't being sneaky. Whomever it was seemed to be tracking David and Jasmine's trail. *But who?* He wore a mackinaw. Was he a logger?

The sound of pounding hooves grew louder.

The horseman came closer.

The gun never wavered from being pointed at Riley and Jasmine.

Heather strained to see both the rider and the gunman. Was the horseman more danger or help?

Liza let out a curdling scream—more wild than a war cry—as she leaped off the wagon onto the gunman.

He pulled the trigger.

Smoke plumed out the end, before Liza and her clawing fury collided with him and took him to the ground.

Heather flinched at the loud report.

Jasmine, who had moved even farther away from her husband, came to a slow stop and slumped. Red brighter than chokecherry juice bloomed a crimson flower on her back.

He shot Jasmine.

Heather screamed.

The sound of the pounding hooves and Jiggy's voice yelling threats met her ears, a hot contrast to Jasmine's silence.

Ignoring David, Heather leaped from the wagon and ran past the scratching, hissing Liza on her way to Jasmine's lifeless body. "Riley! Dear God!"

He shot. Her legs wobbled with every step.

Heather gulped for air. None came into her lungs.

She rolled Jasmine, who clutched Riley safely in lifeless arms.

She scooped up a perfect Riley, his mouth full open, his face purple, the biggest scream of his life caught in his throat. When he finally managed air, he let the world know his anger at being so jostled.

He's alive.

And the dam of tears finally broke on a sob.

Heather felt her son over as she kissed his screaming face. She wailed almost as loud as her son. Tears fell down her face and dripped on her beloved son. She clutched him to her chest. His warm head snug in the crook of her neck.

Then, still on her knees, she rocked him.

The legs of a coffee-colored horse came to a stand beside her, and a pair of boots slid into her view. The stranger who provided the distraction was there. She tucked herself around Riley to protect and shelter him from whatever was coming next.

Heather peered up.

Recognition penetrated even as her thoughts grew more muddled. Then anger like she'd never known tore up out of her belly. As if her legs were coiled like twin snakes, she stood, keeping Riley safe, and slapped her father across the face so hard her shoulder and hand ached, startling them both. She ignored the trickle of blood that pooled at the corner of his mouth as he shuffled back.

"Heather." His hoarse voice saying her name was both familiar and strange.

He said my name. He is here.

Anger kept her on her feet, barely as she adjusted the still screaming Riley. All the years he was gone. And he came now? He found her? How much did he know?

To be here, he must know about Mama and Riley.

Like that, all the strength she possessed spilled away.

Her son was alive.

Tears poured double and dripped down her cheeks.

She turned to run away from her father, she couldn't face him now. Where was David? Was he going to shoot again? She ran from the pain and relief that battled for her heart. She tripped over the bleeding woman at her feet. Straightened one arm, bracing for impact, protecting Riley with the other. A warm strength caught her around the middle before she connected with the earth.

Zeke's strong arm was around her.

His beard scuffed her face as he caught her and Riley and pulled her up and away. He settled her on her feet a few steps away from the worst and best moment of her life—Riley was alive.

She could only watch as Zeke turned away from her long enough to punch Pa and drop him in the dirt next to Jasmine. "Pa!"

"He's your pa?" Zeke stared at her. "I hit your pa?"

"Is she your Jasmine?" she called back.

"Yes." They answered in unison. If they were going to understand each other, they would have to talk.

Now was not the time.

Twelve oxen bellowed behind them. Each huffed to catch their breath.

The faint rise and fall of Pa's chest gave her a measure of reassurance. *He was here.* He came just in time to distract the shooter. If he hadn't been there, just then, Zeke and Jiggy wouldn't have made it in time. The shooter would have taken better aim.

The shooter.

Liza?

Pa gave Liza the chance to spring. Pa saved Riley's life. *Liza?* "Liza!"

Zeke was close. He laid an open palm on the back of Riley's soft curls. "She's over there helping Jiggy detain David. If you're good, we should go to them. Jiggy needs my help. Liza may need yours. Cookie too. But I need to know you're all right first."

She reached to support Riley's head and her hand found Zeke's. A flood of strength swirled its way to her with the gentle touch.

He was studying her face for a reaction.

She nodded, and they walked over together to help.

Jiggy was tugging Liza off the shooter. She continued to scratch and claw like a cat trapped in a pillowcase.

"Liza! Stand." Jiggy finally got her away and stepped between her and the man on the ground, his dueling pistol aimed at him. "Explain yourself, sir, and fast. My finger feels a mite twitchy when left waiting."

Heather came behind Liza whose hands were propped on her slim hips. "I should've brought my rolling pin. I told you I'd scratch the eyes out of anyone who tried to hurt you."

Zeke spoke, never taking his eyes off Heather. "This is David. He is the man responsible for framing me for murder in Auburn. I believe, but have no proof, he killed a man with a stick similar to the one he hit Cookie with." He pointed to the offending tool where it lay next to David's boots in the dirt. "He wants my inheritance—Price Mansion."

Cookie was sitting with his back against a wagon wheel, rubbing at the lump on the side of his head. "As far as I'm concerned you should shoot him, Jiggy. He ain't worth the hay we'll have to feed the horses to travel his sorry hide to the sheriff."

David spoke over Cookie. "I killed a man in Auburn? That's rich. You think you can frame me for what you did?"

"And I suppose Jasmine shot herself in the back." Liza scoffed and pointed to the woman in the dirt.

Pa sat up and rubbed his jaw, but he was only looking at her. The anger that swept her was nearly cooled, but she couldn't take the layers of questions and unknowns that rushed in in its absence.

For now, she ignored her father. What on earth was she going to say? She couldn't even look him in the eye.

Zeke spoke to them all, "David's been scheming for a long time. Any chance you recognize him from your wanted posters, Cookie? His name might not be David. I suspect that Auburn wasn't their first town." Zeke forced the empty gun from David's hand while Jiggy continued to hold his weapon to David's head.

Liza was clutching at the back of Jiggy. Nails out and ready to scratch David if he didn't surrender.

David's face held several red streaks—Liza's doing. "Fine, take my gun. But you should take Zeke's too. I'm telling you, he's a murderer. I happen to know his face is on a wanted poster with a hefty reward. And I didn't kill Jasmine. That fiend jumped on me and knocked the gun."

"Tie him up. Even if you're innocent of murder, you ain't innocent of whoppin' me upside the head and endangering little Riley. And…" Cookie huffed as he ran a hand through his gray hair. "…there *is* a wanted poster on Zeke, but I'd bet it isn't worth the pail of pig slop I threw it in. I know it after meetin' the likes of you."

Liza gasped and turned her blazing gaze on Zeke.

"Man from another camp brought a copy to me." Cookie nodded his explanation toward Zeke.

Heather stepped closer to Zeke as if to lend him the strength to stand, like she had Cookie.

Cookie went on, "For now, Zeke, give Jiggy the other gun, and we'll get the sheriff in Oregon City to put in his widow's mite. But I trust you."

Zeke nodded and pulled the gun from his belt and gave it to Jiggy.

When Heather found his face, to see what he was thinking, his eyes were on her, pleading for her to understand.

Her heart fluttered.

How could she give him reassurance when she was still reeling from Riley being pulled from her hands, and from her pa still lying still next to that dead woman? Not to mention the tears streamed down her face and clogged her throat, making up for their missing days.

But Zeke must've found what he wanted in her eyes. He came so close that the fabric of her calico brushed him as he made his way to find a length of rope from the back of the wagon. He moved behind David. Jiggy waved the gun for David to stand still.

David fussed, "If I'm to be accused for a murder in Auburn, then you need to take me there to accuse me. You can't prove a thing out here in the trees." David twisted to look at Zeke. "If you know what's good for you, you won't return to Auburn unless you want your neck stretched. The whole town knows it was you that murdered an innocent. They'll never believe I had anything to do with it."

Zeke pressed his lips into a thin line and tugged the knotted rope to tighten David's bonds.

Heather watched David's face as he spewed his venom. He was like a cornered animal. But was he stating the truth? There was a wanted poster, and Zeke knew it. Zeke was here hiding instead of in Auburn clearing his name. She liked Zeke and found him to be warm and caring—but could he still be a killer? Could she be trusting a dangerous man?

The strength he'd shown her when Riley was born would never be forgotten, but could she trust her own judgment? She needed to know the truth even if it was the worst of news. She believed what Zeke told her. Was there more to it? She didn't have to like David for him to be saying something that was possibly true. Weariness swept over her. She was too tired to decide what the truth was.

Zeke's voice was dull. "I think they will change their minds when they see what you've done to Jasmine."

"They'll think it the accident it was. And you will all be my witness."

Heather stepped into the conversation, "But you stole my baby and threatened him for the deed to some house."

"What house? What deed?" Liza came to her defense. "I heard what you said too. You kidnapped the baby."

"*Jasmine* took your son. I never touched him. Once I tell

them she was a two-bit whore that was possessed with a desire to please you, Zeke. To take you back and call you hers. That she was obsessed with having your baby, then they'll think no more of it. The whole town saw how you made eyes at each other." He made to sweep his hands over the whole scene before them, but they were bound behind his back.

"Unfounded accusations—all of it. Your word against mine. Release me now or take me back to Auburn to stand trial and watch as they start up a celebration to hang your friend. Are you his whores too?"

Both Heather and Liza gasped.

He was looking at them both when he said it. "Why else would two single women be living with a bunch of men in the middle of nowhere."

Zeke pulled his fist back to smash David's face the way he had Pa's. David ducked away and never saw Jiggy's clean right hook connect.

"You beat me to it," Zeke said to Jiggy.

"Figured you was in enough trouble as it is. Besides, I've done worse to protect a lady's reputation. But I think he is right on one score. You need to go back to Auburn and look your troubles in the face."

"But you don't have to go alone," Liza said. "I'll go with you. And I'm bringing my rollin' pin."

"If she's going, then make room for me. I'm going wherever she goes," Heather added.

Cookie, still rubbing his head, said. "I say we skip the local sheriff and take Jasmine and David back to Auburn. We'll go slow and careful for you, Heather."

Pa came to and sat up.

The whole group looked at him. Heather was glad he stayed silent. She wasn't ready to think about all the changes his presence brought, or how many things he didn't know that she would have to tell him, that she wasn't ready to think about with Riley finally sleeping in her arms.

She only cared about whether Zeke was worth trusting or if he was simply a better liar than David.

She had to know.

She had to know if he truly was her friend, and she had to know if her intuition could be trusted.

She'd gone months feeling withered on the inside. Zeke slipped past the guards of her heart and carved out a place of friendship, but if she couldn't feel with all her emotions, how would she know for sure if she should trust herself? If she went with him, she would find out.

Zeke touched the back of Riley's head like he had moments before. "Are you sure you are up to traveling that far. I mean you just had him."

Did he have an affection for Riley, or was he trying to get her to stay behind? "If the wagon is made as cozy as it was for today's journey, then I should be fine. I can sleep as we roll along when I need to."

Riley gathered a breath and gave a tiny shudder and coo. He'd exhausted himself with all his crying earlier.

Chapter Twenty-Five

When David staggered to his feet after being punched, he glared at them all. Dirt smeared the side of his face and the wet of the earth soaked his clothes. His jaw throbbed. His body cold, but his mind worked fast.

Let them all talk around him—in front of him.

Maybe they would let something slip that he could use.

The power of accusation was a sword that needed to be swung and thrust fast and first. They had him dead to rights with killing Jasmine, but he'd deflected that as an accident, and no one seemed to think twice about it.

He was sad she was gone. That surprised him.

I'll find another—one that doesn't want marriage and a family. He couldn't think about that now.

The fingernail scratches the she-cat gave him latticed across his face would actually help his defense, if they got him to Auburn before they healed completely, which sounded more and more like a real possibility. He could complain to the lawyer about his rough treatment and win some points.

But really, he hoped he wouldn't be with them when they got there. He had to plan.

If they all traveled to Auburn together, then things would get harder—more people watching him. But if they didn't get a sheriff, then there could be ropes not irons. Ropes were less forgiving and gave less second chances. *No matter.* He took a deep breath to settle the intensity of his situation. He'd gotten out of stickier spots than this.

Should he go back to Auburn and take his chances—see if his

web of deceit would hold his weight? Or should he fly and begin again? He had choices. He had options. Things weren't as bad as the last time, and he'd weaseled his way free then.

This would be no different.

They were all blundering idiots and they underestimated him. *That* would be his winning hand. It would take them a little more than a week to return to Auburn, if they traveled hard and fast—would they do that with a newborn babe in tow?

He could have a plan in that time. Or something would come up.

It always did.

Two days after the attack and Jasmine's death, Heather held the squalling Riley to her chest as the wagon rutted and bumped along a new road, little more than a path, heading away from Camp 13. In the other wagon, Jiggy held the reins with Zeke in the back alongside David—both men bound. Liza rode beside Jiggy on the wagon bench.

She was grateful not to be sitting on the hard bench with her friend. She liked her spot comfortably lounged on a stack of bear furs and blankets in the back of the wagon. She and Baby Riley spent the long days nestled like birds in a nest. The only mar on the journey was sharing her space with Pa.

Pa spelled the drivers, sparing Cookie the need to drive. He drove her now, making things easier for Liza and Jiggy—since there were two wagons to man. But Pa offered her no relief. He offered her no explanation or excuse or apology for his arrival. He just sat there and traveled in silence even when Cookie was trying to start friendly conversations. She'd held her tongue. There was no way she was going to start a conversation with Pa.

He's finally here.

Yet he was still absent. His silence made her heart squeeze with all the years he was gone. His return, so far, hadn't been anything like she wanted.

How could anyone stand this much silence when they had enough unsaid words to choke a horse? He was more a stranger than Zeke.

She held her unhappy son and spoke loud enough for both wagons to hear. "What is the matter with you? Why so fussy." Riley cried as they rolled over the sagebrush and prairie grass all green with new growth until she found the perfect combination of pressure on his tummy and support for his little bum and tucked up legs.

The noise didn't seem to bother Cookie. His head leaned over his shoulder, and he was snoring louder than the wheels of the wagon over rough trail.

Pa spoke from his place at the front of the wagon. "You are much like your ma, you know? I still can't believe she's gone. It doesn't seem real."

Heather nearly dropped Riley. Tears sprang to her eyes as Pa spoke about Ma. Since the dam broke on her tears two days ago, she could hardly stop them. The simplest thing had her eyes flooding. She didn't want Pa to see her tears. She wanted him to hurt, like she had hurt all those months, those years.

She'd watched Mama mourn her husband and slowly die at the same time—a double death—crueler than any judge's sentence. Mama's pain was his fault. He had a choice. "Her death would seem real enough, if you were there to hold her hand and kiss her cold cheek. You left. You left us."

"I was dying with her. I just couldn't." He bowed his head.

His words were empty to her. She was the one who fed, washed, clothed, and cared for Mama. How could he say *he* was the one who was dying? Where was he when she breathed her last?

Heather wiped the wet from her face with Riley's blanket and then turned her back more completely on her father. She adjusted her clothing to feed her son. Pa could think she turned for privacy, but everything in her hated her father for all the added pain he'd put her through.

"When I asked about you and your mother, I heard. Did you love Riley? I remember him being a kindly neighbor kid."

With a few measly words, Pa flayed her open. She might as well be laying naked with nothing hiding her secrets. She didn't love Riley, but she would have. She could feel a sage quote of Mama's rising to the occasion. She squashed it down.

Her mind casted for every old memory caught with pain—she didn't want to soften. If Pa had stayed when he should have, then she wouldn't have had a reason to marry Riley. She would've never met either Liza or Zeke or any of the others…even Mo.

And you wouldn't be holding Baby Riley. Somehow, Mama's words that should never know about Riley, did. The sound of her voice in her memories had caught up with the present.

Without Pa seeking her out here and now, her baby wouldn't be here. She wilted into the furs. Her shoulders bent over her baby.

Could she really hold Pa accountable for his missing years when he came in time to save the most precious gift she'd ever possessed? Grunting and rooting to better find his meal, her son was alive and well because Pa interrupted David just long enough to spare his life.

She wished she could lean into Zeke as she had done when the birthing pains were on her. Zeke would brace her. But he *wasn't* with her. He rode in the other wagon.

She turned her head, so she didn't have to answer Pa's question or look into his sad brown eyes. So, she studied the wagon Jiggy drove. Liza beside him. David and Zeke sat separately, arms bound, in the wagon bed.

Zeke was tied willingly and David by force. David's back was up against the wooden coffin that held Jasmine's body. A shotgun lay across Jiggy's lap and poked out of the side of the wagon. Its presence said Jiggy wouldn't think twice about being judge and jury, if either man tried to run.

Pa's words interrupted her distraction, "I loved your ma, Heather. I'd like to say that I loved her more than my own life. But watching her fade." He shook his head. "Dying would've been a mercy. I'm sorry. So very sorry I wasn't there. I'm a cow-ard. That's why I hid in the trees and watched all those months. I was afraid you'd send me away because of what I'd done."

She could punish him by staying silent. It would take years, but she could burn him slowly, like his abandonment of her had done. But that meant she had to care what Pa thought and felt. Who had time to care when Zeke might be facing a fate as sad as Mama's? Who had time to care when it took all her energy to tend Riley Moses?

She didn't have the energy to hate. Her body still ached in all the soft spaces. She blotted her face again. More tears. She wasn't numb anymore. Had she come full circle, back to herself, like Riley said that night in the tiny shack? She would feel, then heal. That's what he said.

It was finally here in all its ugly sting.

If she let the bitter hate win out, would she fall back into the numbness? What kind of mother would that make her? Numb would be worse than abandoning her child.

She turned to Pa, letting all the pain and hurt show in her face. Tears coursed unchecked. She could barely breathe through her flooded throat and nose. "You left us. I needed you."

He nodded. He knew it to be true. "Yes. I did." Then he looked forward at the road. The rest of the wagon ride was silent.

She had no more to give. She was as limp and lax as her sleep-nursing newborn. She needed Zeke's strength.

Riley slept in her arms, and eventually she slept too.

A while later, when she woke again, the wagon was stopped, and she could see treetops. Unusual for the open terrain they spent the morning traveling through.

Zeke was at her side of the wagon as she sat up. "Would you like me to take him, so you can climb down?" He reached his arms for Riley, who was bundled and tucked to keep the spring chill from touching any of his pink skin.

"Please." Riley was so small and fair against Zeke's heavy black beard. He held Heather's hand and guided her down from the back of the wagon and cared for Riley easily. "I had all afternoon to tell him everything. He even read my letters from Patrick. He still needs proof, especially after coming this far, but he knows I won't run and I'm no threat."

She looked around and saw Jiggy working to tie David to a tree. "Did David stay silent for all that?"

"With the help from a strip of Liza's petticoat, yes."

David sat with his back against a tree, swath still jammed between his lips and tied at the back of his head.

Still holding his hand, she looked back up at Zeke. "I'm sorry about Jasmine."

His grip tightened. "I don't think I knew her very well. I think I wanted family so bad, I was willing to see it where there was none." He looked around and up into the treetops. "This place. This is where I first met Moses. It feels like a long time ago, but it was only at the beginning of last fall." Zeke smiled from behind his beard as he watched Cookie prepare the ashes to build a fire.

She wished she could freeze time and hold on to the strength in his grin. "I was thinking, if Pa hadn't run off, I never would have met Moses." She let her words quiet enough only the two of them would hear. "Or you."

She stayed close to his arm that he'd used to help her from the wagon.

"The waters are still too murky to see our way through, but I hope you'll stick with me. If things get cleared up, then maybe we could talk about the future? Maybe I could help you with this little guy? But I have no right to ask or hope, yet." Zeke held little Riley in the crook of his arm and lifted his tiny hand in his own.

"Right or not, I will hope." She could give him that. She could stand with him as he went through his own trial. "I could use the help. Especially, if I have to cook for all the men and keep up with this little guy. I don't know how I'm going to do it. I could barely keep up before."

"Do you have to? Cook, I mean? I'm not sure if Price Mansion will stay in my possession. Even if it does, I don't want to live there with all that's happened. But I don't know if I'll go back to

Camp 13, except to take my leave. I'm not sure my knee will let me keep doing that kind of work."

"Plus, it's too dangerous. We *know* that." She planned aloud with him.

"If all goes well, I should be able to get my surveyor's tool kit back. I was forced to leave it behind when everything happened. I could do that job anywhere. So, it's just a matter of choosing where to go."

They walked to a ring of rocks, ground uneven beneath her boots. A ring of rocks black with the dregs of a firepit.

"Moses and I camped here. Kinda nice to remember. It feels like a long time ago. I think we might have met your pa. I'll have to ask him."

Heather didn't respond to that. But she was thinking about her pa. "Having Pa here makes me remember. Makes me angry and sad. I want to get mean and then I can't, because of Riley. I wish I could tell my friends about Baby Riley, about all of it."

Zeke looked over at Liza who was bustling about gathering firewood.

She added, "Liza already knows. I mean my friends Rebecca, Cora Mae, and Rose. The sisters of my heart. I came to camp to earn enough money to move closer to Rebecca. She lives in some place called Eagle Creek, which is closer to the logging camp than Auburn. But I don't know where exactly. I just know, I don't want to live alone. I need family. I can't be like Pa and disappear to cope with the loss. I'll probably go back to cooking and stick with my original plan. Until…"

He was looking at her like he wanted to say so much more. She hoped he wanted to say so much more. Words of hope. Words about a future. But she knew, he didn't even know if he would be alive next week. *I suppose I don't know if I'll be alive next week either. Life was unpredictable.*

She sighed.

Zeke snuggled Riley closer. "I'll keep holding him if you want a minute to yourself to go down that path to the lake to wash and freshen." He pointed. "It's been a long couple of days, and I suspect there will be a couple weeks more just like them."

His life was hanging in the unknowns and still he offered comfort. He couldn't promise, but he could be helpful. How could he be guilty? How could she doubt him?

She leaned close to Zeke, savoring the warmth of him as she checked on her son. "That sounds lovely. Thank you." She let her fingers trail across Zeke's shoulder as she left them to be on her own by the waterside.

David saw it all. He watched Heather separate from the rest.

Some lessons only need to be learned once. Like when you feign sleep against a tree, it's best to rest your head against the trunk, instead of leaning forward—better to secretly survey the possibilities—better to time his movements for the moment when no one was paying the least heed.

He wished for a whiskey toast to his success. He knew the small pocket he sewed into every pair of his pants, to house the slimmest blade, would someday save his life.

He'd yet to own a pair of trousers that he didn't alter with the hidden pocket. It was handy to peel an orange or pare his nails, but this was the moment he anticipated.

Zeke and the older man—Heather's pa—were having a serious talk while Zeke studied the infant as if he held all the answers to his troubles. Jiggy and Liza were being industrious about the wagons and finding dried limbs for the supper fire.

David needed a hostage—leverage.

If he simply ran, they would chase, and there was no strategy in that. But if he had the baby or Heather, they would be as careful as a harlot with a client with a hair-trigger temper. If he had leverage, they would do nothing but turn him up sweet.

He'd waited until they were well away from Camp 13—no risk of a posse being set on his trail. Should he try for the baby again, or her?

His tied hands worked slow until the knife slipped from its hidden pocket and felt warm to his hand. The rope took seconds to sever, even with the care he took not to slice himself on its fine edge.

No baby. Hard to travel with after you took him. The mother would do the trick better, and she was unguarded, at the moment.

He would wait the she-cat made her next pass into the trees to find dry wood, and then he would slip into the brush that surrounded the lake and would hide him from view. Everything slow. Drawing no attention.

Then he could come up behind the fair lady and slide the blade under her chin.

He could tame her until they got away. They would take a horse and be off, and then he would disappear as he'd done so many times before. He'd call this particular game to forfeit. He would start again with the most important chess piece—his life.

Starting over was always work, but what other options did he have? After listening to Zeke weave his pathetic tale of woe, he knew that he needed to be off and running before they returned to Auburn. It was annoying to leave all he built behind, but there would be no building a future there, even if he convinced them Zeke was at fault.

They would always wonder and watch, and he couldn't have that. There was no advantage in that.

Liza came back to the fire carrying more than most men. She had her arms so full she couldn't see around to the firepit without turning sideways, effectively blocking her view of him.

She was a sharp one.

She was used to thinking and fending—he could tell. She might be able to see it in him, if she slowed down long enough to notice.

But she wouldn't.

Her kind knew work was always at hand. To stop moving and hustling was akin to a guttering candle—no flame, no heat. No heat, no life. She would keep working.

He watched her through barely slit eyes, keeping his mouth open for effect. Let them think he was exhausted. Let them forget he was a concern at all.

When Liza had the fire going, the waterpot on, and finally trotted off through the trees on her quest for more wood, David tipped his head against the tree enough see Jiggy leading the second set of horses to be hobbled in the shade. Zeke rocked the baby. Heather's pa fussed over something in the wagon bed.

This is it. My turn.

As quiet as a whisper, he was up and behind the first tree. Moving behind Heather's father's back and out of Zeke's sight. As easy as busting Jasmine free of that brothel, he slipped out of sight.

The grass was long and coarse to the skin on his hands, but he stayed low and moved through it. He could see Heather's flyaway hair blowing in the breeze if he came up slightly taller, but it wasn't worth the risk of being seen by her or any of the others. He moved low—closer to her.

He only had seconds before one of them noticed, and he needed to get to Heather before she spun around and left the water's edge.

And then he was behind her.

Chapter Twenty-Six

$\mathcal{H}$eather stood at the edge of the blue water and savored the sight and the sound. How long had it been since she was alone?

A great long-legged bird, with the feet of a helpless frog sticking out from his beak, leaped into the air and flew off.

She shaded her face from the setting sun, so she could watch him fly away. She'd been uprooted from all she knew and moved to different waters, but at least she was alive and well—unlike the frog would be.

Zeke's troubles would either come or go. She needed to think like Cora Mae. Assume the best possible outcome. Assume a gumption would be found that would sweep in and solve everything.

"*Worry will only make your stomach hurt—it changes nothing.*" Mama's voice again, so dear.

Yes.

That was her choice.

In this moment, her gumption would be to take Mama's advice, and be like her friend and believe something would come through. *Jesus, help.*

Prayer wouldn't hurt either. Peace unfurled inside her. It'd been awhile since she felt so at ease. *Help me find my way to Rebecca. And help Zeke find—*

A hand clamped over her face, blocking the air from going in or out of her nose and mouth.

She clawed at the clammy strength of it. The voice in her ear was ugly-familiar. "I left your son back there, but I won't hesitate to take my revenge on him, if you give me away. Keep quiet, and I won't kill you."

The prick of a blade came to her neck below her ear. The peace in her being traded places with panic and a cloying desire to scream. Before she could act on it, she heard Pa and Zeke shouting. "He's gone! David is on the loose!"

David whirled her around, using her as a shield, as he stepped backward—lake behind them. The blade bumped against her skin and bit her flesh. "I meant every word I said. Jasmine knew my metal. She tried to run from me and look what it got her."

Thinking of Jasmine as she fell with Riley, horrid red spreading over her back, made Heather begin to wriggle against David's restraint. She now knew what Jasmine was thinking before she started to step away from her man's side. Jasmine knew he *would* do what he said.

He *would* kill her baby.

Jasmine gave her life for a newborn she'd never met—a newborn that might end up motherless by sunset if she didn't figure out something.

There would be no running.

Zeke and Jiggy came down the trail. Zeke got the closest. She could see the outline of Pa's cowboy hat on the other side of the thick grass. Riley must be with him because he held back—but he was there. Her pa stayed.

Jiggy was pulling the shotgun around and pressing it in front of Zeke who stood his ground only feet in front of them when David shouted in her ear. "Stop! If you know what's best for her, you *will* stop! Just let me go away, and I'll release her when I can fade into the hillside. If you let me go, then there will be no one to accuse you Zeke, making you one decision away from being a free man."

Heather knew David was lying. She could feel his bluff in the hard lines of his body behind her. He would kill her—just to spite them all. Did the man even know how to tell the truth? Certainly not when he felt trapped.

But he wasn't the only one feeling trapped.

She stood by when Ma was dying. What could she do for her other than make her comfortable? And she'd gone along with Riley's dreams because she had none. She'd stood by and watched as he tried to hoe a living out of the rich earth. Then she was so busy cooking for the loggers that her dreams and plans took low priority again. Then she was trapped by the growing babe in her belly. That was the most confining thing of all, though worth it. But she was done taking in life without a fight. She'd fought to keep her sweet son safe two days ago. She would fight for him again now. She would protect her love.

She could feel David trying to maneuver her to the game trail that lined the edge of the lake behind them. He would drag her away from Zeke, Riley, Liza, Jiggy, and even Pa—all she loved— if she let him. Her friends could do nothing as long as David held her life at the point of the knife in his hand.

She would take a chance he was too busy watching all the others to manage a closer attack. Before the thought was fully formed, she kicked out. She clonked him in the shin just below his knee then sagged to her knees. David came forward with her, his hold tightening. The blade cut into her neck before she jumped back up with all her might, crashing her head into David's face. She shoved backward into him, making them both lose their balance and fall into the lake.

Cold wet swallowed them both.

The water dropped from shallow to deep within feet. Heather rolled away from David and managed to get the wet clump of her hair out of her face in time to see Zeke jump headfirst, with his boots still on, onto David who was still wallowing around for footing.

Water splashed white and frothy about the tumbling men.

Pa came to her, clasping Riley to his chest, and offered her a strong arm to climb from the lake. She took it and joined Jiggy and Liza as they watched from the shore.

A flood of red flooded the water as Zeke cried out, choking.

"Look out!" Jiggy yelled.

Zeke made space between himself and David. Enough to face

David, keep the blade away, and plan his next move. David raised his arm to bury his blade deep in whatever part of Zeke he could connect with. He leaped for the kill.

Bang!

A scream ripped from Heather's throat. Riley joined.

A puff of smoke exploded from the end of Jiggy's fancy gun.

David's arms went limp, and he fell back, floating in the water.

Liza nearly threw herself on Jiggy's chest. "You did it. Finest shooting I ever did see."

Jiggy caught her in his free arm.

Liza bounced with delight until she found her celebrations silenced by a sound kiss on the lips.

Her friend went nearly as limp as David for a moment before she slung her arms around Jiggy's neck and drowned him in kisses.

Zeke was on his feet, making his way to shore and dragging David by the arm. "I'll need help with him."

Pa handed her Riley. She tried to protect her son from her wet clothes, but it was useless.

"Are you sure he's dead?" Liza was breathless when she asked.

"I'll check." Pa stepped in and aided Zeke. "He is most certainly dead."

"Good riddance. He wasn't worth a cow pie," Liza said as she let Jiggy put an arm around her waist. He blocked the grizzly view from both Liza and Heather's sight.

"What now?" Jiggy asked.

Heather wished she could lean into Zeke's comfort. Her body was sore everywhere. Jiggy asked a good question. What *would* happen now?

They would roll into Auburn with *two* bodies. Would the town dole out their version of justice? A life for a life? *A life for two lives?*

"With all you told me, with the letters, with all that happened back where Jasmine was killed, I think we will stand excused," Pa spoke. "If we stick together. Each of us saw plenty. Our witness combined will free Zeke."

Pa's words were filled with protection for Zeke, but he looked at her. "You two go get warm and dry. Jiggy, you help me put him in the box with Jasmine. The lid won't fit but they might as well take their last ride together. Bring the Hudson Bay five point—the blanket will be big enough to cover their box and keep the flies off until we make Auburn."

Pa came to her side before he went to work. He ran his finger over the cut that creased her neck.

She'd forgotten she'd been cut until he did that.

"Take your son. Take care. He needs you. I couldn't bear it if I lost you too." Pa pulled her into a mighty hug—wet dress, baby, and all. She wouldn't have denied him that even if she had the strength and energy. She let him hold her. The kiss to the top of her head flooded her eyes with a million tears.

Her pa would never leave her again unless he was going to the grave. She knew it. Felt it in his hug. When he pulled back only to grab Zeke's shoulder to tug him before her, she knew he wanted what was best for her, even if it meant sharing her.

Before Zeke took Pa's place, he looked at her pa. "You were the one. You were here. Moses and I gave you coffee—you said you were looking for someone."

Pa smiled and nodded before he walked away.

Zeke pulled her close with the wailing Riley between them. He was smoothing her dripping hair back from her face with the flat of his large hand.

The warmth of his wet soaked through her chill as soon as he stood close. "The town is good-hearted. They will understand. They will set me free, if David isn't there pouring his lies in their ears. Do you know what that means?"

She cuddled Riley to her neck. He bobbed his tiny head in search of food. His cries turning to small whimpers. She couldn't take it all in. "What does it mean?"

"It means we…we can settle up and go to Eagle Creek as a family. Do you think your friend will welcome all three of us? Or four, if your Pa does what I think he will?"

"Rebecca will. She would love it as much as I would. I can't think of anything better."

"I can." His voice lowered.

She looked at him.

He inched even closer. "Will you marry me and make me the happiest man this side of the Blue Mountains? Will you be my wife and make me the father of your sweet son and fulfill my dreams? I miss being a part of a family. I want you, no, I need you as mine."

She saw the longing in his face and knew her answer on the moment. But before she could say it, another thought bounced around and jumped in front. "Mama would have liked you."

"Is that a yes?"

"Absolutely. But!" He was about to scoop her up. "Do you think you can wait to marry until we are together with Rebecca? I'd like to share at least one of the two best days of my life with one of my sisters."

"Two best days?"

"My wedding day and the day you helped me say hello to this little man."

He kissed her gently, so as not to crush Riley, then he pulled her to his chest and rested his chin on her head with Riley tucked between them. "Same two for me as well. Let's get you back to your wagon. Liza can help you into something dry, and I will try not to think too closely about the details of that, my love."

She smiled up at him. Her numb tears broke free from their frost only days ago and now the sunshine, warming her soul, came forth. Her fresh tears were tempered with joy and a love so much bigger than the beat of her heart. She understood Pa's absence now.

She could forgive him.

Zeke scooped her and Riley up in his arms and carried them back. He had to stop in the middle of the path when she blocked his view of the trail with her face nose-to-nose with his. "I love you. I'm not sure when it crept into my heart. But it's as real as the son in my arms." She laughed and kissed him full. He kissed her back until they were both plenty warm.

"Never put off until tomorrow what you can do today." Her mother's voice offered nothing but sweetness. And as always, her mother was right.

She leaned in close to Zeke's ear. Her lips brushed his skin as she gave him the news of her heart. "Never mind Rebecca. I can tell her soon enough, let's not waste a day. We should get married. Rebecca can be there for the birth of our next child."

"Yes, ma'am. I like how you think. After we're married, I'll give Price Mansion to Patrick, if he wants it. Then when you are rested and well enough, we'll be off." He kissed her again.

Epilogue

Meramec, Missouri
October 1848

On the way out of the finest restaurant Meramec had to offer, the postmaster gave Cora Mae a letter. She thought her knees would buckle right there in front of Father and Archie. The darkness of the autumn evening spread around them and covered her response—thankfully.

Cora Mae never felt so alone. But she had a letter.

Archie kept a firm grip on her elbow, and Father droned on and on about something at the mines as they walked the boardwalk back to the house.

She pressed the letter into her pocket and rested her hand over the top.

She would wait until she was alone to find solace in news and updates—the last two that came together were shockingly short—finding out Riley was dead and Heather had to make her way alone was terrible.

Archie claimed her elbow, like he owned it. Like he owned her. *He hasn't asked me to marry him yet.* She imagined his face when she said no. Wishing she actually could say no. Hoping he didn't ask any time soon.

He probably will soon. I'm running out of time.

She needed her friends right now more than anything.

She wished she could roll back time and call her sister-friends to her house to stay the night and catch up, like they'd done when they made their sister-pact. How dear that time was to her now.

She needed their advice and comfort and possibly their straight-talking sense. Rose was gone now too. If her stupid brother, Cecil, hadn't dragged her away with him on his moronic, prideful adventure Rose would still be here. She'd sent both Rebecca and Heather letters to let them know, but there hadn't been enough time for their response to get back to her.

Cora Mae went through the motions expected by the two men who were more interested in each other's company and business chat than her. She burned with impatience to be away from Archie, who kept trying to claim her affections. Finally, the night was coming to an end, and they were at her front porch.

"See you tomorrow night. I can't wait to see you bedecked in loveliness." Archie's words slimed her.

"I'm not pretty enough for you as is?" She shook him off her elbow under the guise of rubbing a crease out of her full skirts. If she could just shake free of the town party tomorrow. She had to if she didn't want it to possibly turn into her engagement. She didn't know if he would ask her tomorrow or not, but she'd been putting him off for so long now.

Tomorrow night. Her life could end tomorrow night if she wasn't careful.

Lord save me. Help my father to see.

She breathed a sigh of relief and touched the letter in her pocket when Nanny was there to open the large wooden door.

"I'll leave you two to talk shop. Night, Father." Cora Mae kissed her father's cheek. His beard so familiar and comforting when he normally saw her and listened to her. Not so, tonight. It hadn't been a comfort in a long time.

"So early to bed? Are you feeling ill?" he asked.

"Ready to contemplate all the possibilities with me?" She answered with a question. No sass in her tone.

Her father patted her hand.

She wished she could slap the patronizing grin from his face, but what daughter did that? He was forcing her to solve her own problems.

Is that what Mother had done?

Was there more behind the reason she left than letting her passions consume her with a lover other than Father?

There was no time to ask.

The party was tomorrow. She had to miss it. Her clothing had been picked; her meal was being prepared. If Archie asked the question, the answer she must give was known to the whole town.

"Sleep well, my girl. Tomorrow's a big day," Father said.

"One filled with the first of many dreams come true." Archie arched his eyebrow in a knowing way that made her want to swing her reticule at his head. Archie shouldn't pretend to be smart when he was standing in the company of two people that could run circles around him with their intelligence. It might be arrogant of her to say that of herself, but truth was truth. "Night, Father." What else was there to say?

She had a letter to read.

Archie trotted up the steps to kiss her before she ducked inside. She timed it so his clumsy kiss was followed by a step on his foot. She may have turned her cheek to him with a demure smile, but she didn't have an ounce of surrender in her. "I do beg pardon. Until tomorrow."

She dipped a curtsy to them both, went into the only home she remembered, and raced down the hall toward the stairs. She took the steps at her normal unladylike charge. If she could run from them both, she might find her sanity.

But how could you run, if you'd never been anywhere before and had nowhere to run to? Her head throbbed with the same question over and over.

Father would have a solution if it was *his* trouble. He always had solutions to the impossible problems. She loved him for it, even if he didn't see her or value her. She'd tried so hard to impress him and see that look in his eyes that he gave to the business partners he respected.

But no, besides her accidental idea of buying the mercantile and giving it new management, she'd never felt his respect. And that decision took Rose from her when he acted on it.

Where was Rose now?

It would be weeks before a letter came from her. Cora Mae didn't like that she'd be sitting here in Meramec always the one waiting to hear from her sister-friends. How was that better than what she had before the pact?

She unlaced her boots and kicked them off in a heap before flopping on her bed and tugging the pins from her hair. Once her hair tumbled thick and free, she unwrapped the letter and read—she could feel sorry for herself later.

> *Dearest Cora Mae and Rose,*
>
> *I dare say you thought, with this address, this would be Rebecca's writing when you opened the letter, but it is not. It's me, Heather. Boy, do I have news, and lots of it.*

How could that be Heather's handwriting?

Cora Mae looked at the return address and could easily see Rebecca's handwriting. How was it that Heather's fine script was flourishing inside? Did Heather meet up with Rebecca? She sat up.

> *Yes. You guessed it. I'm here with Rebecca. We are neighbors. In fact, my husband, NOT Riley, and I are living with her and Clark while our farmhouse is being built. No, I'm not going crazy. I'm sorry I haven't been able to keep up as fast as my life has unfolded. I should have sent you another letter when I found out I was in a family way.*

Cora Mae gasped. Heather was married again already? And a baby?

> *I'm married. Zeke is a fine man inside and out. He loves me and Baby Riley as if we were pirate's treasure newly found. I've never been so happy. Baby Riley is the*

last kindness Riley gave me before he passed. He is such a perfect little man.

    Another piece of news is to tell you that Pa found me. He came back just in time. But before I tell you more, Rebecca has news, and I figure you need to see both our writing side by side to fully believe.

Rebecca's handwriting took over.

    It's true. We hug each other every day and dream of the day that you two can both come to visit. Wouldn't that be dreamy? Though I don't recommend walking the Trail if you plan on returning back there. It's a long ways to walk. I'd never make it a second time in my condition.

    I wish you could see the smile on my face as I write this next sentence. I'm to be a mother. Can you imagine? Me. A mother. I figured if I wrote it on here to the two of you—those who've seen me from the beginning—it might feel a little more real. I'm so glad to have Heather here with me.

    Especially since she has gone through all of this already.

    Hope you two are well and healthy with hopeful husbands finding their way into your hearts. What I wouldn't give to see both face-to-face.

A tear dropped from Cora Mae's face and splatted on the page, smearing the ink. The loneliness ached into her bones. She wished she was with them too. She would give anything to be free of her situation.

She snapped up and turned the paper over to see the sending address.

This is it.

She held the answer before her. It had niggled at her a time or two in the past. She could remember announcing it when Rebecca left, but that was two years ago—and she'd meant it only in jest. She could never have known then, how truly stuck she was.

But they were together now—her sister-friends, and she was older and wiser.

She knew where to go.

It was October. She'd have to plan for early spring. Maybe by then she would hear back from Rose wherever she ended up with her idiot brother and have a choice of destination.

Plans started to wheel in her mind. This would be her biggest gumption of all. She would make her friends proud.

Before she hadn't been desperate enough. But now—with two of her sisters in one place—she could do this. Something clinked down inside her like a bolt being set in a lock. She had the seed of a plan, now she needed to plant it and watch it grow—only it had to grow fast. And it had to be smarter than her father.

Tomorrow she would definitely be sick. There was no way she could risk Archie proposing. She had to get Father to push it off until spring. She could do that.

She went to her closet and slipped on her sturdiest old shoes and moved to climb out the window and down the big tree that Archie had used to spy on them all those times.

Father and Archie would have their heads together over business and fine port, in Father's office, for a few hours more.

She could get things rolling with them none the wiser if she hurried. Finch, Rose's nice uncle, would help her. He always worked late, and then she would find the blacksmith. Things had to be perfect.

Nothing could give her away.

Acknowledgments

To my editor Naomi Rawlings, David and Roseanna White, and the WhiteFire publishing crew for their patience, editing helps, and amazing cover design. I love working with you.

To my critique buddies, the best on the planet, Savanna Kaiser, Cynthia Roemer, Kathleen Denly, Audra Kearney, Stephannie Hughes, and Tara Johnson. You fuel my passions in so many creative ways.

To my mentors, Kate Breslin and Darlene Panzera. I trust you.

To my chief encouragers and my sister-circle, Cheri Faulhaber, Tricia Halverson, Jodi Halverson, Ronya Davis, Vanessa Snowley, and Lizz Grandle. Writing each book is a long, hard, and glorious journey. I'm so glad you all help me keep on going.

To Danielle Kendall, for your inspiration.

To my family, my heart is ever yours. Especially you, Tim Grandle.

To my Savior, I'm so very thankful.

Author Notes

One of my editing steps as I prepare for publication is to read my story out loud. When I hit the part about Mo and Liza, I cried every time.

Being forgiven is the breath in our lungs. It sustains us until we find heaven. If every sin and mistake of our life was rolled into one, it would be but a rain drop compared to the ocean of Jesus' forgiving love.

You are forgiven.

We are forgiven.

If life has thrown you messy curve balls, if the grief you've survived still haunts you, if self-reliance and survival is the only mode of operation you know, then I hope these pages bring you waves of fresh hope, full faith, and new love as you experience the fullness of our Savior.

He never leaves.

He never forsakes.

You are His beloved.

Discussion Questions

1. Does love feel risky to you? Did the vulnerability and possibility of pain, when falling in love, turn out to be worth it?

2. Has your life ever been redirected after the loss of a loved one?

3. Have you ever had to move cross-country and start over without knowing anyone? What would you tell someone facing the same?

4. Would you be good at the hard work needed to live in 1846?

5. Have you ever had to wait a long time for a dream to come true? What was your dream? How long did it take?

6. Do you like to play detective and figure out cozy mysteries? Do you watch, listen to, or read crime drama?

7. Have you ever delivered a child without pain medicine? Have you ever delivered a child outside of a hospital?

Also by Cara Grandle

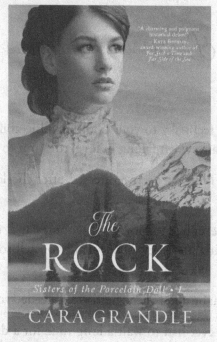

The Rock
Sisters of the Porcelain Doll, Book 1

After a whiskey still explosion destroys her home and nearly her life, Rebecca Packwood and her father must leave Missouri and her dear friends behind. After crossing The Oregon Trail, she sets out to discover her famil's secret history and to forge a home and community out of the raw farm land of Eagle Creek, Oregon Country, never suspecting a ruthless enemy is seeking to thwart her plans.

CPSIA information can be obtained
at www.ICGtesting.com
Printed in the USA
LVHW090849200522
719152LV00003B/14

9 781941 720875